I0613779

# KUDZU SUMMER

**A River Bend Chronicle Book**

*Renee Kumor*

ABSOLUTELY AMAZING eBOOKS

Habent Sua Fata Libelli

**ABSOLUTELY AMAZING eBOOKS**

Manhanset House
Shelter Island Hts., New York 11965-0342

bricktower@aol.com
absolutelyamazingebooks.com

All rights reserved under the International and Pan-American Copyright Conventions. No part of this publication may be reproduced, stored in a retrieval system, or transmitted in any form or by any means, electronic, or otherwise, without the prior written permission of the copyright holder.
The Absolutey Amazing eBooks colophon is a trademark of J. T. Colby & Company, Inc.

**Library of Congress Cataloging-in-Publication Data**
Kumor, Renee
Kudzu Summer, a river bend chronicle book
p. cm.

1. FICTION / Romance / Suspense. 2. FICTION / Thrillers / Crime. 3. FICTION / Mystery & Detective / Private Investigators.
Fiction, I. Title.
ISBN: 978-1-955036-50-4, Trade Paper

Copyright © 2023 by Renee Kumor
Electronic compilation/ paperback edition
copyright © 2023 by Absolutely Amazing eBooks

November 2023

# KUDZU SUMMER

Number 20 in the

River Bend Chronicle Series

*Renee Kumor*

For Angela Tarry
and all women pilots
who touch the sky

Books in the *River Bend Chronicles* Series

# CHAPTER ONE

Lynn Powers looked over the gathering in her backyard - her dedicated mask-free zone. "This is like a kudzu summer," she mused. "Can't you feel it? We're all wearing masks, and everything seems to be hidden." Like the pervasive kudzu vine that chokes and cloaks unsuspecting areas throughout the southern states, the world-wide pandemic had crept into River Bend, smothering life.

It was an eerily quiet, lockdown summer all around town. Lynn assumed it was that way around the country as well. She watched the news and heard from colleagues. 'Sanitize' and 'mask-up' were the bywords of the day. Lynn's dining room table had evolved into her home office. To stay in virtual touch with the local non-profit community, she liked using the large table surface in the dining room as her office in her role as the executive director of the River Bend Philanthropies. Dusty, her husband and chief detective of the James County/River Bend Investigation Unit, used her father's old office on days he worked from home.

Her best friend and sister-in-law, Piper Zubov, flopped in a lounger. "I can't go through a whole school year like those last months." Piper, principal of a local elementary school, was working with the school board planning for the delivery of education in the upcoming year. There would be an effort to have the elementary grades in classrooms. Distancing and masking were going to be the biggest challenges. Will, Piper's husband and owner of a good-sized manufacturing facility, had his company working in two shifts so he could keep everyone employed at a safe distance. But he was starting to grumble about lack of materials and increasing prices.

In a small act of rebellion, Piper threw an old mask at the dog. He was enjoying himself. People seemed to toss masks daily. It was a new game. Of course, Lynn hadn't been happy when the dog had to spend time at the vet's while he passed a mask. The vet had muttered something about a whole new sideline in animal preventive health. He had treated birds, ducks, cats, dogs and one ferret for maskitis. He was certain someone would find a mask in bear scat while hiking in the forest.

In the initial weeks of the virus pandemic, Lynn had declared her backyard a mask-free zone. All attendees just had to social distance. No one seemed to sit still long enough at any distance. She didn't know how a virus could find anyone in her yard. The teen and college crowd were always working in Will's vineyard under the direction of Piper's father, Bri Llewellyn, or playing soccer out in the field behind the barn. With the adults working from home at intervals and students of all ages going to classes online, her house and yard were always in flux.

This evening's gathering was becoming routine for the virus summer now that the school year had ended. The college kids had been online learning from home since April. And high school graduation ceremonies for Piper's son, Jeff, and his friends had vaporized. Ricky Mitchell, Jeff Hanby and Ryder Plummer had had a strange high school graduation. Everyone had tuned in for an online version of the event, but as a celebration it had been tepid. No one even wanted to talk about the end of senior year events that had been abbreviated or erased, and always masked. They all wondered if there would be a college freshman year in their future. Ryder had been recruited for his basketball talent, but no one knew if there would be an ACC basketball year scheduled. The thought of a 'no basketball' season almost made some hearts threaten to stop.

And then there was college graduation. Dusty's nephew, Way Reid, had graduated from the state university with his criminal justice degree. That ceremony had been as lackluster as Jeff's high school graduation. And Way had been turned down for a slot in the James County sheriff's office because of his relationship to Dusty. The sheriff continued to see Dusty as a political challenge in the next election. Much to Way's delight, Dusty had helped him get a position with the sheriff in a neighboring county. The young man was now enrolled in the basic law enforcement certification program at the community college as a requirement for his job.

Patti Ann Seymour, the only young woman in the college crowd, had also graduated from college and was preparing for her first year of medical school at East Carolina in Greenville, North Carolina. She and her sisters were making plans for her move. Lynn was always charmed by the way the four Seymour sisters took care of one another. Patti Ann was the youngest and her three older sisters mothered her to distraction.

In the early days of the pandemic the community had lost several residents, three touched Lynn's family. Robert O'Hara, her father's law partner succumbed early, and he was followed by Mrs. Cohen, Lynn's next-door neighbor. Finally, Eddie Erhardt, one of the brewers at River Dog Brewery, a wheelchair bound veteran, had been lost. Those deaths had caused Lynn and her friends and family to take the health warnings seriously. To that end, although there was a lot of activity, the family tried to observe all advised health precautions.

Lynn's father, Jim, and his wife Marianna were being very cautious in their exchanges with others in the community. Marianna liked to joke that grocery shopping online and ordering carryout meals and clothing from her laptop had improved her typing skills. And zoom had become the new, enhanced American verb.

Jason had given up his summer job at the bakery for a summer job working for his grandfather. He had become a courier and messenger between Jim and the law office. Since Jim's partner Robert O'Hara had died from the virus, Jim and Marianna were living very quiet, secluded lives. It had been a difficult decision for Jim to withdraw into lockdown. He had always valued his independence and freedom. He weathered some negative responses from old friends, but in the long run decided that a few months in quarantine outweighed the other option - death.

"Life is certainly different than it was a year ago at this time. We'll survive," Lynn declared, "no matter the conditions." An optimistic declaration!

Piper rolled her eyes at her longtime friend. "But will we recognize ourselves?"

\*\*\*

Teniquia LaMont, a detective with the James County/River Bend Joint Investigation Unit, knew that as a young black woman she faced challenges as a law enforcement professional. But none of those challenges compared to mothering and policing online in a pandemic. Dusty Reid, chief detective of the unit, had organized what he called half and half office duty. She and the other detectives, Mars Healey and Danny Valeri, alternated days in the office and days working from home. Fortunately, crime was in lockdown, too. Things were slow in bad guy world but managing three small children while working from home had Tee wishing for a crime wave.

Staring at her computer screen, just staring because she had finally gotten the kids to nap, was hypnotic, but she knew she had to be somewhat productive. Nothing was pending from the office. However, under old cases, she scanned her file on Bill the hobo. Over a year ago Tee met Bill as a hobo who wanted to return home after twenty years on the road. She helped him reunite with a wife and daughter, only to learn that Bill was not their missing husband and father. After confessing that he had traveled with Wayne, the missing gentleman, Bill admitted that at Wayne's death he had promised his friend to look after his abandoned family. That explained the false identity Bill had promoted as he was united with the family. In spite of his deception, he became a man the two women had grown to appreciate for himself. However, he hadn't expected Wanda, a police officer and Wayne's daughter, to become interested in his past.

Wanda's observation skills led her to question Bill's true identity and then become curious about his past. Wanda asked Tee to help her quietly look into Bill's background. When she was sidelined on maternity leave, she urged Tee to continue the background research. As Tee uncovered Bill's identity, she also learned that he had been a person of interest in a twenty-year-old murder investigation. That information led Tee to contact Des Moines PD and Rose Marie Jaeger, a Des Moines police officer. Rose Marie surprised Tee when she confessed that she suspected that Bill was her biological father. Over time Tee introduced Wanda to Rose Marie and they kept up an email stream as they all got acquainted. One day Tee suggested, "Let's meet on Zoom. I'm working from home." Both women agreed and the date was set. The mystery of Bill's past life was shared among three curious law enforcement officers in three states.

Today was the zoom day, they were meeting Rose Marie in the digital flesh. The shy Des Moines rookie looked out from the screen into Tee's home office space, a room that was, depending on the time of day, the playroom, TV room or home office. "Tee?" The eager officer greeted her new friend and received a nodding grin in return. Her eyes rolled across the screen, and she said, "Wanda?" The other woman nodded. "You brought the baby?"

Wanda kissed the baby's forehead. "She wanted to be in on the girl talk." Everyone grinned. They talked about what brought them together and began to relax in this new method of building partnerships. They turned to Tee as the more experienced member of the group to begin the discussion of what they would do next.

Tee said, "I know from all those emails that you both want to clear Bill's name. Rose Marie, why don't you send us copies of the cold case file? We'll see if we can figure out anything new and help you develop a plan of action."

"I don't want to say anything to Bill," said Wanda, "until I have more information." She smiled into the screen, balancing a sleeping baby on her shoulder. "We've talked about his history once I told him we had found his true identity." She rubbed the baby's back. "He says he was a drug user and is embarrassed by his past, but he never said anything about an investigation."

Tee enjoyed these women as her e-friends. "Maybe we can come up with some threads to pursue. If he was into heavy drugs, he may have no memories."

"I can justify sending you the file because you both have an investigative connection with a person of interest." The experienced officers rolled their digital eyes. Rose Marie grinned at their silent comment. "Maybe mentioning the name Darla Somerall to him might get a response." Rose Marie studied her new friends on the screen. She was a rookie, younger than the other women, an eager blond Midwesterner. "And it is a cold case, who cares?" She gave them her still optimistic rookie smile.

They talked some more about issues common to women in law enforcement, complained about the pandemic, and in Tee and Wanda's case, talked about babies and husbands. Rose Marie waved as Wanda turned the baby's face to the camera and Tee invited her three children who had finished napping to mug before the computer screen.

Finally, Tee, the informal leader, said, "Here are the tasks. Rose Marie, you get us the file. Wanda, you go into more detail with Bill to see what he remembers. My unit is involved with some guy who just tried to kill his step-kids in March. I'll be doing real work to wrap the case for the DA. So my time will be limited."

All of them, pleased to be building new friendships with colleagues, ended the meeting.

\* \* \*

A few months ago Michael Janic, wealthy Des Moines developer, had heard talk in the locker room at the club. The professor's daughter was snooping into Darla Somerall's murder. Of course, only he knew she was the professor's daughter. Over the years Janic had decided that building a close relationship with investigators in law enforcement would be his first line of defense should his past life become interesting to anyone. Was today the day? He had taken a stab at acquiring more information. As they walked toward the locker room, he had asked his sometime racquetball partner, "You guys don't have anything to do, so you're opening cold cases?"

The mellow detective looking to retire in four months had said, "Not me. One of our rookies. Part of their training is to get them familiar with the files. The victim in this case was some drug dealer. A woman if you can believe it. The kid asked me for background, but I told her I was still working in Cedar Rapids at the time." He had wiped sweat from his forehead. "You been practicing? I usually win one game."

Janic had laughed. "When you said cold case, I thought you were getting ready for that TV show." Janic had to dig deeper. Was this investigation going to get legs after all this time? Had he covered his tracks well enough?

"Hell, no." The detective dropped his sweats and headed for the shower. Over his shoulder he had said, "It was a boring case. Drugs, junkies. I don't think anyone even remembers, or cares."

Both men were soon back at their lockers dressing. "Will this virus shut your office down?" Janic had asked as he finished tying his shoes.

"We run twenty-four seven. We'll get protective gear," the officer had laughed, "you know, masks with our badge over our mouths."

It was summer now and the country was under wraps, or in quarantine or sheltering in place. Janic didn't care. He worked from home most of the time. It was amazing the way the internet had streamlined businesses, especially ones that managed property. He was proud of his migration over the years from drug middleman to real estate developer. He had taken his drug cash and bought property on which he had been able to build apartments and small strip malls. Rental income was legit. He paid taxes and he wasn't worried that some underling would off him in some coup attempt. Like poor old Darla.

Janic sat back in his expensive digs and thought about the night he took control.

# CHAPTER TWO

*Twenty years ago*

Michael Janic, a handsome, muscular young man, had found a job in tough times. He had accepted the position as boy-toy for an older, well-connected woman who happened to manage a successful drug distribution operation. Was this where he wanted to be at twenty-six? Hell, no! But a guy had to eat. The woman was a slob, but savvy. She had worked hard to get her operation running. He appreciated that she was succeeding in a man's world. He just didn't like that he was the toy and not one of her lieutenants.

He would soon be taking over this distribution business, he could feel it. He was ready. He was tired of being Darla's on-call sex partner. He wanted to run the operation. Each time he hinted that he would like more responsibility, she would sneer, slap his bare rump, and suggest that he do what he was good at. His stud service gave him some privileges. He always got through her guards. He had a credit card for his needs, but he never had cash. If they went to dinner, he paid with the credit card she gave him. If they went out on the town, here he sneered - Des Moines? - he drove her fancy car. When he left her place, he drove his piece of crap car. He had promised himself time and again that things were going to change. And he wanted to be ready. She was getting cocky. And he had heard rumors. Some rival might be planning to take her out. He just had to be certain he wasn't nearby. Or that he got to her first.

His best fantasy was him, Michael Janic, doing the taking out and stepping in as the head of operations. The last time she scoffed at his hint of more responsibility, he began to learn all he could about the operation. Using his status in the organization as the dumb fucker, (he knew that's what her guards called him), he began to read and study her

8

files. Soon he knew the game and all the players. He just needed opportunity. He'd be patient - but ready.

One evening he greeted the guard in the front yard, "Hey, Ray," tossed him a candy bar and walked into the house. It was a big place on a couple of acres. She always said she liked neighbors at a distance. It was situated so that no one saw the guard in the front or back. All buyers and supplicants came to the back door. The dumb fucker always came in the front.

As he entered the house he heard voices in the kitchen. He walked back to watch and listen. Darla Somerall always seemed to get a high by demonstrating her power. She was shouting, "You loser! Get out! You owe me ten grand! You lost your big college professor job, and you don't even know that you have a daughter out on some farm."

"Daughter?" whispered the supplicant looking for credit, looking for a fix.

Janic stepped into the doorway. His eyes met the strained and pleading eyes of some needy bastard. Darla loved this shit, but by her tone of voice Janic knew that this supplicant was being cut off. That's what happens when you can't pay, Janic mused.

"That waitress you banged," Darla taunted, "Her family took her back. They're raising your kid to be some dumb farmer." She pushed him out the back door. "Jimmy," she shouted into the dark yard, "take the professor here on a train ride." The backyard guard came to the door, nodded to Janic who was leaning on the refrigerator, and pulled the bastard into the night. She slammed the door.

"That was harsh," Janic said as he walked all the way into the kitchen.

She turned and smiled always ready to admire and possess his hard body. "Come here, Mama needs some sexy ass."

He moved closer. "Who was that guy?"

"Someone who owes me money."

"Where's he going?"

She reached for his crotch and massaged. "You and me got other things to do. But if you're interested, I'll give you the short story. He's some professor. Lost his job, owes me money he can't pay, and got that waitress at Harry's pregnant. Jimmy's tossing him into a boxcar at the train yard. He may wake up in Minneapolis or Chicago. Or they'll find his body in Minneapolis or Chicago. Depends on Jimmy." She grabbed him harder. "Now let's get busy."

Only one guard outside, thought Janic. Opportunity met anger and ambition. He moved in to kiss her in the rough way she demanded and grabbed her throat, twisting quickly until she went limp in his grasp. He held a few minutes more, then let her body drop. He found her small pistol and went out front to deal with the remaining guard. "Ray, can you help me get something out of my car?"

"Sure." The man followed Janic to the back of the piece of crap car. Leaning over he stretched into the open the trunk, twisted, and shot Ray first in the stomach and then, once he fell, shot him in the head. Stashing Ray inside the trunk, he returned to the house, collected her supply of drugs, cleaned out the files, opened her safe and took the cash. He decided not to go for any of his clothing. Everyone knew he would have items at her place. After all he was the dumb fucker.

The drive back into the city created an opportunity to dispose of Ray's body. Leaving the road and driving into the parking area for an old, deserted fishing spot, Janic pulled the body out and rolled it into the river.

It was done. He was the new boy in town. He called the next guy up the line. It was time to inform the chain of command. "This is Janic," he whispered. "I was just at Darla's. Someone killed her. I got out. I took all her records so no one finds out about the operation."

"Pretty smart for a dumb fucker," came the voice on the other end.

Janic cleared his throat and used his real voice. "Not so dumb. I'm ready to keep the operation going."

"I guess she didn't die from no accident."

"This is my show now. We don't have to talk about her anymore."

"You sure you can keep the operation moving?"

"Yes."

"You got one month."

And that was all he had needed to step into Darla's shoes and flip her crew to his. He had two worries - Jimmy the guard and that spaced-out professor knew he had been there. Janic chuckled to himself. That dumb farm boy had probably dumped the professor at some rail yard and had gone for a late date. Maybe that professor who had seen him in the kitchen would survive his beating. He thought about the pregnant waitress. Maybe he'll show up at her place if Jimmy let the guy live. Janic decided to track the waitress and keep an eye on her and her child just in case the professor came back.

* * *

Life went on. Janic watched as the waitress married some farmer and over the years had other children. No professor. And Janic, prosperous and legit, became a wealthy businessman and local political operative. His best friends were in law enforcement and the court system. He positioned himself to know if anyone ever raised Darla's cold case. And he wanted to know if the professor was ever resurrected. He knew what had happened to Jimmy. The former guard was another fellow who didn't want the cold case arousing interest for anyone. That dumb farm boy had morphed into general counsel for the big medical center.

It wasn't just the old murder and twenty-year old witnesses that concerned Janic. He had new sidelines that might interest police if he became a person of interest in a cold case. He had given up the seedy side of crime when he gave up his drug business. But he had become sort of a criminal financial advisor. Or as the FBI might say, a money launderer. Once his colleagues in the drug trade watched him move with his cash into real estate, they asked for help. Over the years he had developed a very successful method of partnerships and buyouts, allowing local criminals with cash from all sorts of endeavors to shift cash, minus Janic's cut, into legitimate bank accounts.

It had been smooth sailing until one day Janic learned that the waitress's daughter, known to him as the professor's daughter, and now as law enforcement rookie Rose Marie Jaeger, was interested in Darla's cold case. Janic smiled to himself. Years of focused friendships were now going to pay off.

# CHAPTER THREE

As usual when Lynn ran errands she always checked in with Marianna. "Do you and Dad need anything?" she asked over her cell as she walked out to her car.

"No, thanks," came the reply. "Jason and those new delivery services keep us supplied."

"How are you doing?" Lynn was concerned about the isolation Marianna and Jim were imposing on themselves.

Marianna chuckled, "We're busy enough masking to accept deliveries, unmasking to eat what we ordered." She sniffed into the phone. "Some days are a little difficult. In fact, some days I have to check my iPad just to be sure of the date. Days sort of blend together." Her voice became more upbeat. "On the other hand, I'm more in touch with my children than I have been in months. And I'm meeting online with several old friends and some professional groups."

"How are your kids?" Lynn hadn't seen Marianna's two adult children in a year or two. Jim and Marianna had visited the son in California just last year.

"My daughter and her husband are having challenges with their restaurant in Chicago. They have started a carry-out service. My daughter says they're learning to adapt their popular dishes to popular boxed meals. My son says the entertainment world in LA is on hold. But we already know that from Bryce and his Broadway experience." Piper's son Bryce had returned home after his job as a member of the chorus of a popular musical disappeared when the play closed for the duration.

Lynn leaned against her car and stared at her garden as she spoke. "Your folks seem to be doing things just like the rest of us."

"But," Marianna jumped in, "my son has suggested that I work with some of my friends to develop some scripts. He says he sees this lockdown as a time to redefine movies and TV series' directions. I'm not sure what he means except that he says there is going to be a market for small series on all these pay-for-view services like Netflix and even some opportunities for online movie releases." Marianna chuckled. "I feel like I'm a bystander watching the whole industry reinvent itself."

"You're developing shows?" Lynn knew nothing about the industry.

"We are. Some of my pals and I have started tossing out ideas during our online chats. Three of us have moved to more private talking and," here she lowered her voice, "I've even started the first script. They're reading my outline and first scenes."

"How exciting!" Lynn stepped away from the car and said, "Keep me informed. Since you don't need anything from me, I'll let you get back to your writing."

"Thank you, dear. I do think my son gave me a good suggestion even if he just did it as a ploy to keep me busy."

The women signed off as Lynn pondered the alterations to life made necessary by a pandemic. She thought about the challenges to restaurants while the evolution of home delivery services exploded. One thing she was certain, home delivery options and the rise in online shopping of all sorts would allow many homebound folks relief from lockdown isolation, and these were services that would be welcome even as the world spun back to some version of normal.

\* \* \*

It had been a while since Janic had heard any more rumblings about Darla's cold case review through his Des Moines PD sources. He wondered if anything was happening with the professor and his daughter. He decided to check in with his racquetball partner. "How are you guys working the street? On Zoom?" Janic laughed into his phone.

"I don't give a shit," growled his friend, "I got one month and I'm gone. This is the best way to finish my time."

"No crime?"

"The younger guys are doing patrols." Papers shuffled. "I'm assigned cleaning and filing."

"More cold cases?"

"Nah, just that one from before. That rookie thinks she's on to something. Something about her father." A chair squeaking. "I don't care. I'm leaving town in two months. With this lockdown I guess we've played our last game."

"I'll miss you buddy. I always liked a sure win."

"Asshole." They both laughed and that was the end of a relationship in the time of masks.

Janic would have to give some thought to developing his next PD informant.

\* \* \*

"How was Hilton Head?" asked Dusty as he met Doug Fiore along the stone wall that separated his yard from Emily Jacobs' new place. It was another evening on the lawn. Lynn and Piper were lounging in the mask-free zone while Dusty walked the property with the dog. He was happy to find Doug, a recently married Highway Patrolman, ambling through his great-aunt Emily's recently purchased property.

Doug smiled. "Since I met my lady, life keeps getting better." Doug had met Emily's niece, Connie, through an online dating service in December. Challenges with ex-spouses and three children had caused them to marry within months of meeting. They had been happily adjusting to combining their families into one family that included one small boy, Toby, and two young girls, Annabeth and McKenna. But life called for a readjustment when Connie's great-aunt Emily Jacobs asked Connie and Doug to accept guardianship of her great-grandchildren at her death. Three more children would be joining the family at some future date.

Doug and Connie decided to encourage all the children, already cousins, to become better acquainted. It seemed that exploring Emily's property in Hilton Head had offered that opportunity.

"I remember when you found out about that property," Dusty chuckled. "Ms. Jacobs has a lot to offer you and your family."

"Going to Hilton Head was a perfect opportunity for us all to get better acquainted. We had a great time at the beach even with all this virus and masking. The house is on the water and has a pool. It was big enough for all of us to quarantine in place with a lot of activity to enjoy. We even brought Lucia and Juan to help out." Doug suddenly frowned.

"What?" Dusty was concerned by Doug's change in demeanor.

"I think I have to resign from the Highway Patrol," said Doug. "Life is getting busy. I think I need a day job, not shift work. I feel really pressed to do all I can for Emily and these kids. But I still need a job. And with schools online, Connie doesn't know if she'll have a job in the fall." He shrugged. "She thinks she may become the official tutor for all the kids if they have to attend classes online. But she's up to it." He grinned at Dusty. "I got the best of this marriage deal." Doug pondered his new life and said, "Emily is very generous. All the kids get along. Even Connie's parents have welcomed me."

Dusty studied the younger man. "When I married Lynn, I got a lot more family than I expected. I can understand your concern about time for everyone." He leaned against the stone wall. "Have you thought about asking the sheriff if he's got anything?"

"Your sheriff?" Doug was confused. "I thought you were going to run against him."

So much for secrets, thought Dusty. "I'm thinking about it. But we're talking about you. I do his budget. I know he's got some administrative openings he's never filled."

"Like what?"

"Someone to monitor certifications and organize trainings. Tee does the in-house training for new hires. She's happy to do that, but that's a small part of the monitoring and paperwork involved for the whole department. Someone should be taking responsibility for advanced training and reporting to the state boards. There's also a budget officer position he never fills but gives me the chore. There's a PR position that needs someone. There's no one focused on daily releases and managing coverage for big stories or emergencies or to interface with other community agencies."

Doug was thoughtful. "I've handled chores in all those areas for the Highway Patrol. I've even had some special PR training for highly charged community risk events."

Dusty stood, brushed off his jeans. "Check it out. I'd like to see you in the department. Just don't mention my name."

"Really?"

"Really." Dusty gave him a wry smile. "I'm Dunwoody's nightmare. He spends a lot of time working against me or trying to set me up for fiascos." Dusty thought about a few months ago when the sheriff directed him to arrest Piper for operating a school during the initial lockdown. He shrugged. "Dunwoody wouldn't even accept an application from my nephew, Way. He got himself hired in Henderson County."

"I don't know," Doug demurred, "I am your friend. You and your unit. You folks have helped me a lot, especially through my family problems." Doug's young son had shot Connie's ex-husband in a near family tragedy. Dusty and his staff had taken over the investigation easing the burden for Doug and calming all family members. "I owe you a lot."

Dusty said, "I appreciate that. But the sheriff needs smart folks like you. Some of his administrative choices are clowns. Whether I challenge him in an election or not, someone with brains needs to keep the department functioning professionally. I think you can be a big help."

"Thank you for saying that," said Doug, feeling touched by Dusty's regard for his skills. "I think I'll go in and talk with him." He grinned. "My life is too good. I need a challenge."

* * *

On the other side of town Sean Hennessey, retired Coast Guard Chief and secret millionaire, was sitting in his living room reading. During the spring he had gotten the gardening bug as unsolicited seed catalogs assaulted his mailbox. With lockdown and a restricted work schedule, he had thought, "Why not?" He was now enjoying the determined flowers that had sprung from the mulched beds around his yard. This had been the first year he ever tried his hand at gardening.

What a success! That's why he was sitting this evening reading about perennials and annuals and ground covers. He was already planning for next year. After staring at a picture for a few minutes he finally thought the variegated Hosta, one of many varieties, as the book reported, just might grow well in the back corner of his yard mixed in with some ferns. There was a knock at the door.

To his surprise Lee Stahlmeier, unmasked, stood on his porch holding a dish of something. He stepped back to allow her in. She was an old high school friend. They had renewed their acquaintance on his return to River Bend. During the winter and spring Sean and Lee had spent some time together and had, to Sean's surprise and delight, begun a quiet, intimate relationship going much further than their high school friendship. In those days Lee had been the pesky younger sister of Sean's best friend. However, after sharing Sean's bed on several occasions, Lee had told him that she was uncertain about her feelings. He had tried to talk with her for the last three months and she had avoided him with determination and skill, using the virus and her hospice clients as excuses. Now she was in his living room.

"I brought you a coffeecake." She carried the plate to the kitchen. She was a small woman and always dressed as though she were ready to work on the farm - boots, jeans and a t-shirt or flannel shirt depending on the season.

Sean never knew what to say to her. During their brief affair she had been two people, a loving woman in the evening and a sad, somber woman at breakfast. He found himself regretting that he had not had more experience with women in his past. Other men, he was certain, would have known how to handle Lee and her moods.

He followed her into the kitchen and asked, "Do you have time to share a piece with me? I can make us some coffee or tea." He watched her place the plate on the table.

She stood with her back to him, raised her shoulders, let out a sigh, then said very quietly, "It would be good for breakfast, too."

Sean held his breath. Her tone suggested that she was back. He touched her shoulder and she turned to lean against his chest. They stood in the kitchen embracing one another in silence. Finally, Sean guided her through the house and up to his bedroom.

They came together in the soft, warm exchange that Sean treasured.  Lee spoke his name over and over in a sound that thrilled him.  It was a great way, in Sean's opinion, to spend a summer evening.

* * *

It was the same dark landscape, the same dark terrors.  Lee was frightened.  She tried to run, to scream.  Something held her.  She struggled.  She awoke with a jolt.

"Are you having those dreams again?" asked Sean as he pulled her to him and arranged the covers to keep out the night air.  He drew her into his arms and spoke soothing words in a soft, hypnotic voice.

Tonight Sean did as he had done before - made her feel safe. Resting in his arms she thought about his kindness and attention.  He was protective, warm, and affectionate.  She was thrilled with the soft and gently persuasive reality of Sean.  Staying very still in his arms she gave lots of thought to him, to his welcoming qualities and finally to her own life-long quest to find such a man and such a relationship.

Not fully awake, she only knew that she wanted to sleep against him tonight - to feel safe.  As she moved closer, he murmured, "Having another nightmare?"  He didn't wait for an answer but held her and whispered soft protective words.  "I'll take care of you.  Nothing will hurt you."  He spread his hands across her back, slowly rubbing up and down her spine as he continued to whisper.

She couldn't speak.  He asked again, "Did something frighten you?"  She relaxed under the warm blankets, settling into his welcoming arms.  Nestling into him, she raised her lips and kissed him.  "Are you okay?" he asked.  She kissed him again.  He understood her need.

Waking the next morning Sean found himself alone in his bed.  He walked down to the kitchen.  It was empty and the coffeecake still sat on the table.  He blew out his breath, realizing that nothing had changed. Lee was still two different women.

# CHAPTER FOUR

Beth Seymour was walking on air. Six weeks ago she had completed her flight training. A month ago she did her solo. She had taken advantage of the maximum training level the program offered and was licensed to help her instructor in his charter business. That was why two weeks ago Butch, the flight instructor, had offered her her first charter. This virus was making folks think a quick flight on a private plane was healthier than using a common carrier. And some enterprising person in the state had organized an online mix and match flight service, or as Butch called it, e-dating for passengers and pilots. He told her someone wanted a quick hop to Raleigh. She took the charter and told him she didn't need to be paid. So he allowed her to fly Patti Ann to a medical school orientation at East Carolina. It was a longer flight and she had stayed overnight. That delighted Butch because he was able to snag a charter from Greenville to Hickory. And the e-dating worked again when Patti Ann was ready to return home. This will be an exciting summer, thought Beth, the new attorney and newer pilot.

She was so involved with her flying lessons and new charter pilot option that she was neglecting her role as parttime CEO at her father's recycling business and was skimping on time with her law clients as well. Guilt was threatening to eclipse the excitement. She pushed the guilt down deep. What if she missed a few days at the recycling yard, or maybe a few weeks, or a month or two? She was busy - flying every minute she could while being assigned more clients in her law practice. She was bringing in a lot of business for her brother-in-law's law office. Unfortunately, she was nowhere to be found in the other business, the recycling yard. When Greg Chou pleaded for help, she had no choice but to visit the recycling office. "What is it that you can't solve?" she challenged him. "You're perfect." Greg the Perfect sat at a desk covered in paperwork, scowling.

Greg had come to River Bend a few years ago as an environmental engineer. He was at loose ends when his job evaporated after a colleague had been murdered. But fate smiled on him when he met Hank Seymour who needed Greg's environmental knowledge in the industrial waste recycling business. The young engineer scowled at Beth, again. "I'm drowning in admin stuff and we're going crazy with new clients."

"We are?" Beth, the AWOL CEO of the family recycling business, was surprised. She had replaced her father in the executive role because he wanted more time with his new wife, Dr. Rita Rutherford. As her law practice took off and she gained more opportunities to fly, Beth paid less and less attention to the recycling business.

Greg's eyes bugged out. "Don't you read all the memos I send you?"

She blushed. "I sort of scan them."

He blew out his breath. "The hospital and doctors' offices are going crazy dealing with this virus safety gear disposal. The hospital has asked us to help them manage their in-house incinerator and is offering local medical practices use of the facility." He fell back in his chair. "We would pick up old gear - sort out recyclable material from burnable." He shrugged. "It's a whole new world and job opportunity. I need help with admin. Someone here to handle this." He tossed a few papers into the air. They watched as the sheets drifted to the floor.

"I can't help, I have a day job." Her voice said she wasn't interested in paperwork either.

And I gotta fly, she thought.

"That's what I want to talk about. I need help, another person to handle this paper. Maybe create a new job? Maybe Hank could come back?" Greg stood to pick up the papers he had thrown.

"I think Dad might like coming in a day or two but nothing full time." She hoped he would be willing to give a little of his free time. After all Dr. Rita was up to her armpits in virus.

"Let's just get him here and ask him to help us design a new position." Greg was desperate as he pleaded with her. "I think this job is bigger than a day or two every few weeks."

Beth nodded. "That's an idea. We can all figure out what you do, what I do, and what a new person would do." With that plan Beth set out to find her father. As she left the recycling yard, she called his cell.

"Yeah?"

"Where are you?" she asked.

"I'm helping Bri at this vineyard. He convinced Will Zubov to buy some of the equipment I used in my gentleman farming days." Beth laughed. Hank's idea of farming had been to buy small pieces of machinery that his daughters could operate. It kept them busy, and he allowed them to organize a small farm stand during the summer and make extra spending money.

"That junk?"

"I'm in the recycling business. My junk is Bri's vineyard equipment."

"Stay there," she said, "I want to talk with you."

\* \* \*

Dusty was in the office today, door closed securely so he and Danny could take off their masks. Danny was wishing the masks were back on because Dusty was turning the air blue with his angry language. Finally, he turned to the young detective. "What are we going to do with that crazy man?" Danny shrugged. The crazy man was the old sheriff, Bergy Bergman. "He's trying to break his contract with the retirement community."

"I don't understand how that place works," said the man decades away from thinking about retirement.

Dusty glared at him because there was no one else in the office. "Bergy and Thel paid an entrance fee to get in and it was hefty but guaranteed care for the rest of their lives. If he leaves now, he loses a good portion of the money and he doesn't have any place to go. He's in a wheelchair and Thel can't care for him." Dusty gave a grim chuckle. "She refuses to leave their cottage, telling him he's on his own."

"Did you get him to listen to you?"

Dusty had spent a good part of the morning arguing with the old man. "It's hard to be scary when I have to wear a mask and the staff at the retirement center keeps an eye on germ spreading behavior." Translated that meant Dusty had to keep covered or leave. "I got him to agree to let them set up some computer chat with Janet. I promised a bigger monitor so he'll be able to see the grandkids better. That should keep him calm for a few weeks. I did tell him that even if he got out of the center, he couldn't fly to Japan and visit. They wouldn't let him in the country."

Danny laughed. "Is he declaring war on Japan?"

Dusty rubbed his forehead. "Probably. I think I'll contact Tim and make certain he understands the problem." Tim was Bergy's son-in-law. "Maybe if he sets up a twice weekly online visit on the bigger monitor, we can keep Bergy calm for the duration."

Mars and Teniquia, the working-from-home-today detectives, were on screen on Dusty's computer. Dusty had asked both of them to listen in. The calls from the retirement community asking for help to contain Bergy were happening weekly. He turned to the screen. "Any other ideas?" Two digital heads shook. Mars moved his lips. "You're on mute," growled Dusty.

"Sorry," Mars grinned out of the computer. "The kids want to go outside." They could hear his two small children singing in the background. They caught a glimpse of Trina, his wife, trying to hustle them from the kitchen, better known as Mars' home office.

To which they heard Tee's son, Moses, call out, "Hey, Brian," to Mars' son, as he crowded out his mother on the screen in her home office, formerly the playroom.

Dusty glared at the screen and the little heads disappeared leaving the laughing parents behind. "Sorry, chief."

He began to chuckle himself. "Tell the kids I'm not upset with them. Bergy is just driving me crazy."

"I think you have the right idea," said Mars. "Get in touch with Tim for a long talk. He needs to understand that we need some help."

Tee nodded. "It's unanimous. They may be thousands of miles away, but they need to weigh in."

Dusty nodded to the screen and glanced at Danny. "Thanks, I think you're all correct. Tim and Janet are going to have to give us more help." With that he began composing another email report to Tim about Bergy's latest escape attempt.

\* \* \*

After several summers working for Umberto at the bakery, Jason finally had a career path job. He was errand boy, copier, and messenger for his grandfather's law firm. Of course, he spent a good bit of time, masked, helping his grandfather manage things from his home office. Grandpa Jim was old and one of those groups susceptible to this virus. Jason understood and would do anything necessary to protect this man he loved. So today he was following Kevin's, IT consultant to almost everyone in River Bend, instructions to hook up a second monitor on Jim's hurriedly extended desk surface.

"Wires!" complained Marianna. She adjusted her mask and stood holding the extension cord. "We need more outlets."

Jason winked at her over his mask. "I brought a power strip. Old houses never have enough outlets." He pulled the strip out of his bag and tried to corral the wires. He looked over the electronics to make certain he had enough sockets. Monitors, computer, printer, speakers, six sockets, five plugs, check. Until he noticed that there was one plug left and he still needed to plug in the desk lamp, the cellphone charger, and the scanner. Which caused him to wonder if old houses had enough electricity for modern technology?

Since he wasn't clear about electricity and old houses he gave a quick call to his Uncle Carl, the general contractor. "Yo," came the un-professional response.

"Uncle Carl, this is Jason."

"Yeah, my phone told me. What do you want?"

"I'm adding some more electronics to Gramps' office at the house, and I wondered if he has enough electricity."

"You're fine," came the reply. "When I rehabbed that house for Dusty, I upgraded the wiring. It's a good thought, though. You might just amount to something someday." Click.

Dusty had bought the bungalow years ago and had his brother turn the small home into charming bachelor quarters. When Jim met Mari-anna and Dusty married Lynn, everyone agreed that switching houses was a great idea. Lynn, Dusty and Jason took over the big house in The Heights while Jim and Marianna shared the charming bungalow.

"What did he say?" Jim came into the room with another power strip.

"He said he upgraded this house when Dusty first bought it."

"Good," said Marianna, "because I want one of those big monitors and a new printer."

Jim's eyes rolled across the top of his mask. He pulled out a credit card and handed it to Jason. "Whatever she needs."

"Hmmm," came a mask-muffled sound from Marianna. "I might need a bigger desk and maybe a more comfortable chair."

Jason was grinning, but because of the mask who knew. He took the credit card and said, "If I can't get this stuff at the store, I'll order it online. But you," he turned to Marianna, "can search for your own desk and chair. I know you've figured out how to order online."

"Has she ever!" moaned Jim. "Some delivery person shows up every day with something."

Marianna blushed even behind her mask. But her eyes twinkled. "You eat all the food they deliver." She had learned how to order dinner and even grocery shop online.

Jason enjoyed these moments with his grandparents. He knew he was lucky to be the one they trusted to solve their problems. With that he picked up the folder of contracts and other work that had needed Jim's signature or review and left the house.

* * *

Arriving in The Heights Beth waved at Lynn who was directing some young men and Emily Jacobs' grandchildren in a gardening project. She marveled that the definition of working from home allowed a lot of flexibility. Here she was, a working-from-home attorney, chasing her father in a vineyard. There was Lynn managing the Philanthropies and also getting her gardening done. Was this multi-tasking?

As she climbed from her car Emily Jacobs' kids ran over to greet her. Several months ago, she had represented them in a child protective hearing and succeeded in dissolving their stepfather's guardianship. Because he had attempted to murder them, he lost some credibility with the courts. "I'm looking for my father," she explained to the kids. They looked puzzled. "Hank."

They understood. Cody said, "Hank's with Bryce. I can drive you there." He pointed at the repurposed golfcart, now vineyard transport. Smiling at her young clients, she followed Cody and took her seat in the contraption. His skill was still a little choppy, but she had nerves of steel now that she was a pilot.

They raced across the property and into the vineyard where Hank and a fellow Beth didn't know were gesturing to one another in some deep discussion. The younger man must be this Bryce that Cody had mentioned. Beth squinted. He was a handsome guy, slim, average height, blond. Cody slowed and allowed her to scramble off the cart before he whizzed away to answer a wave from a vineyard worker across the field.

"Dad?" she called. Hank turned and waved her over.

"This is Bryce, Piper's son," said Hank as he introduced her. "This is my lawyer daughter, Beth."

"As opposed to the IT daughter, the CPA daughter, and the pre-med daughter?" The young man gave her a charming smile. "I'm Piper's unemployed Broadway chorus son."

Beth laughed. "Dad didn't mention that I just got my pilot's license?"

"And I'm still unemployed." He oozed charm.

Hank interrupted. "What's so important that you came out here to find me?"

She took his arm. "Greg needs some help. Business seems to be booming and he wants some office help. We thought you might come back a few days a week and help us figure out just what we need."

Hank shook his head. "That money I spent on you learning to fly is costing me a lot." Beth blushed because Hank knew she was spending more time flying than working on the family business.

"Ahem, ahem." Bryce loudly cleared his throat. They looked at him. "I haven't much skill with office work, but I have less with vineyard work. Can I apply?"

"Have you held jobs in River Bend?"

He replied, "I've worked for Will, and I've worked for my grandfather most summers." Will was Piper's husband and Bryce's stepfather.

"Why aren't you working for Will now?"

Bryce shrugged. "Will says I have food and shelter. He's trying to keep his folks employed who need those things." He thought quickly wanting to demonstrate that he had more than vineyard experience. "I have a master's in fine arts and have assistant stage managed a few Broadway and off-Broadway productions."

Beth was a skeptic. Lawyers were biologically that way. "Working in the chorus taught you how to manage a recycling business?"

"I work in theater." Bryce rocked on his heels. "A year ago Marianna got me a job interview and I've been employed on Broadway ever since." He held up his hand to stop her next question. "Before you ask. I had a regular job in the chorus. When I was not on stage, I was in production."

"What's that mean?"

"I was a gofer. I tracked down props, chased after costumes, sobered up actors." Bryce finally smiled, "I made sure the show went on." He frowned, "Until this virus made sure no show went on."

Hank grinned. "I like the keeping everyone sober part." With that remark Beth knew that Bryce had the job whatever it would turn out to be. Her father continued, "See, I solved your problem without giving up my retirement." Beth sputtered and Bryce tried to look businesslike in dirt caked cut-offs. "I'll come in and help this young fellow learn the ropes, then I can go back to retirement." He slapped Bryce on the back. "Monday morning, eight." Bryce nodded.

"That means, Dad," Beth spoke in a voice Hank knew meant he had better listen. "You and Greg and I have a few days to design this new job that Bryce has accepted." Hank hung his head. She was correct. Father and daughter went off to plan the future.

# CHAPTER FIVE

A scream came from Lynn's home office. Dusty didn't even blink. He would be screaming, too, but she did it first. The internet was out again. How can you work from home when your ISP keeps flipping you on and off? Dusty had asked that question of any number of folks. And no one had an answer. He had been paying attention to the discussions of the federal funds coming to communities, and the talk about improving broadband was a priority. It had his vote.

Lynn staggered into his office so angry she could hardly walk. "A year ago I didn't know who our ISP was. Now I want to kill him."

"Him?"

"Who but a man would interrupt my internet service while I'm shopping online?" She watched as Dusty moved his mouse and some internet site flashed onto his screen. "The internet is back?" She moved to look over his shoulder.

"No, I just made my phone my hotspot."

She stared at him with suspicion. "Hotspot?" She pulled her phone from her pocket and stared at it. "This?" She wiggled the phone at him.

"Yeah, Danny showed me how because his internet is spotty, too."

As they discussed this deep concern, Piper barreled through the front door. "My internet is out. Do you have it?" She was holding her laptop to her chest as though it were an open book. "I was in the middle of a Teams meeting with regional principals." Clutching her laptop she paced Dusty's home office ranting, "How are we supposed to work when our SPI-

"ISP."

"- ISP keeps floating in and out like the sun behind a cloud or something?"

"Dusty says we can use our phone."

"I hate to use my phone for an online meeting. I can't see anything, and no one can hear me."

"They probably just mute you," offered Dusty.

She stopped and thought about his statement. "They can mute me? I thought I could only mute me."

"You're special. I'd want to mute you." He taunted her by tapping his keyboard.

"Stop it, both of you," growled the referee. "I want to get back to that shopping site. They were having a great sale."

Dusty got up, took Lynn's phone, and motioned the women to follow him. He got to Lynn's office at the dining room table, punched the screen on her phone, punched some more and finally used the mouse to click a few things on her monitor. "There." He stood back and watched the shopping site blink on.

He walked away as he heard Piper say, "I like the blue. But get both. They're on sale!"

As the two women scanned clothing options, they were distracted by someone speaking. Piper was still clutching her laptop. Pulling it away she noticed that the household wireless network had returned and had reconnected her to the meeting because her laptop held password access to Lynn's wi-fi network, too. Piper pulled a chair up to the dining room table and rejoined the discussion, first making certain everyone understood that her PSI had disconnected her.

Lynn heard several voices echo, "ISP."

\* \* \*

The Heights had become a closed neighborhood. Everyone stayed in touch while holding the outside world at bay. Half the neighbors were retired and had dug in like Jim and Marianna. The other half were working from home. As summer progressed folks eased into a familiar routine in the long warm evenings. There were strollers and porch sitters. One calling to the other. Lynn thought the neighborhood was returning to the atmosphere she remembered as a teen. A lot of vegetable gardens had been planted in spring. And flowers burst from every yard.

It was a melancholy feeling. Happy to stay in touch but wondering if everyone was safe enough.

This evening Lynn sat on her front porch thinking about life, reviewing the changes she had witnessed on the street during her lifetime, when Abe Cohen, unmasked, stomped through her gate, climbed onto the porch, and perched on the other rocker. He looked at her, rubbed his face with a handkerchief, and sighed.

"Iced tea?" she asked. His family had owned the house next-door for decades. His mother had been one of the first virus victims.

"Got anything stronger?" He was a man closing in on sixty - short, muscular with thinning hair. In their younger years he had delighted in teasing Lynn, and she had spied on him when he dated one of the older girls in the neighborhood. Needless to say, adulthood altered their relationship.

"You know I have. What do you want?" She still owed him for the water balloon assault from several decades ago. But he was a charming man who had taken good care of his mother.

"A cold beer." He slumped in the chair as she went to fetch the brew.

Handing him the cold bottle, because she knew he didn't need a glass, she asked, "How is the house cleaning coming?" Abe's mother, Lynn's long-time neighbor, Mrs. Cohen had died in the spring from the virus. Abe was selling the house to Emily Jacobs and her three great-grandchildren. Lynn's brother-in-law Carl was doing remodeling to accommodate the new family while Abe cleaned out years of Cohen family memories.

"I didn't know she kept so much stuff." A long drink. "She kept all the school papers from me and my sister. And every trinket the grandkids ever gave her."

Lynn looked at him with sympathy. "From experience I can tell you that you should prepare yourself to find some family secrets." Years ago, Lynn had found her mother's diary about Helene's orphan origins as a survivor of bombings in Great Britain during World War II and eventual adoption by her deceased mother's American pen pal. Then Lynn had found photos and letters that indicated that as much as Jim had tried to hide his indiscretions, Helene had known that Will Zubov was Jim's son. She had befriended Will's mother and helped him in his early years, even allowing Lynn and Will to meet as children. The attachment faded when Will's mother had become ill and could no longer continue the meetings. Lynn remembered the day she and Will had discovered those secrets. Warm and sad.

"Really? You learned some stuff?"

"I did. All the secrets seemed to be squirreled away in strange places. I don't know if I was meant to find them, or they were supposed to be lost forever."

"Are you sorry you found those things out?" Abe took another long gulp. "Because I'm trying to figure out if I want to know what I found today." He rocked on the chair and stared at the street as the reason for his visit became apparent.

"Do you want to talk about it?" Lynn had to offer, but she would understand if he declined. Sometimes family secrets should stay secret.

He took a deep breath. "I think I do, that's why I came over." He sort of smirked at her. "When's the last time we had a talk?" He paused. "Never?" She nodded. "That should show you how confused I am. Here I am talking to that pesky kid from next door."

"Hey, I was a sweetheart. You were the evil one." Abe was about eight or nine years older than Lynn and always liked teasing her during their youth in The Heights.

He laughed. "Those water balloons scaring you and Piper on Halloween. You guys were so cute and so little and so ripe to terrorize." They both laughed.

"We got even. Remember when you tried to kiss some girl and we told?"

"She's my wife now. I don't know if you kids helped or not." He put aside the beer bottle and pulled some papers out of his pocket. "Enough old memories. I gotta tell someone about this and you win." Smoothing out some papers on his thigh, he began, "According to these papers, my father was a former rabbi."

He looked at Lynn for a response. She nodded and said, "I don't remember him. He was always at work when I visited your mother."

Abe continued, "It seems he met my mother who was not Jewish - maybe Catholic from her family name. I can't pronounce it, something eastern European. I have a marriage certificate from some church with a saint name." He took a last gulp from the beer bottle. "Anyway, he was drafted into the war and when he came out, he went into rabbi school. They met in Missouri when my father was sent west to serve a small Jewish community."

"I never knew you were Jewish. Your family always had Christmas decorations." She shrugged. "But I was just a child observer. I wouldn't have known anything about your religion."

"We didn't have a religion." He thought a moment. "Or we had two. We were raised in very private religious beliefs by our parents, sort of taking some rites from each of their heritages. I'm sure you never saw us celebrate Jewish holidays, but when I was young, we did. I remember Seder and other things. But Dad got older, and we had our lives and I think their religious attachments faded. When he died Mom just had a military ceremony at his grave."

"What about family? Certainly any of your relatives would have shared holidays."

"We have no relatives."

She gasped. "How can you not?" Then she remembered her own mother who had lost all record of her birth parents during the London blitz.

Abe pressed the papers on his leg again. "I think there are relatives. Once Dad died, I think Mom tried to find folks. She left some notes. She must have sent letters to old addresses and kept the letters that were returned because that person was no longer at that address. I have no idea if there were letters that were not returned. She left a short list of names. I think they're her siblings and Dad's. He had two sisters and she had a sister and two brothers."

"Internet?"

"I typed in some of the names, but you know how the internet sucks you in and you really don't know if you're randomly picking the right name. I think I need help looking."

"Yolanda Valeri is an expert at that stuff. She volunteers at the genealogical society. She can help you look. Or teach you how. Or help you evaluate the information you find." She stood. "Want another beer?"

"Yeah."

When she returned with a beer for herself and another one for Abe she said, "Yolanda is on her way over. She was happy to get the call. This virus seems to have ended her volunteer life."

"I remember her from high school. I don't see her much in town."

As they reminisced about high school and the old days in River Bend, Yolanda arrived and waved from her car stopped out on the street. "Yolo," shouted Lynn from her front porch, "pull to the back and sit at the picnic table, our mask-free zone. We'll meet you there." She instructed Abe to make his way to the mask-free zone while she went through the kitchen where she picked up more beer. She also picked up some crackers, chips, and a random dip from the fridge.

Yolanda and Abe were seated at the table when Lynn arrived. Yolanda helped set out the snacks as she remarked, "I hope this is worth my time." Before anyone could comment, she continued, "Who am I kidding? Anything that has me face-to-face with real people is worth my time." She rolled her eyes, "Zoom? Teams? I can't focus on my computer screen without getting hives."

"Here," said Lynn diving into the soliloquy. "Have a beer." She looked around because Yolanda always brought something from the bakery.

"In the back seat." People had expectations when a bakery owner visited.

Lynn walked nonchalantly toward the car imagining all her favorite treats. And she wasn't disappointed. "Tres leches!" she squealed. Umberto made the popular Mexican cake for Pedro's dessert menu.

"Dave sent it back. A day or two old," explained Yolanda. "He said some days he sells out and some days no one wants cake." She shook her head in puzzlement of diners. "I guess doing carry-out confuses folks about dessert." She placed the cake on the table while Lynn ran into the house for plates and forks. "The bakery is about to explode. Everyone seems to want fresh bread and donuts," she confided to Abe while Lynn was gone. "We can't bake enough." She squinted. "You came by yesterday for black bread and cannoli."

"Guilty," he admitted while Lynn began slicing the cake.

Miraculously, hungry dessert fanatics appeared. Dusty was at her elbow holding a plate, Will close behind. Emily Jacobs' great-grandchildren were closing in as the eldest, Meg, held up her phone,

"Gran says save her a piece." They could see Bri Llewellyn driving the agri-cart filled with vineyard helpers.

"I'll get Gran," called Cody as he jumped in the cart as the vineyard workers, better known as Piper's sons and assorted friends, fell out.

Yolanda scanned the crowd and sent out a quick text. Before the cake had disappeared, leaving unsatisfied fans, Danny drove up in his car, followed by Mars and Lonzo, Tee's husband. The men had been out entertaining their children, giving moms a break. Dads and children piled out of the cars. Another bakery sized cake, random cookies and paper plates appeared. Piper's sons ran into the house for an assortment of drinks, both adult and child beverages.

Lynn and Yolanda dragged Abe back to some privacy on the front porch. "So why did you call?" And Yolanda answered her own question, "It wasn't for the tres leches."

Lynn flipped her hand at Abe, and he handed Yolo his notes. "Abe found some information about his parents' families and was wondering how to track down and verify the information."

Yolanda read the information and raised a questioning eyebrow at the man. "Are you sure you want to learn all this information? The notes suggest some family secrets and hurt feelings and grudges."

"My parents are both dead," he said, "I haven't a grudge against anyone, but this is like the tip of the iceberg. They have a story I never knew. I'd like to respect and learn their history."

"Meet me at the genealogical office in the morning. We have access to services we pay for." She squinted at him. "You can give us a donation tomorrow, too. Bring a mask."

"Done."

As her two friends made plans for tomorrow, Lynn heard laughter and giggles coming from the mask-free zone. Time to investigate, she thought as she also wondered if there was any cake left.

* * *

"I don't understand it, Mom," Jason observed from his spot in the mask-free zone. "Gramps is very concerned about getting the virus and Mrs. Jacobs ignores all the warnings." He shrugged in confusion as he watched Emily Jacobs gather her great-grandchildren after their evening dessert frenzy in Lynn's backyard.

Lynn gave his observation serious thought before she answered. "It's the difference in their life situations."

He looked more confused. "They're both old."

"Emily is years older than Dad," said Lynn. "She just got guardianship of her great-grandchildren and she wants to enjoy every minute with them. She knows she hasn't many years left. She's made arrangements for Doug and Connie to take the children at her death. She sees every day as a gift. She's told me that she is so happy, the virus could grab her and squeeze out her life and she'd go with a smile."

Jason caught sight of Cody giving Emily Jacobs a ride in the agri-cart. He laughed. "She sure enjoys life. But Gramps has cut himself off from living."

That was a harder question for Lynn to explain. She also was concerned that Jim and Marianna had withdrawn from the family. "I think Dad is more concerned that he's not ready to leave us. He was very shaken by Robert's death." Jim's long time law partner had succumbed to the virus in the initial days of health warnings from the government.

Jason nodded. "Mr. O'Hara seemed to die before we even knew the risk. I guess I can sort of see what worries Gramps."

"I'm happy that you see him so often."

"I think he and Marianna take advantage of electronic media." He chuckled. "They always have questions that aren't related to law office work, like how to use an electronic coupon when they shop."

Lynn laughed. "I guess they're like the rest of us, shop, check in with friends, and maybe get some work done. We do it all from the same computer."

Jason looked at her and she saw the young man he was becoming. "I'm glad Gramps is cautious. I'm not ready to lose him." He seemed to gather his thoughts. "I'm glad you had us move here when Dad died. If we were quarantined without our family, it would be miserable." They heard Emily and the children whoop and laugh. He smiled. "And I'm glad we can help Mrs. Jacobs enjoy those kids."

Emily brought the children over to say good night. "Lynn, dear," she chirped, "we had another delightful time. I wish Carl would finish the remodeling so we can be here full time." Emily and the three children seemed to come by every day to check on Carl's progress then return to her house in the country.

"Thank you, Miss Lynn," echoed the children. The oldest youngster, Meg, helped Emily to the car, as the other two waved and climbed into the backseat.

"She even drives," marveled Jason.

"She told me she only drives from her place to my place. Juan drives her shopping and other things." Lynn watched the car disappear. "It won't be too long before the remodel is finished." She tousled Jason's hair. "Then you'll have those kids back here full time, following you around."

He moaned.

* * *

Sean waited weeks to hear from Lee after her surprise coffeecake visit. She never returned his calls, nor stopped by again. One evening he drove out to her trailer which was nestled at the edge of a field on her brother's farm.

He could see her inside, bundled on her small couch watching TV. He knocked at the door. When she answered, he said, "I'm returning your plate." He walked past her into her tiny kitchen and put down the plate, then he sat on the couch. All this time Lee remained at the door.

"What movie is this?" he asked.

"*The African Queen.*"

"You have cable out here?"

"No, I borrowed the movie from the library." She sat beside him because she had no other seat in her living room.

Sean picked up the remote. "I guess I could pause this, and you wouldn't miss anything?"

"I guess."

He pointed the remote at the TV and turned everything off. "I'll turn it back on when we finish."

"Finish what?"

He took her hand and moved closer to brush his lips along her cheek. She shivered and pressed into him.

\* \* \*

Lynn sighed heavily into Dusty's shoulder as they settled in for the night. "Wow!" he said, "that sounded like a deflating balloon."

"That's how I feel," moaned Lynn. "Where is all this going? Piper says we'll be so different when this is over that normal will be unnormal."

"Huh?"

"You know, we used to shake hands. Will we do that in the future? We used to hug."

"I still hug you." He pulled her closer and nibbled at her ear.

"But what about everyone else?"

"You want me to hug everyone else? What if that gives me a virus and I give it to you and you die or I die or something?"

She pulled away and asked, "Are you giving me germs from some criminal you arrested?"

"No, I spray them down before I arrest them," he replied, reaching for her again.

"What do you spray them with? I don't smell anything." He heard her sniff loudly.

He sighed and reached out to stroke her hair. "This is getting to you, isn't it?"

"Do you think I'm going crazy? Dad and Marianna have really isolated themselves and every time I see someone without a mask I panic that germs are just waiting for me." She let herself be drawn into his arms. "Then I see Emily, who's not a bit worried about getting sick. And Nathan worrying about giving a virus to Buck's children. And Yolanda mad that she can't go to South Africa to see her friends and help their orphanage." She kissed his cheek. "So, am I crazy?"

Dusty was quiet for a while as he traced circles on her back. Finally he said, "I think you're cautious. You respect the virus, but you aren't giving in to panic. In fact, I think you set the standard for our friends and family when you declared the mask-free zone."

"I did?"

"Yes, you let everyone know that caution was important but so was staying in each other's lives." He gave her a kiss that promised the talking was almost over. "I think that you allow us all to remember what normal is, while reminding us that we should respect healthy practices."

"I do all that?"

"And you do it without thinking."

She pinched his arm. "Are you saying I'm dumb?"

"No," he pulled her close, yet again, "I'm saying that you are a natural at keeping us all calm and connected, but safe."

"That's better."

"No, this is better," he whispered in her ear.

And it was.

# CHAPTER SIX

Sean woke up in Lee's small bedroom in her little trailer - alone. She did it again, he thought. Then he heard a noise. Jumping from the bed and finding his jeans, he tiptoed out to the kitchen anticipating coffee and maybe another fresh coffeecake. Instead, her brother was standing in the doorway.

"I'll be damned," said Jasper. "What are you doing here?"

"None of your business," Sean replied to his old high school friend.

"Where's my sister?" Jasper stared at the barefoot and bare-chested man in his sister's trailer.

"None of your business."

"She's my sister."

"She's been your sister for over fifty years. I think she's old enough to look out for herself."

"What have you two been up to?" Jasper raised his eyebrows. Sean blushed. "But you're an old man," sputtered Lee's brother.

"No older than you," Sean reminded his old high school chum.

"I'll be damned," said Jasper, then he left the trailer.

* * *

It was the beginning of another week. Last week they had celebrated a quiet Fourth of July. Summer was happening, masked or not. Lynn stared at her computer. She had just sent out e-mail to her board members with an invitation to join the virtual meeting in a few days. She marveled at how everyone seemed to adapt. And they were sharing stories with her about family online gatherings. One board member was in raptures over getting to see a grandchild only a few days after birth. "He is so cute," she had bragged to Lynn. "My daughter even got my mother to join the Zoom gathering. We all decided to Zoom once a month."

Lynn smiled to herself. She was hearing that more and more. Although folks had started Zoom and Teams as a way to meet for work, the apps allowed for more informal meetings such as family gatherings, reunions, weddings. People were adapting, life was conspiring against disease.

She also had heard folks were talking with their docs via a concept called tele-health. How did you take a pulse, or check reflexes online? At least using this method docs made certain patients were still alive - unless it was a delayed broadcast! Lynn pulled herself together. She was certain she was on the brink of a 'crazy as a loon' diagnosis - live or via Zoom. Her mind continued to wander, thinking about changes in daily life - there was Bev, her hairdresser. Her salons and spas had taken a financial hit during lockdown. You couldn't tele-a-perm!

Just thinking of Bev and she popped up in FaceTime. "I saw you at that Teams meeting," said Bev, the hairdresser/county commissioner and owner of Bev's Spas. "Your hair looks terrible."

"I thought you would be busy with the baby."

"His hair is cute and curly." Bev's son, Dave, and his wife had recently presented Bev with her first grandchild. Dave's carryout, Uncle Chicken, had been running a celebratory special, the Baby Bundle - two jalapeño chicken wraps with crispy fried onions. The new grandmother squinted out of Lynn's monitor. "I heard you have a mask-free zone. I'll be there at two with my scissors." The screen went blank. Bev always said Lynn's hair reflected on her hairdressing skills. Lynn was humbled or insulted, she wasn't certain which. But she couldn't argue. Pandemic or not Lynn's hair had a mind of its own.

A text message popped up from Bev. *Wash your hair at 1:50.* When Bev made a house call, she didn't waste time.

Lynn took another sip of coffee and planned her day around her hair appointment. That was normal, sort of.

\* \* \*

Sheriff Dunwoody and his minions looked over the unexpected job application. "Boys," he rasped, "I like this guy Fiore. He's clean cut and has that new wife. He'll be an asset in Verona for my next election since he's a local."

"Which job?" asked a minion.

"I think we should put him in the community PR position. If folks like him, it'll be good for my campaign in two years."

"Do you know him well? Will he work with us?"

A sheriff could hire and fire at-will in North Carolina. Sheriff Dunwoody wanted to hire people for his inner circle who would be an asset during an election and hopefully do a passable job in between elections. He had well-trained staff like that asshole Dusty Reid to do the real work. It was just a matter of getting the most votes during an election and keeping Reid and his team in place to do the hard work.

The sheriff nodded. "I never heard that he caused any trouble at the Highway Patrol. His wife's aunt is that rich lady. He's just looking for work until she dies and leaves him all her wealth. He'll keep out of our way, take the heat as my PR guy when things go wrong, and be an asset for votes 'cause he's local. He'll go along." Practical politics led the sheriff to accept Doug Fiore as a new hire.

\* \* \*

Piper walked into Lynn's home office munching on a pastry she had found in the kitchen. "I'm having my end of summer party," she announced. She looked at the food in her hand. "Have Yolo and Abe been meeting here again?"

"What?" Lynn had been deep in thought. She watched Piper lick her fingers. "Yolo brought the day-old stuff as thanks because Abe gave the genealogical society a nice donation." She seemed to rewind a mental tape of Piper's comments. "Your summer party? But we can't," sputtered Lynn. She waved her arm. "Gatherings, masks." She ran out of nouns.

"It will just be family and our bridal party. I didn't have it last year. Maybe next year it will be back to normal. But this year, I'll keep it small. Just twenty or thirty of us in your backyard."

"My backyard?"

Piper gave her friend a disgusted look. "Of course your yard. No one will arrest Dusty for violating any group assembly in your yard." Piper glanced out the window. "Besides, with all the trees and shrubs, no one will notice."

"Piper, you're being silly. People will understand why you aren't doing a big gathering this year."

Piper looked belligerent. "It's a themed party. My anniversary!"

"Right, your anniversary and school starting, kids going off to college."

Piper sort of wore a puzzled, surprised, happy smile. "No, just my anniversary! Will and I went through some tough spots last year." Will had had business problems and Piper had thought he was having an affair. "I want to celebrate that we came out stronger."

Lynn's eyes misted. "It was bad. I was torn between the two of you." Then she scowled. "And Dusty knew but never said anything."

"The bastard!" Piper always enjoyed finding fault with Dusty, except when he was helping her look after people she cared about, like her students. In the pandemic he and the other detectives were keeping a close eye on students Piper thought might need services or protection during this isolation.

"Okay, I understand your reasoning," admitted Lynn, "but a party?"

"We have to celebrate," stated Piper, sounding like she was making foreign policy decisions. "We need to stay positive and keep up family life and connections, especially now."

"I can't argue with that." Lynn was thoughtful. "How big?"

Piper began to enumerate. "My family, or as we're known - the bridal couple and sons. Miguel and Justine. He was Will's best man. His family of course." Lynn was making notes on a small pad. "You and Dusty. And since this includes our kids, I guess a few of their friends may show up." She looked at the list. "Don't include Doyle or Lori. They're both working in Raleigh."

"What about our parents?"

"My parents will come. They're here almost every day." She considered sharing some information. "We've been talking about them just moving in here. Will met with Carl about that plan we had for turning the garage into a suite of rooms for them. I think this is the time. They said they feel alone at their house, and like the activity at our place."

"I thought it would be difficult to get them to move," said Lynn. "I remember when you brought them into town from the farm."

"This is different." Piper nodded. "This virus has them changing their thinking."

"I guess that's a good thing."

"But Carl is busy. He said he can at least start because he has a crew here working on Emily's place." Piper shook her head, causing her blond curls to dance. "My parents will be here. What about Jim and Marianna?"

Lynn shrugged. "I don't know. We text and Zoom, but Dad seems committed to quarantine. He was frightened by Robert O'Hara's death."

"We'll just zoom them for the party and Jason can deliver some food."

Lynn checked her list. "We'll only have about twenty people." Then she smiled. "Of course, with junk food, we can expect Emily and her grandchildren to drop in."

Emily Jacobs was earning a reputation as a real junk food addict. As she said often, "At my age, it isn't junk food that'll kill me."

They laughed at the memory and began planning Piper's anniversary party.

\* \* \*

Lynn looked at her email. An online meeting invitation. The notice was from her brother-in-law, Tim Powers. She squinted, was it Zoom or was it Teams? It didn't make any difference, her computer dealt with both. She couldn't decide if she looked fatter on Zoom or Teams. But a digital visit from Tim was always welcome.

After Lynn and Jason moved to River Bend, Tim had been a frequent visitor because he and Lynn had agreed to place his father in a local nursing home in his declining years to better manage his health and have family close by. They had agreed that Tim's Navy assignments made care for his father difficult but sharing the responsibility with Lynn made it an easier task. For those few years that Mr. Powers lived in River Bend, Tim, Jason, and Lynn developed a caring bond.

On one of his visits during those years, Tim had come to town a bachelor and left with a wife. He had married Janet Bergman, the local IT genius and daughter of the retired sheriff. Janet needed Tim to help her manage life. She knew technology, but she sometimes forgot to look when crossing the street or forgot to sleep when involved with a challenging technical problem. She was a consultant to the military, helping them with very secret work. They had been delighted that she married Tim and they were able to place her in government housing at secure locations as Tim served his time in the Navy. At the beginning of their marriage, they had agreed to become guardians for Polly Carmichael. Polly's mother, Susan, a county commissioner, had been murdered leaving Polly orphaned. Janet and Susan had been fast friends and Tim was happy to accept the young teen into his married life. Polly was delighted to leave River Bend and its bad memories to join Tim and Janet in their naval assignment in Japan.

Lynn looked at the time. Dusty pulled a chair up beside her at the dining room table which was now Lynn's office desk. "Almost time," he said. "Why do you think Tim wants to talk live?" She shrugged as she clicked on the 'join meeting' button.

Tim and Janet came into view. "Sorry to have to keep you up so late. It's the time difference here," Tim explained, "And I wanted Janet to be able to join us." He gave a teasing look toward his wife. She grimaced. "She has a hard time juggling babies and national security." Janet had had baby number two while in Japan.

Dusty and Lynn smiled into the computer. Janet said, "I hope everyone is okay there."

"We're fine," replied Dusty. "I hope we're here to talk about Bergy."

Tim grinned. "There's no fooling a detective." He exchanged a look with Janet. "Is Bergy really that bad?"

"Yes." Dusty had been called out several times during this lockdown to calm the old sheriff or yell at him or threaten him. Nothing seemed to work. The man wanted out of the retirement community.

"We've called with a solution," said Tim.

"You want us to mail him to you?" Dusty was desperate.

"Almost. How about if we come home?" Tim grinned at them from the monitor.

Lynn squealed, "Really? When? Does Sara know?" Sara Margolin was Janet's partner in the consulting company. Janet worked military and Sara worked regular clients.

"We're talking to you first," said Tim. "I want you to tell Bergy that we will only come home if he promises to behave. I'll make certain he sees his grand-babies. We can visit along the fence at the greenway, can't we?"

Dusty nodded. "I think everyone would be happy with that if it keeps him contained."

"What about your career?" asked Lynn. She wasn't certain about Tim's years in service.

Tim looked at Janet again. "I'm coming up on twenty years, and Janet's business, both military and civilian, has grown with this lockdown stuff. Sara needs us home to help with clients. Bergy needs us home, and I think we need to be home."

"What about Polly?"

Janet shrugged as Tim said, "She says she wants to go to a small college away from River Bend. She has been refining her drawing skills here, working with local artists and graphic novelists. She's really good. She isn't interested in returning to River Bend to carry on her life."

"She won't come home with you?" asked Lynn.

"She says since everyone is in lockdown, she can ignore everyone." Tim shrugged. "She'll survive. This has been good for her. But she does have to attend a college with a fine arts program that can help her grow her skills."

Lynn thought about the sad little girl. Polly's orphan future had challenged everyone until Janet and Tim took her into their family which now included two toddlers. The young woman was a very talented artist who consoled herself by drawing sketches of her mother when she needed guidance. Lynn kept a special card Polly had designed to thank Lynn for creating Susan's garden on the cul de sac near Lynn's driveway entry. Lynn had replanted many of Susan's perennials promising she would save them until Polly had a garden of her own. Polly's card showed the garden with an angelic Susan watching over the plants and life in The Heights.

All the faces on the computer monitor grinned. "I think that's a great proposal," said Dusty. "I think Bergy just needs to know that seeing you all in person will soon be a reality."

The call ended with Tim's promise to keep everyone informed and to move as quickly as pandemically possible.

# CHAPTER SEVEN

Lynn's mask-free zone was very popular in the neighborhood. Abe and Yolanda had met there today for an early morning information exchange. They had been eager to bring Lynn up to date on the ancestor search. They had found some good leads and would keep her in the loop.

One guest who seemed to materialize every few days was Emily Jacobs. Dusty's brother Carl was remodeling Abe's old house for Emily and her great-grandchildren. They were currently living in Emily's secluded country house, but Emily and the kids found lockdown and seclusion didn't work for them. The bustle of Lynn's mask-free zone and Will's vineyards were frequent options when country living felt isolated.

"Emily," called Lynn from the kitchen porch as the older woman settled at the picnic table. "Can I bring you something?"

"Coffee and surprise me."

Lynn brought out the coffee and a small dish with a few chocolate covered pretzel bites. It was somewhere between breakfast and lunch. Lynn knew that Lucia, Emily's housekeeper, had already fed Emily and the children a five-star breakfast. Emily liked Lynn's place for the available junk food.

Lynn sat across the table with her own coffee. Working from home meant a lot of breaks. Of course, Emily was a generous donor to the Philanthropies, so maybe coffee with Emily could be considered work. Hmm. Too early in the day to splice that thinking. She'd have to have another bedtime conversation with Dusty. He seemed to help her work out these crazy days. "How's the house coming?"

"Carl says we can move in any time if we don't mind the noise and interruptions." She nibbled a pretzel bite. "And it seems we haven't much choice." Emily hung her head. "When I bought the Cohen place, I put my house on the market. I didn't realize the market was so hot. Inventory is flying off the shelves." She stopped to think. "Houses can't fly off the shelf, but my realtor says even at my listed price buyers are plentiful. I got an offer yesterday. And they want us out in two weeks. I counter offered," she nodded, "just waiting for their response." She looked over her shoulder, checking for real estate spies, Lynn supposed. "I think I'll hear soon, but I think they will be firm on two weeks."

"Wow," Lynn laughed, "they really must be in a hurry."

Emily shook her head. "They're coming from a big city and will be working from home. They want us out so they can get the house ready with all their technology so they don't miss a day's work."

Emily took the last pretzel. "My bedroom suite is almost finished. I haven't told Carl about the offer." Lynn raised an eyebrow waiting for her to continue. And Emily obliged. "He'll probably be upset when I tell him he only has two weeks." She chuckled. "He's had some delay working on the master suite upstairs. That's where Lucia will stay until the garage is finished." A sip of coffee. "You know, of course, that Lucia and her son will be living in the rooms over the garage? It's got a bathroom and air conditioning. Lucia says they can wait for the other work to be finished once we finish the house."

Lynn laughed. "You must have a good idea of what living with those kids is going to be like. You've all been together for months now."

Emily used a conspiratorial whisper. "You won't believe all the potions all three of them seem to need for hair and skin and" she giggled, "under arms. I see them as perfection, and they see themselves in need of assistance." They sat quietly and listened to the activity of the neighborhood. The grandkids could be heard shouting, the agri-cart revving, Bri Llewellyn swearing and a few dogs barking. The old woman smiled. "Having them so close has added years to my life."

"Just keep that virus at bay, Emily. Take care of yourself," Lynn cautioned.

"I intend to," she replied. "But things are all in place if something happens. Doug and Connie have signed the papers in anticipation of guardianship. You and Penny and Babs are officially the trust board. I'll just enjoy whatever time I have with them." She thought more.

"Doug and Connie could move into this house if need be. They could take the master suite upstairs and the kids could spread out in the other three bedrooms. Did I tell you how much fun we all had at Hilton Head?"

After the trauma of the last months when Emily's grandson-in-law tried to orchestrate her murder to be followed by the children's murder, Emily had taken steps to ensure that the children would be cared for and she could enjoy them for as many years as she had left. She was happy with the plans and thought that removing those concerns also added to her remaining years. She was happy that Jim Hoefler had insisted that she get the future in order. He had been correct.

"I hope I hear from my realtor soon," Emily said as she stared at the empty pretzel plate. "I have to get Carl moving."

* * *

Bryce had finished his first week as the recycling business administrator. He, Greg, and Beth were slouching in his office. "Man, I feel great. Who knew there was so much drama in trash?"

"Recycling," Beth and Greg said together.

"Yeah, recycling." Bryce grinned. "I enjoyed this week. No one asked me to dig a hole or weed around the vines."

"I'm just glad you're here." Greg stood. "Just be back next week. I gotta run." He tossed keys to Bryce. "Lock up."

"Where's he going?" Bryce watched his new boss jump into a pickup and speed from the recycling yard.

Beth smiled. "He's got a girl. Kew -

"At the Chinese carryout?"

"She's a physics professor at the community college but helps at the family carryout. Greg helps, too, trying to impress her father."

"Isn't Mr. Lee happy his daughter is interested in another Chinese guy?"

"It's not that easy."

"It never is." He had a thoughtful frown on his face.

"Mr. Lee is very traditional, and Greg's parents are affluent west coast Chinese. They're both very well-known and respected physicians."

Beth leaned back in her chair. She was finally relaxing, certain that Bryce could handle the job.

"That's a long way from making dumplings."

"They'll work through it."

"What about you? Any guy?" Bryce looked relaxed in his khakis and company shirt - *Seymour's Industrial Recycling*.

"No time." She felt comfortable with this young man and felt pulled to explain herself. "When I came back to town I was fat. I entered therapy and I attend a bi-monthly support group for sexual assault survivors. I've been building my practice and I've lost a hundred pounds and got my pilot's license. No time for a man."

"Wow!" He sat up. "You sound like a dynamo."

She shrugged then asked him the same question he had asked of her. "What about you? Anyone?"

He became guarded. "I'm not an appealing package. No job until this week. I've been tied up with grape vines, and now I'm into trash."

"Recycling." Beth stared at him. "Why did you leave River Bend?"

"I wanted opportunities that aren't here." He toyed with a pen on his desk.

"I think you're brave to strike out on your own. I wish I could leave. My father gave me a business to run. My brother-in-law gave me a job in his law practice." She looked at him. "I don't belong here."

"You handled it all, right?"

"Yes. I've done quite well. I just feel empty." She was silent as she wrestled with that admission.

Bryce asked, "Do you want to go for a ride?" He wasn't interested in going home to another Friday night hanging at the edge of the social life in Lynn's backyard.

"Why not." Beth sounded as though she had no better Friday option either.

They locked up the office, secured the gates to the yard and drove off. "How'd you lose a hundred pounds?" he asked.

"I quit eating and exercised. I ran a five K earlier this summer."

"I have a friend who carries a lot of extra weight. I think he's depressed."

"That's a factor. That's why I was in therapy and currently attend the support group. My stepmother, Dr. Rita, figured me out and got my health and mind organized. The hard part was sharing it all with my dad and sisters."

Bryce drove into river park and stopped the car. "Sharing things with your family is hard." She opened her mouth to ask what he wanted to share, but he spoke first. "Let's go for a walk. This is one of the things I miss. You don't hang out in parks late at night where I live." He surveyed the welcoming park draped in setting sun creating the long shadows of a summer evening.

"Do you plan on returning to New York?" asked Beth as they walked toward the river's edge.

"I don't know. I was in a new relationship. I had some friends, but I wasn't at home there any more than here." They sat on a bench. "I've learned that I'd like to be a theater manager one day. You know, like manage The Met, maybe start with a performing arts center in a middle-sized town, or regional center." They watched sunny ripples float on the water as the fishermen glided through the current for late night angling. "I've never told anyone that before. Does it sound stupid?"

"I don't know. I don't know anything about the entertainment industry. But it sounds exciting. Learning recycling administration should help. People have to try out a lot of opportunities before they find what fits."

"I know what you mean.

"So far, I only know what doesn't fit, and that's River Bend."

It's too bad because life here seems so safe and storybook, even in a pandemic." He smiled into the setting sun.

"My mother was murdered a few years ago. Some crazy woman attacked and tried to kill my brother-in-law. I was molested when I was a child. What kind of storybooks do you read?"

"Is that why you want to leave River Bend? Bad memories?"

"I don't know if I want to leave or if I want to make it into what fits me."

"That doesn't make any sense," offered Bryce.

"I know. Becoming a pilot has changed my horizon."

He laughed. "Come on, Ms. Pilot, let's see what's happening in The Heights." Two young people in the pandemic were building a new friendship. Maybe The Heights won't be so bad on a Friday night if you have a friend, thought Bryce.

* * *

"You're really planning a party during this pandemic?" Will asked his sister as they lounged in the mask-free zone.

"That's what your wife says," replied Lynn. Piper winked at Lynn. Marriage to Will had been a great idea for everyone involved, especially the bride and groom.

"Yes." Piper placed a bottled of wine on the table. "Marriage is something to celebrate. Look at us. We all haven't been married very long. You'd think that at our age we would all be celebrating silver anniversaries," observed Piper.

"Speak for yourself," Dusty opined from the lounger. "There's no silver in my hair."

"So what's your point?" asked Will bringing the cooler from the porch.

"I don't know. Marriage isn't what I thought, I guess. Remember when we got married the first time?" she asked Lynn. "Didn't we think it would be forever?"

"I'm planning on this marriage being forever," said Dusty as he walked over to the table to join the discussion and find some food and drink.

"I wasn't talking to you," said Piper. She handed him a beer.

"No matter how hard you try to get rid of me, I'm staying." He tousled the curls on the top of Piper's head. She brushed his hand away.

"I'm not trying to get rid of you. But Lynn and I both thought our first marriages would be forever." She looked at Dusty waiting for a response.

"I'm not going anywhere, so it'll have to be Lynn." He found a stray cookie under a napkin.

"I think what Piper's saying is that at this time in our lives we didn't think we would be on our second husbands." Lynn poured some wine for Piper and herself.

Will had been listening to the discussion. "We're having an anniversary party because you're surprised we're still married?"

"Our wives have started planning for their next husbands." Dusty looked around for more food.

"How?" asked Will, "Taking applications? Working on the internet? Stalking guys who look interesting?" He found a beer in the cooler.

"You're missing the point of this discussion," frowned Piper as she filled her glass with more wine. "We're just having a philosophical talk about our marital status and how it's different than our expectations were twenty-five years ago."

"Twenty-five years ago?" asked Will.

"Last June would have been my twenty-fifth anniversary," mused Piper.

"Are you regretting things?" Will waited for her answer, holding his beer midway to his mouth.

"No, I'm marveling at how different life turned out." She took Will's hand. "How much better it turned out."

* * *

"What did Jasper say to you?" Sean asked. It was dusk. He found Lee in the park near his home, almost like she had been waiting for him, at a spot they had enjoyed last summer.

"He's distracted by your, our, implied sexual activity." She pushed some cookies toward Sean along the battered picnic table surface.

"What do you mean implied?" He ignored the cookies and held her hand.

"I'm not admitting a thing. But his wife has indicated that something has inspired Jasper to think that acting his age includes renewing their sex life." Lee grinned. "All these years and that's the first time I ever heard them admit to having sex."

"How many kids do they have?" He gave in to the cookies.

"Four, and seven grandchildren." They both laughed.

"Are you thirsty? You can come up to the house and I'll make us some tea." He took her hand again. "We could talk."

Within minutes of entering his house, Sean had her in his arms. When he caught his breath, he said, "You have to stop this disappearing. If I go to bed with you at night, I want to wake up with you beside me in the morning." He didn't give her a chance to speak but kissed her and tugged at her clothing. Pulling her upstairs, they tumbled into the first open doorway.

"I thought it was just me," she whispered.

"Just you what?" He undressed and began helping her out of her jeans.

"The one who was loving."

Sean held her tight as they stretched out in his guest room bed. "You don't think I love you? You think, what, I just use you, take advantage of your offer of sex because I'm lonely, or shallow, or a louse?"

She turned away from him as he moved to bury his face in her hair. "I don't know. You never said anything," she whispered.

"You never said anything," countered Sean. "You let me enjoy you, then the next morning you're angry and silent. Sometimes you just disappear."

"No, I don't."

"Let me tell you." And he chronicled all their times together, and Lee's behavior afterward.

"But you never said anything."

"Did I have to? Couldn't you tell how I felt?"

"I didn't trust you," she admitted. "I need to hear words, because I know it's possible to have sex without love."

Sean turned her so he could see her face. Almost sixty years old and his inexperience with women was going to ruin everything. He hugged her until he thought she would break, then he said, "I don't know how to say things that women want to hear. I never found anyone before that I wanted to say anything to."

Lee rolled onto her back and stared at the ceiling. "I love you, Sean. When I'm with you I have no nightmares. When we're apart, you come into my dreams and keep me safe." Several months ago Lee had confided in Sean her history of survival as a victim of a gang rape many years ago. The nightmares were a legacy of that time. Several times in their relationship Sean had cuddled her at night chasing away the horrifying dreams.

"Isn't that love? I protect you wherever you are."

"Do you feel that it's love?  You have to let me know how you feel."

Sean placed his lips to her ear, "I love you, Lee.  Will you marry me?"

# CHAPTER EIGHT

By morning Lee had disappeared. Sean was furious. Last night she had never answered his proposal but was still her usual loving nighttime Lee. Again it was morning, and again he was alone. Dressing quickly, he raced out to her trailer. She wasn't home. He drove to her brother's place but didn't see her car at the farm. He returned to town and drove by the Rape Crisis Center. No car. He continued on to the hospice care facility. No car.

He returned home in a foul mood. And there was Lee's Prius in front of his place. He raced into the house and found coffee brewing and Lee placing some pastries from the bakery on a plate.

"Where did you go?" she asked.

"I went looking for you." Sean tried to be calm. He sat down and waited for her to speak.

"You didn't hear my cell last night?" she asked as she placed pastries on the table.

He shook his head.

"I was on-call for the Crisis Center. A young woman was raped last night and brought to the ER. I got the call." She put a cup in front of him and poured some coffee. "I thought I would be home before you noticed."

Sean let out a deep sigh. "How often do you get called out like that?"

"Between assault victims and my hospice clients, probably three or four nights a month."

Lee sat at the table and took his hand. "I'm still thinking about your proposal, if you haven't changed your mind."

"What's to think about?"

55

"I want to stay involved with my volunteer work. I can't walk away from counseling assault victims," she said.

"I understand."

"Both of my volunteer commitments take an emotional toll. And I can't give them up. I don't know what that would do to a relationship."

"You don't have to give anything up. I have things I do. I work at Will's place and have coffee with Nathan and help Piper at her school."

Lee's eyes tracked over to the drawings on his refrigerator that expressed gratitude to Sean from an assortment of third graders for new playground equipment at the elementary school. She smiled at him. "Maybe we wouldn't have time for each other."

"Yes, we would. You can volunteer all day as long as you share my bed at night."

"You certainly get down to basics."

"We aren't getting any younger and I like you in my bed." The coffee pot let out a little hiss and the sun came out from behind the clouds to brighten the kitchen. "I have an idea. Why don't you just move in here for a few months and see how things work out." Sean gave her such an eager and disarming smile that she saw the boy she remembered from high school.

"What will people say, especially my brother?"

"We don't owe anyone an explanation. Let Jasper stew. He'll never come out and say anything."

Lee laughed at Sean's conclusion. "I want to keep my place."

"Why?"

"Sometimes the late-night calls leave me with so much sorrow."

"That's when you need me most. You just come back here and I'll hold you until you feel better - like when you used to have those dreams." Sean took both of her hands. "You'll see."

\* \* \*

Dusty walked into the kitchen needing a break from his computer in his home office. He was working on a routine monthly report. Not many crimes, but he noted that suicide, through drug overdose or other, sometimes messier methods, seemed to be occurring more frequently. Folks were responding in some very negative ways to this lockdown.

He glanced out the window and saw his brother, Carl, sitting alone in the mask-free zone. The popular general contractor was staring at nothing and seemed to be startled as his phone interrupted his reverie. Taking the cell from the clip at his belt, he scanned the screen and tossed the offending electronic device into Lynn's impatiens.

Oh, oh, thought Dusty as he grabbed two beers. On the porch he called out, "I got a beer. Need anything else?"

Carl looked up and scowled at his brother. "Maybe three more." He took the offered bottle and gulped. "This world is crazy."

Dusty nodded agreement and sat at the table. "What crazy thing has you going?"

"I've got more work than I can handle. It seems everyone locked down has decided to make all the improvements they've been putting off. Bathroom upgrades, kitchen rehabs, extra bedrooms, add-ons." Carl gulped the rest of his drink. Dusty took the bottle before it joined the cellphone in the impatiens.

"Can I help?"

Carl growled, "You aren't safe with a hammer, remember? That's why you chase crooks."

Dusty did remember. His construction skills were limited. "What do you need?"

"About fifty workers." He walked into the house and got three more beers. Returning, taking a long drink, he said, "If I spoke Spanish, I could at least hire some guys with basic skills."

"Illegals?"

"I don't care if they come from another planet. I need workers." He gave Dusty a threatening look. "And if I hire anyone, I don't want to see you sniffing around for papers."

"Not my job unless they murder someone." Dusty slowly sipped his drink. "Have you talked with Juan who works for Ms. Jacobs? Maybe he can help you recruit and translate."

"I thought he works for her and goes to school."

Dusty was thoughtful a moment. "He might like to earn a better salary. I think he's pretty sharp and would learn fast." He and Carl were silent, thinking about employment options. Dusty finally suggested, "I think Ms. Jacobs would encourage him to work for you. You should talk to her first. And work something out."

"That's a thought. A little negotiation." Carl smirked, "She doesn't think I'm moving fast enough to get this house ready."

"Sounds like you can scratch each other's backs."

"Hey, there's a virus going around." Carl finished his second beer in a happier mood and went to find Emily. But first he had to find his phone.

\* \* \*

Carl drove out to Emily's country home. "Just the man I want to see," she said as she answered the door.

"I saw you called," said Carl. He didn't mention that he had thrown the phone into Lynn's garden. "What do you need?"

She walked outside and led him to a bench near the garage. "My house sold. I have to move." She smacked his arm. "Soon!"

"You called to tell me that?"

"I called to tell you that you have two weeks to finish the new house."

Carl thought he heard Dusty laugh and whisper, "*Negotiate!*" He settled on one of the concrete benches. "Now, I'd like to help you out," the wily contractor began, "but I'm short of workers. I've been trying to hire some of these guys who speak Spanish, but I have a difficult time communicating. If I just had a foreman who spoke the language." He tried to look as pitiful and helpless as he could.

Emily became suspicious. She was an old elementary school teacher. She had dealt with prevaricating seven-year-olds in her day. "I wasn't born yesterday, you con artist. What do you want?"

Carl looked at the elderly, spritely, smiling woman. He grinned back. "I was thinking that your guy Juan might be able to help me. Dusty thinks he's a smart fellow."

"He's taking classes and working for me. I need his help, especially his driving."

Carl looked around the lovely gardens and saw three kids dashing through the trees. "I know you rely on his help."

"I pay good money for his help." Emily opened the bidding.

"I would, too."

"I think I might be convinced if you paid better." She dared him to see her and raise.

Carl took the hint. "Whatever you pay, I'll go three dollars an hour more to start."

"I'll need a driver if you hire him." She looked around her yard. "And gardener and someone to help pack up and move."

"You know you're going to hire professional movers. I know you and Bonita," his interior designer sister-in-law, "have been picking out things to move and things to sell."

"I still need a driver."

"I bet one of those kids that help Bri would be happy to drive for you. It's got to be easier than working the vineyard."

"But my gardens?"

"Aw, shit, Emily, you're moving. These gardens did their job. They sold the place."

She laughed. "Your mother would be unhappy if she knew you talked to me like that."

He turned red. He tried to redeem himself. "Besides, once you live in The Heights, those boys can help with your garden, too. They work for Bri and Lynn all the time. At least *you* would pay them."

She slapped his knee. "Let's see if Juan is interested."

Emily called to the young man who was cleaning out the garage, getting items ready to be moved, or sold, or in some cases just identified. There were things that had been in the garage since the day Emily's family moved in. "Juan," she motioned, "please join us."

The young man put down yet another unidentifiable 'thing' and responded to Emily's request. "*Sí?*"

"Carl has a proposal." She nodded to the contractor.

He stood and shook Juan's hand. Even though that was a no-no in these virus days, Carl thought it was important to establish his regard for the young man. "I was telling Ms. Jacobs that I'm having difficulty finding workers. Those willing to work often speak Spanish. I told her that I needed a foreman who could help me recruit and supervise a crew." Juan looked at the man, trying not to look confused. But he said nothing. Carl continued, "My brother, Dusty, thinks you're a smart fellow and that you could handle a job like I described."

Juan was shocked and his faced showed it. "I . . . ah . . . . he is kind. But I don't know building."

"I know building," said Carl, "but I don't know Spanish. We could be a team." He was thoughtful a moment. "I know you attend classes at the community college. If you're of a mind, you might think about some night classes that teach basic carpentry and electrical work or HVAC."

Juan had just completed his second semester of the healthcare curriculum. "That is not what I study."

"I know, but I told Ms. Jacobs I need help and I would pay you three dollars more an hour than she does. And I would pay for any construction related classes you take."

Juan sat on one of the other benches while Emily said, "Juan, you can put your training classes on hold for a semester or two and help Carl. That way you would save more money and pick up other skills."

"You need a driver." Juan had never had so many opportunities knock in his short life. Good fortune was a challenge.

Emily smiled at this loyal young man. "Carl suggested that I offer that job to the boys who work in the vineyards for Bri." She nodded. "I agree with Carl they would be happier working for me than working in the vineyards for Bri."

Juan grinned his agreement. Then he got serious. "I know many who want work. Some may not be legal." He challenged Carl.

"That's not an issue for me."

"And I know those that would be good and those that you should not hire."

"That's what I expect from my foreman."

"I would like to try this opportunity," said the serious young man. He held his hand out to Carl to seal the deal.

\* \* \*

Sean found Lee staring at his mother's portrait in his living room. He had found the photo in his father's things that he had claimed on his return to River Bend. When the house had been remodeled Sean had made certain that a space on his built-in shelves was the perfect fit for the portrait in its lovely frame.

"Talking to my mother?" asked Sean.

Lee continued to study the portrait. "I was looking at her earrings."

Sean pulled the photograph from the shelf. They peered at it. "She wore those earrings every day." He smiled at Lee. "She always touched them for, well, she always said she touched them as a blessing because her grandmother had given them to her." He chuckled. "She told me that her grandmother got them from a leprechaun because she did him a favor." He shrugged. "I don't know what favor." Tears gathered in his eyes. "They didn't help when she got sick."

Lee put her arms around his waist as they stared at the picture of Moira Hennessey. "I can see her love and her joy," said Lee. "I remember her. She would come to the vegetable stand when Pops ran it. She and Mom would talk. She always gave me a smile and told me my life would be long and filled with wonder." Lee stepped away from Sean as she smiled. "Mom always shook her head when your mother left. She would mutter, 'Those papists are strange folk. But kind.' I thought your mother was pretty."

"A lot of years have gone by since then," sighed Sean. He replaced the photograph on the shelf. "Why are you noticing those earrings?"

With a tiny gasp, she remembered what had caught her attention. She ran from the room. He heard her in the kitchen making a shuffling noise. She returned with a wrinkled, creased envelope in her hand. She shook something out and, as she returned to his side, she held out her hand, palm up. Resting there were earrings with entwined hearts and shamrocks - the same earrings as those Moira Hennessey wore in the photo!

"They're just like hers!" he exclaimed. "Last time I saw them was in her coffin. I think Dad buried them with her. Where did you get yours?"

"They were a gift from one of my hospice patients." Lee gave him the earrings and pulled a paper from the envelope. "Let me show you what came with this gift." She opened the letter and handed it to Sean.

*Dearest Lee,*

    *Luck and love will be yours. Your demons will be chased away. All will be as you deserve. Just be patient.*

    *Forever, Sonny*

"Sonny?" asked Sean. "I've heard Nathan speak of her. I believe he told me you helped nurse her at the end."

"I was one of her volunteer hospice nurses when she was in her last weeks."

"That's right," he said, "Nathan speaks of her often. Wait here." He disappeared into his small office. She could hear him searching through drawers and cupboards. When he returned, he was waving a DVD at her. "Just look at this." He put the disc in the player and pulled her to the sofa. He placed an arm around her and clicked the remote.

*"Hello, Mr. Hennessey,"* said the image on the screen. Sonny Bosco peered into Sean's living room. *"If you're watching this you must have returned to River Bend. We met one day as I was sitting in front of the mall. Do you remember? You picked up my walker and returned it to me."* Sonny licked her lips. *"As you can see, I'm much closer to death today than I was on that beautiful, sunny day. It's a funny story. I don't know why I had to be at the mall that day, but I was determined to get there. My young nurse, Patti Ann, was very unhappy. But she did as I asked. When I saw you come along, I knew you were my mission. I had to give you a message. That message was - come home. Maybe one of your parents used me. These last months of my life, the spiritual world keeps intruding."*

Sonny smiled. *"But you came back. Your happiness is here, Sean."* Sonny seemed to swoon, then she looked out from the screen as though she were hypnotized, *"May the Virgin Mary smile on you, Sean Michael Hennessey."* The screen went blank.

Sean and Lee looked at each other in front of the dark screen. He cleared his throat. "My mother said that very same thing to me every morning as I left for school," stated Sean. He handed the earrings to Lee.

"I keep these in my purse at all times." She removed the plain gold studs she usually wore and inserted Sonny's gift. "I wondered about the gift and why Sonny gave them to me." Lee had been mystified.

"Fate? Leprechauns?"

"What?"

"We're supposed to be together. It has been ordained by some power." He looked smug.

Lee snorted. "That sounds so papist!"

Sean laughed out loud. "Why? Because your friend Sonny seemed to know something? Communed with the angels?" He was thoughtful. "Got instructions from my mother?"

"I'm Presbyterian, Sean. We're realists." She gave him a starched look.

"So no spiritual influence? No managing deity?" He hugged her then cupped her face in his hands. He kissed her gently. "No angels or magic, Lee?" He looked over her shoulder at the portrait. "My mother sent you to me. She knew you would make me happy. She sent you for me to love." A tear traced down her cheek and he caught it with his thumb.

# CHAPTER NINE

Janic had been thinking about the last comment of his former racquetball partner. *"The rookie thinks she's on to something."* It was coming to the last month of summer, and he had heard nothing more. He was reluctant to keep badgering his contact in the Des Moines PD. Was the rookie still looking at that cold case? It had been months. He didn't want to be surprised. He had thought for days about how he could approach some of his friends on the force - just to be reassured. But he didn't have to worry. Fate came calling.

"Hello, Mr. Janic?" came a gravel voice over the phone. "This is Lt. Mel Carlson. We met about twenty years ago when I was new on the force and I interviewed you about a murder."

Janic took a breath. "Of course, Lieutenant. It's not every day a guy gets asked about a murder. Do you want to interview me again after all this time?"

"This is a courtesy call, sir. I know you have some friends here in the office, so I wanted you to know that during their training we have our rookies look over cold cases." Carlson was slow coming to the point. "A rookie is working on that case, you know, doing research and stuff when she has time. She has made a list of folks we interviewed, found out who's still alive and in the area. You may hear from her. Heh, heh. It's not like we have any new information. My boss, I think you play racquetball with him? He wanted me to give you a heads up."

"I understand, Lieutenant." Janic tried to sound casual and unconcerned. "I'm only a phone call away. And twenty years older. I don't know what I can add to the information in the file. I remember you as being very thorough."

"Thanks for that," Carlson sighed, "it was a puzzler. We finally figured it for a power play."

"Power play?"

"Yeah, someone wanted her territory, something like that."

"I understand." Janic wondered how bold he could be since Carlson already knew he had friends in high places. "Is it possible for me to review the notes from my interview?"

Carlson was quiet. Janic heard him cover the phone and mumble to someone. He returned. "Sure, I can let you have a copy of your statement. Remember, you signed it?"

"Thanks, it'll help refresh my memory."

After a few pleasant exchanges, Janic asked if Carlson wanted to step in as his racquetball partner since his boss was retiring. "No racquetball, but I do play golf," replied the officer.

"So do I," said Janic in a friendly chuckle. "I'll check back with you in a week or so."

"I'd like that," said Carlson, and they ended the call.

* * *

Janic sipped that expensive scotch he bought, because it was expensive, not because he liked it, and recalled that one month was all he had needed to step into Darla's shoes and flip her crew to his. He had taken care of Ray. Jimmy, the other guard, had been no problem, he had been getting rid of that professor that night. Janic didn't know what Jimmy did to that professor, the needy guy who had seen him in the kitchen. He had never asked. He thought about the pregnant waitress again after all this time. In the early years Janic had been concerned that the professor would show up looking for that waitress, if Jimmy had let the guy live. Janic had decided to track her and keep an eye on her and her child just in case the professor came back. A loose end, only one. Janic thought he had been pretty lucky that night. Jimmy had been, too. But old Jimmy might also be on the line for murder if that rookie kept digging. Neither of them needed someone looking for the professor.

The investigation had been an easy ride. Everyone knew he was the dumb fucker. The investigator had smothered a smirk at the interview. Janic had even fashioned an alibi. In the end no killer had been caught. No trial. No impediment to his success. Only one loose end.

Over the years, life went on. Janic watched as the waitress married some farmer and had other children. No professor came back. Janic became prosperous and mostly legit - a wealthy businessman, local political operative, and secret money launderer. He cultivated friends in law enforcement and the court system. He wanted to be in the loop if anyone ever got curious about his secret business or raised Darla's cold case. And he wanted to know if the professor was ever resurrected.

And that's how through those years of false friendships and generous political donations he learned that the waitress's daughter, also known as the professor's daughter, who was now in law enforcement, was interested in Darla's cold case. And that meant there might be more than one loose end.

\* \* \*

"You have how much money?" Lee seemed to cower in the corner of Sean's kitchen.

"Enough." Sean's face suggested he had just admitted to a murder.

"Sean, you have more money than everyone in town added together."

"I don't think it's that much. Nathan and some of his friends have plenty." Sean had initiated this discussion because his attorney and accountant had suggested a pre-nup. He and Lee were planning a small, maybe Zoom, wedding. But there were things that had to be faced. He was against any 'pre' anything. What's his would become hers!

"I don't know if I can marry that much money," said Lee as she refilled her coffee cup.

"I told them we didn't need a pre-nup."

"A pre-nup?" The question came out in sort of a puzzled affront. "You think I want to steal your money? I didn't even know you had so much."

Sean hung his head in regret, balancing his elbows on the kitchen table. "I told H. Lawrence and Michelle that you wouldn't care, but they said you should sign an agreement that looks out for your future but keeps my investments, property and estate distribution intact."

"H. Lawrence and Michelle!" This time she screamed in indignation. "Since when is our, my, private life gossip for some youngsters?"

"They're my attorney and accountant." Sean was in misery. He had very little experience dealing with women and each encounter with Lee just proved it. He took her hand and kissed it. "Lee, I love you, but I have baggage."

"Yes, millions of dollars," she laughed. "I love you, too. And I have baggage. too." She squeezed his hand. "Let me think about this."

\* \* \*

Lynn squinted at her computer screen. She was glad that Dusty had suggested a bigger monitor. Now everyone at her meetings looked bigger than a postage stamp. Of course, when there were only two others attending the meeting, like now, the participants looked like giant heads. The two giant heads nodded in greeting. "Good morning, Lynn." Beth Seymour smiled from the monitor. "Do you know my co-chair, Darlene Porterfield?"

"Of course, I do," Lynn smiled back. "It's good to see you again, Darlene." She looked at Beth's head on her monitor. "Darlene helped Shonda and her son Cooper deal with wrapping up the estate of Cooper's father."

"After he tried to murder them," Darlene pointed out. "And Mrs. Masterson shot him." As an attorney Darlene liked clarity. "Good to see you, too, Lynn."

Lynn studied the two young attorneys. Beth was continuing to lose weight, but still hadn't found her style in dress or hair. Lynn was certain she would find her fashion place with the help of her stylish sisters. Darlene, a few years older than Beth, was a very professional looking young woman with auburn hair cut in a style that needed little attention but showed off her bright, intelligent face. "Why are we meeting so early?" Lynn was still wearing her nightgown under a cotton pull over sweater. Thank goodness for online meeting apps that only showed the head!

"Darlene and I are the education committee of the county bar association," Beth informed her. Lynn rolled her eyes because the county bar association was as elusive as the county ministers' association. Beth caught Lynn's dubious eye. "There are a number of new attorneys in town, and we need to help each other learn more about the community." Lynn seemed to give her a digital smirk.

"Right," Darlene jumped in, "and we noticed that in the past the Philanthropies has always offered local attorneys a training on charity options to consider during estate planning with clients. We thought that topic would be helpful and lend itself to an online presentation."

Lynn grinned. "What a great idea! In the past we've organized breakfast meetings and lunch meetings and dinner meetings, but the attendance was never what we would have liked. Even with free food. I can put together something, maybe even have Penny, the Philanthropies board chair speak if you like." Penny Rawlings was another attorney in town.

"Just keep it brief," advised Beth. "This crowd is still trying to make a living."

"So also keep it simple?" Lynn teased.

"Well, that, too," agreed Darlene. "Remember these are young attorneys. Some of them need your information to advise their clients. They just don't know it yet."

Lynn began to worry about the current crop of new lawyers and then panicked when she realized that her son would be one in a few more years. "I'll do my best. Just give me the time and date. You'll send out the notices?"

Beth nodded. "We have a time to suggest." And they got down to organizing the presentation.

* * *

The sheriff barged into the unit's office. Dusty and Danny raised their masks - a common reflex these days. Dunwoody was followed by his minions and by a new masked face. "I want to introduce my new community liaison," barked the sheriff. "This here is Doug Fiore. He's moving from his job at the Highway Patrol and will be a captain on my staff. I don't want you folks to give him any trouble. He's going to make sure people in this here town know how hard I work."

Dusty and Danny stood. They nodded at Doug because no one shook hands anymore. "Captain," said Dusty, glad that his mask hid his delight at seeing Doug on the sheriff's staff, "we look forward to working with you."

"Thank you, detective," replied Doug. "I'll be working with each department on the new communications policies I'm developing for the sheriff." Everyone nodded. The sheriff spun around on his heel and marched out of the office followed by his minions. Doug was last through the door, sending Dusty and Danny a quick wink over the top of his mask.

"Hot damn," chortled Danny.

"Keep it to yourself," cautioned Dusty. "I told Doug not to admit he knows us."

* * *

Lynn found Piper at the fairy gate, the decorative grillwork in the stone wall separating the old Cohen place from Lynn's property. She was waving at Emily's great-grandchildren. "I was telling the kids about the fairy gate." She smiled at Lynn. "I like to remember our good times here. I hope those kids find the same charm."

"I think they will now that Emily is firmly in their lives."

Piper threw an arm around Lynn's waist. "We have a good friendship. It's lasted a long time."

"Are you ending it?" Lynn the taller one, rested her arm across Piper's shoulders.

"No, I'm just enjoying it. Those kids remind me of the old days, and yet we're still here."

"But older."

"That too." They walked back to the mask-free zone. "I've been watching Bryce and Beth. Is that a friendship?"

Lynn sat at the picnic table and thought about what Piper asked. "You don't want them to be friends? Or do you think it's growing into more than a friendship?"

"I don't know. I find it very confusing."

69

"One thing I have noticed is that they're the only ones in their group. You know, we're older and the college group is younger. They don't fit in except with themselves."

"So you're saying it's not friendship, it's sort of the outcasts hanging together?"

Lynn laughed. "They're not outcasts. They're both in their mid-twenties and have more in common with each other than with any of us. And now that he works for her company, they have even more in common."

Piper was still puzzled. "I just can't figure them out. He's so handsome and she's so . . . . . .Beth."

"Your son is too handsome for a successful attorney and pilot?"

"That's not what I mean, I don't think. They just don't match."

"Look at us," teased Lynn. "I'm tall, dark and calm while you're short, blond and crazy."

"I'm not the one married to-

"I hear you," came a growl from the lounger, "you better end that sentence with a nice word."

"A prince," she said aloud, then whispered, "of darkness."

"I heard that," Dusty grumbled from the lounger.

Lynn laughed as she gave Piper a thoughtful look. "Sometimes friendship comes in different disguises." And Piper began to think of all the help Dusty has given her students when the two of them initiated a program to build positive relationships between her students and police. And how, during the pandemic, Dusty and his staff had personally paid attention to the safety and needs of her students.

Piper glanced at the lounger and smiled but hoped Dusty didn't think she was pleased with him, even if she was.

\* \* \*

Preparing for bed that evening Lynn poked Dusty as he finished brushing his teeth. "You and Piper have an interesting relationship." She hung her towel on the rack and walked into the bedroom. "You pretend to be hostile, yet if she asks for help, you're always there."

"She always asks for help for her students." He hugged Lynn. "I can't say no."

"But you helped her when she found that dead man. Remember when she found him in the roadway and some folks thought she might have killed him?"

"That was easy. Her car didn't have any marks of a hit and run."

She laughed. "You never acted like she was a suspect. You care about her."

He hung his head. "She has some good qualities. As much as I hate to admit it." He pulled back the sheets. "But she can be such a pain in the ass."

"That's what she says about you." Lynn climbed into bed. She snuggled close. "We were talking about friendship. She wondered about the friendship between Beth and Bryce."

"See that's where she's a pain in the ass," he growled. "She should let things alone." He had suspicions, but it was no one's business what he thought. To change the subject he said, "The sheriff hired Doug as the PR guy for the department." Lynn's head popped off his shoulder. He put it back. "We're all acting like we don't know him."

"Won't the sheriff find out that Doug's aunt lives next door?"

"I think we can keep things quiet until Doug has established himself in the job. I told my staff to keep our friendship with him on the lowdown. I'm glad the sheriff has at least one thinker in his inner circle."

Lynn giggled. "Friendship again. I told Piper it comes in different disguises."

Dusty pulled her closer. "I like our friendship that comes with benefits. You know, someone who cooks for me and does my laundry." Nibble. Caress. "Helps take care of the dog."

"How about sexy?"

"Me or you?" His kiss took her breath away.

# CHAPTER TEN

One early afternoon Wanda and Tee zoomed with Rose Marie. "Did you find anything interesting in those files?" Rose Marie asked, referring to the cold case she had forwarded to her friends. Both detectives shook their heads. "Me neither," replied the rookie. "I've made a list of people interviewed and located them. Well, some of them. Some have moved, so I'm doing online research and have found that some are dead. I guess I'll do research on them, too. Maybe locate some family to ask questions. But I have a list of about six folks who are still around." She read the names and watched Tee and Wanda jot them down.

"I read their statements in the file," said Wanda.

Tee looked at her friends on the screen. "Did any of those folks get more attention during the investigation than the others?" Reading the file, she wondered if the perp might be in the list of those interviewed.

Rose Marie shrugged. "I guess I can talk with the officers listed in the case. Some of them are still around. My boss Lt. Carlson was just a new detective then."

Tee, as the most experienced officer, advised the rookie, "Rose Marie, always keep your boss in the loop. Especially since he knows this case. He sounds like a good fellow. You don't want to embarrass him."

Wanda nodded. "My boss always tells me to loop him in." She thought a moment. "And he says do background before you interview anyone."

"Why?"

"It helps you ask useful questions and know when the answers are lies."

Rose Marie's eyes bugged. Tee laughed. "Yes, rookie, people will lie to you during an interview."

A baby cried. "I gotta go," said Wanda.

"Me, too. Keep us in the loop." They all left the meeting.

\* \* \*

"Sir?" The quiet rookie tapped at Carlson's door frame. "Do you have a minute?"

"Yes, ma'am." He was charmed by her blush when he called her 'ma'am.' She was about the age of his daughter. "You solve that cold case?"

"Not yet."

"I like that attitude, rookie." He signaled her to a chair in front of his desk. "What can I help with?"

She straightened in the chair and collected her thoughts. "I think I should let you know everything." She frowned. "I'm interested in the case because it's personal. And you can tell me to stop if you think I'm too involved or distracted or not on the right track."

He made a calming gesture. "There's no problem. Things are quiet with this virus. I have time to listen."

"One of the people of interest in the case is a man my mother identified as my father."

Carlson nodded. "I think you told me. Or someone did. Is he in your life now?"

"No, sir," she replied. "That's why I'm interested. He seems to have disappeared that night." She took a deep breath. "But several months ago our office got an inquiry about him from a department in North Carolina." She looked hopeful. "It seems he did a good deed and he asked to be reunited with his family."

"That means you've found him? Met him?" This was the intriguing part of police work that Carlson enjoyed.

"Not exactly. He was lying about who he was and was reunited with the family of his travel partner, a man he had been on the road with for twenty years. He tried to say he was that man."

"He killed that man?" Carlson was alert.

73

"No, he had promised his partner who died of cancer to take care of the family he had abandoned." She gnawed at her lip. "His daughter," she used finger quotes, "suspected that he wasn't her real father. She and the detective in North Carolina who had united them figured out who he was. He told them the whole story. They love him." She stopped. "Oh, I forgot. His daughter is a police officer in Indiana."

"This is becoming a travelogue, rookie," Carlson teased.

"Yes, sir," she blushed. He made a signal for her to continue. She nodded. "I sent the file to both of the women because they were both interested in this case." He raised an eyebrow. "Did I do wrong?"

He shrugged. "I can't see why, but I wish you had asked just to protect yourself."

She nodded. "Tee, she's the North Carolina detective. She said I should be thoughtful in how I proceed now that I have some names to interview. And that I should keep you in the loop."

"You're going to interview folks from that old file?" He thought she already had.

"Is that OK?"

"Why don't you do phone interviews to start and see where it gets you?" He sat forward and spread his hands across his desk. "Can I see your list of names?" She handed him the list. He didn't see any names that he thought would cause her problems. "Just be polite. Anything else?"

"Thank you, sir. My friends want me to be cautious also." She blushed again. "And they want me to always keep you informed."

"They sound like good friends and smart professionals." He shooed her from his office.

\* \* \*

"Mr. Janic, my name is Rose Marie Jaeger," came the soft voice over the phone, "and I'm with the Des Moines Police Department. I'm researching an old case and your name is in the files."

"You sound mighty young to be in law enforcement," he flirted into the phone.

"Sir, I'm a rookie. You can call my supervisor."

"That's okay." Janic decided to play it as a successful, very helpful businessman. "My name is in a file?"

"Yes, sir. The Darla Somerall murder case. You were one of the people the police interviewed. Do you remember the case?"

He gave an embarrassed laugh into the phone. "Those were my crazy, stupid days. When she was murdered, I was frightened into changing my ways. I had never known anyone who had been a victim of a crime before."

"What was your relationship with the victim?"

"We dated some," he admitted. "Are you checking in with all the folks from those days?" He might as well learn what he could.

"I've found, or accounted for, everyone in the file."

"That's interesting," he observed. "I sort of suspected she dealt drugs, but I couldn't afford that habit in those days, and she told me I wasn't so good a sex partner that she would give me anything for free. I thought she meant cocaine or something."

He could almost hear the rookie blush. "Sir, I believe she was a midlevel drug dealer. But the search of her property never found records, money, or product."

"Are you trying to solve this case? Has new evidence come up?"

"No, sir. This is my own, I guess you could say, quest. I think my father was one of Ms. Somerall's clients."

"Really, who?"

"William Halstead."

"I don't know that name." But it was a piece of information he was glad to have.

"He taught at Drake but lost his job because of his addictions."

"If he's your father, can't he tell you about this case?" Janic tried to sound helpful and confused.

"I never met him," she admitted. "He disappeared about the time of the murder. The investigators wanted to talk to him. And I learned from my mother that in her crazy and stupid days," Janic laughed as she used his description, "he got her pregnant. And recently I got an inquiry about him from another jurisdiction."

"He's a criminal?"

"No, sir, he seems to have helped some small-town detectives find a lost child and they have been helping him find his old life."

Janic heard a sadness in her voice as he asked, "You think he killed Ms. Somerall?"

"I don't know, sir. My mother say he was a sweetheart, but a druggie."

He decided to agree with her mother. "I would suspect that the murderer was a competitor, you know, some other dealer. Druggies don't kill their suppliers." He didn't want the young woman digging into Darla's past, nor contacting her father. "Do you plan to go meet him?"

"I'd like to someday, but right now with everyone concerned about this virus, I think I'll wait until life is less contagious. This case isn't going anywhere."

He laughed into the phone. "Sounds like you'll make a practical investigator. Do you need more information from me? I don't know much. It was a long time ago and I wasn't happy with my stupid self from back then."

"No, sir, not today. Thank you for your time."

Janic hung up the phone and stared out the window, thinking.

* * *

Lee had been encouraging members of the sexual assault survivors support group to gather in the park during the summer as soon as they felt comfortable with the virus and lockdown. Each meeting was different: sometimes everyone showed up; and sometimes she sat in the picnic shelter alone. Tonight she was alone, staring at the river and wondering what to do. She needed support tonight - where was everyone? And, finally, Beth walked into the shelter, a six pack of diet soft drink and a container of cantaloupe slices.

Lee grinned. "You're watching everyone's weight." She marveled at the changes in Beth since the winter.

"Invite me to a party and you'll leave healthy and sober." The attorney settled at the table with her treats.

"Tonight I could use the old Beth," said Lee in a soft sad voice. "I could use a pound of chocolate."

"Oh, Lee," Beth was at her side embracing her old friend. "How can I help?"

Lee shook her head. "Of all the people I know, you are the one who *can* help."

"Anything."

Lee gave her a teasing smile. "Do you have time for me with all your other work?"

"You need a pilot or a lawyer? I can't imagine that you have trash to recycle on a commercial scale." She winked at her friend. "That's me, Beth for all seasons." Lee was laughing. Beth opened the container and invited her to dig out a melon slice. She nodded knowingly. "I'm not surprised about anything anymore."

"I'm interested in talking to Beth the calm, focused attorney."

"You're in trouble? How can I help?"

Lee brush her fingers along Beth's cheek in a very un-CDC approved gesture. "I'm getting married."

"It's Sean, isn't it?"

Lee sputtered. "How can you assume it's Sean? We were so secret."

"You delivered a baby at his house. You brought a dead body to his house. You got him to find some cabins for the Sharing Shelter program." She dared Lee to deny her conclusions.

"How did you know it was . . . him?"

"It was my client who had the cabins that Sean found. I had another client who was suspected of the murder of the body you took to Sean's. And the baby was all over town." Beth took her hand. "What do you need?"

"Michelle and H. Lawrence are his attorney and CPA. They recommend a pre-nup."

"My sister and my law partner made a recommendation, and you don't trust them?" Beth stopped to consider what she was saying and needed clarification. "Why? Do you have assets they think you should protect? Or Sean? Or heirs or something?"

"You don't know?" asked Lee.

Beth shook her head. "He's not one of my clients. He's Herbie's. Is there something wrong with him? A disease or another wife, or ex-wife?"

"He's very wealthy." Lee was now stressed. "Very wealthy. More money that anyone can spend in a lifetime."

"And he wants a pre-nup?"

"No, Michelle and Herbie want it." She shrugged. "I don't understand. I'm angry that they think I'm after Sean's money and he's confused about their advice."

"Oh," chuckled Beth, "You misunderstand." Lee scowled. Beth gave her a calming smile and continued, "They want to protect you and Sean and make certain his financial plans stay in place even after his death. I'm sure he's got a very complex financial structure to manage his wealth. You could throw a wrench in things if he became incompetent or died."

"They just want to keep control of a lucrative account!" Now Lee was even angrier.

"Yes and no," Beth waffled. "Yes, Sean's account is lucrative to both of them. But I think they want to protect him and you. When Sean marries you, you become their client, too. They want what is best for you and want you protected should something happen to you, and you need long term care, or some long lost relative tries to come in and claim your share of his estate. They're just doing what they do, thinking of the worst and trying to put things in place to prevent or circumvent bad stuff."

"Bad stuff? Long lost relative?"

Beth shrugged. "The world gets weirder every day. They want to protect you both."

"I'm not marrying him for his money. I didn't even know he had it." She put her hand over her heart. "It was a shock. I couldn't catch my breath when he told me."

"Why don't you let me represent you in the pre-nup negotiations?"

\* \* \*

After hearing from the rookie, Janic decided it was time to reach into his past. "Jimmy, how are you?" Janic called into the phone. "Long time." Jimmy had cleaned up real good. He was now chief counsel at the medical center.

"Who is this?" asked a voice that sounded like it was used to being in charge.

"Janic. We met about twenty years ago." Silence on the other end as he heard the man say, "We'll finish this later, Margaret." He heard a door close.

"It's James, now, Janic. What do you want?" The last time they had spoken was a day or so after Darla's death, and prior to scheduled interviews requested at the police station. Janic had pointed out that they both should stay silent about having been at her house that evening. Neither one wanted the police looking into their lives. Jimmy had agreed.

Janic lowered his voice. "Do you tape these calls? And are you alone?"

"No tape and I'm alone. Get to it." James was not a happy camper.

Janic lowered his voice even more. "I have heard that a young rookie is looking into a cold case involving some woman drug dealer. She's looking because she has a reason to believe that the man sometimes referred to as the professor is alive and happens to be her father."

"The guy didn't die?" James cleared his throat. "It's not my problem. I was only interviewed once by the police in those days. And now you tell me I didn't kill anyone." He hung up.

Janic stared at his phone. Bastard!

# CHAPTER ELEVEN

After the conversation yesterday with Rose Marie, Tee had done some of her own investigating and didn't like what she had found. She had gone into law enforcement restricted records to research a few names in Rose Marie's cold case file. Both James Knudsen and Michael Janic had the background to have been the murderer twenty years ago. Knudsen had military experience and had qualified for some special op's teams. Janic had some juvenile arrests that had been sealed. Tee had only found them because someone had made a mess of the paperwork and the records seemed to have fallen into the wrong file. He had three assaults and a drug arrest.

As she was thinking about this information, Rose Marie called her. "Tee, sorry about not zooming, but I'm so excited I had to talk. I spoke with one of the witnesses yesterday. That Janic fellow." She was breathless but didn't allow an interruption. "He was so nice. He's going to look over his statement and talk to me."

"His statement?"

"My supervisor called him to let him know I would be calling him. He asked to see his statement so he could refresh his memory. He can have it because . . . well, I don't know why. But they're sending it to him and then I'll set up a meeting. Isn't this exciting? Maybe he knew my father?"

"Rose Marie?" Tee tried to sound calm. "Will you take a partner into the interview?"

"Should I?"

"Yes." Tee stopped to form a reason. "You're new at this and having a seasoned officer will help you and will allow him or her to evaluate your technique after the interview."

"Oh." It was a small sound. "You don't think I can do this, do you?"

"Yes, I do. I just want you to be able to learn from the experience."

"Why don't you come and interview him with me? I know I would be comfortable with you." All that rookie enthusiasm!

It was tempting to Tee. "Let me see what I can arrange. Don't see him before I get back to you."

"Really?" Rose Marie was delighted. "I know I can learn good stuff from you. You're so cool."

Tee rubbed her forehead trying to corral her funny feeling. But she was cheerful and encouraging on the phone. "Just hang on a few days. You'll hear from me."

\* \* \*

When Janic answered the phone Rhonda Knox said, "I just had a call from some police officer. She found my name in a file." Silence. He didn't answer so she continued, "Sound familiar?"

"What did you say?"

"I said I had to get to work, and she could call me some other time."

"What do you want?"

"I got bills to pay and that job at the motel doesn't help these days. I'm almost sixty and I think I need a retirement plan."

"Let me think about what I can do." Janic didn't like to hear that the professor's little bastard was digging deeper into that cold case. Darla was dead. No one cared then and no one cared now. That rookie had to be stopped! There were only two people in town who could connect him with that murder: Jimmy and the woman who had been his alibi.

"You got a week." Rhoda ended the call.

Janic shook his head. He should have taken care of Rhonda Knox years ago. She had been working a street corner the night Janic met her. In exchange for becoming his alibi she parlayed the relationship into becoming one of his low-level distributors. She had become a waitress who augmented her wages by selling drugs in the ladies' room of the trendy restaurant where she worked. As she told him in the early days, waitressing and working the lavatory was less mess and a lot more money than working the street. However, Rhonda, who was smarter than Janic had expected, soon realized her role in Janic's life. The newspaper stories about the murder titillated folks for weeks until it devolved to a cold case. Rhonda had kept a scrapbook of the news reports and presented it to Janic a few years later with her conclusions.

He could still remember that night. "I think you know something about this case," she had taunted as she waved the scrapbook. "I think I should get more value for my alibi."

Janic had sneered at her. "You distribute drugs. You willing to give up that income for a chance to become an accessory?"

"What do you mean?"

He had grabbed her by the throat and spit out the words. "I draw police interest on this case, and so do you as my accomplice."

"I didn't do anything." She squeezed the words out.

"You're on record as my alibi." He had released her. "Think about it."

She had withdrawn her threat, and he had kept her on as one of his distributors. As he had gained wealth and moved himself to more legitimate work, she had stayed where she was. But life had gotten hard for Rhonda, and she had approached Janic about five years ago for financial aid. The restaurant had closed, and her clients had gotten themselves hooked on opioids with the help of their doctors who were willing to write prescriptions. Janic pondered that change in business model. Who knew that the medical profession would become a major competitor?

In any case, for old times' sake he had given Rhonda a job at a motel he owned. She worked as night clerk. Her position allowed her to sometimes assist in his other schemes, acting as a receptionist as he played financial advisor to Des Moines' underworld. He had always given her a bonus for those jobs. And now she was trying to blackmail him again!

* * *

Tee liked the idea of Lynn's mask-free zone. It was a great place to take her children to run and play. All local playgrounds were closed and opportunities for them to use their pent-up energy were few. When she arrived in the driveway, she opened the minivan door and three balls of black fire erupted. Lynn's dog stood as the welcoming committee waiting to be adored. The tired mother gave her kids over to the nanny dog and found a comfortable spot at the mask- free picnic table.

Lynn came out with a glass of iced tea. She placed it in front of the detective. "Tough day?"

Tee sipped her drink. One thing about good friends, they always knew how you take your tea - slice of lemon, unsweetened. Her conversation with Rose Marie was bothering her. She didn't know why. Maybe some old detective sense that a rookie hadn't developed yet. "Has Dusty told you about my new girlfriends and that hobo, Bill?"

"Yes," Lynn replied. "He says you're looking into his past and it's been interesting."

"It is. Turns out Bill was a professor in Des Moines who got caught up in drugs. He spent twenty years on the road with Wanda's father. Remember when she came to meet him?" Lynn nodded. "Bill has admitted that he isn't her father but had been his friend and traveling partner. We started to look into his past. We learned that he was a person of interest in a Des Moines murder. When I contacted the police there, I hooked up with a rookie who just happened to be reopening the cold case because," here Tee did a riff on the table, "she's Bill's daughter."

"He left a family just like Wanda's father?"

"Even better," explained Tee. "He didn't even know his lady friend was pregnant. Rose Marie, the rookie daughter, was adopted by the man who married her mother. They all seemed to live happily ever after, but Rose Marie wanted to find her father. So as a rookie she opened this cold case, a murder of some drug dealer."

"What has you concerned? That doesn't sound like it should be dangerous or complex. Was her father the murder suspect?"

Tee looked uncomfortable. "Wanda and I zoomed with her. She's made a list of folks in the file and wants to question them. We told her we would look over the file. This afternoon she called me because she has contacted some of the folks referenced in the file. I just have a funny feeling."

"About?"

"I don't know. I wish I were on the ground to advise her."

"I can help. I have a friend in Des Moines." Lynn sipped her own iced tea.

"Why am I not surprised?" Tee had often heard Dusty complain that Lynn's nonprofit work had allowed her to meet many people who often seem to pop up in investigations.

Lynn frowned at the detective's sarcasm. "Do you want my help or not?"

"Okay," surrendered the detective.

Lynn pulled out her cell phone and found a number. "Kennette? This is Lynn Powers in North Carolina. . . . It's good to hear your voice, too. But I have a reason for calling. I'm putting you on speaker, okay?" Lynn jabbed the phone screen and placed the phone on the table between her and Tee. "Kennette, I'm here with my friend, Teniquia LaMont. She's one of my husband's detectives."

Kennette chuckled across the ether. "Teniquia? Finally, I can hear from someone if all those stories Lynn tells are true."

"Yes, ma'am. All true. And please call me Tee."

"I'm Kennette and why are you calling me? I try to avoid law breaking."

"Kennette," Tee began, "I'm in touch with a rookie on the Des Moines police force and she's looking into a cold case that I have an interest in."

"Are you coming to Des Moines to catch criminals?" Kennette heard Tee's weary sigh. Dialing back her excitement she continued, "If you're calling, it must be important. I'll try to help."

"It's a very complex story," said Tee. "The rookie is starting to contact folks who were listed in the file from a twenty-year-old murder case. Although the case was never resolved, I've been worried that the perp might be on her list of potential interviews. I told Lynn I wish I was there to advise her. And Lynn suggested that you might have background on some of the people on her list."

"Wow," came Kennette's awed voice, "you folks really say perp." She took a breath. "This sounds like it might be dangerous to the rookie."

"Yes," agreed Tee, "that's why I'd like to run some names by you."

"Okay, I'll do what I can."

"Michael Janic, James Knudsen, Rhonda Knox, and Darla Somerall who was the victim." Tee read the list of names across the connection.

Kennette was silent for a moment. "James Knudsen is the attorney for the hospital. I see him often at fund raising events. I like him, great wife, lovely family. Michael Janic is a developer and real estate person. I don't know him well. He makes donations to law enforcement related causes. He's very wealthy. Our paths don't cross. Rhonda Knox, I don't know at all. And the victim is not familiar either." Kennette gave a long, "Hmmmm."

"What?"

"I'm not admitting to anything in my past," she whispered, "but I seem to remember both of those men on the fringes of drugs when I was in college. I'll ask around."

"NO!" shouted Tee. "If they're involved, you might stir up something. Let the rookie investigate."

"I'm sorry." Kennette was contrite. "I understand."

"Kennette, thanks for the information," said Tee. "I appreciate your help. I guess I'll do more online research. And you keep your nose clean."

"If you come to Des Moines," bubbled Kennette, "you can stay with me. It would be interesting to get into one of Lynn's investigations." Kennette sounded determined to get into an investigation one way or another!

"With this virus," Tee replied, "I don't see traveling in my future. But thank you. May I contact you if I have more questions?"

"Oh, yes, please."

Tee rolled her eyes at Lynn who grinned. "Thanks Kennette," she said, "you're always helpful. Talk to you soon." Lynn ended the call. "Well?" she asked the detective.

"I'll see where this goes."

"Mama!" And that ended the detecting part of the day.

\* \* \*

After receiving that blackmail call from Rhonda, Janic made quick preparations to visit the woman to send her off with an overdose of something. He scanned through his old supplies and decided on some heroin. He had scouted out her neighborhood on the county's GIS maps. Even in that cluttered, poor neighborhood her place was isolated. He could get in and out without being seen. He decided to use his old motorcycle; his Mercedes was too memorable.

He knocked at her door. When Rhonda opened it, she gave him a triumphant smile. "You got something for me?"

He smiled back. "For old times' sake." He walked in. "I thought I should ask you what kind of help you need." He looked around the small house. "You here alone?"

"What you got in mind?" She was high on her success. He had come at her call! "We can talk over old times. You can tell me how much I'm worth." She gave a shimmy and hoped it reminded him of the days of drugs and sex they had shared. But she stopped. They had never shared sex and drugs. He had picked her up and paid her for the alibi. He had taken care of her over the years. Rhonda soon realized she had played the wrong card. Janic wasn't a man to appreciate disloyalty. It was the last thought she had.

Overpowering the woman was no challenge. She was skin and bones. Janic tried not to leave a mark, but she did struggle a bit and he was forced to bash her head against the door frame. Once subdued he dragged her into her tiny bedroom, slipped on the current necessity - anti-virus surgical gloves - and prepared the shot. Finding a vein was a challenge. It had been a long time. He completed the injection and left the syringe and other supplies. This had to look self-administered. With one last scan for anything that might identify him, he left, giving a thought to how long it would be before she was found sprawled on the bedroom floor. He shrugged. He really didn't care if she was ever found.

Janic returned home to think about the evolving situation. He had spoken to Jimmy. Had the old bodyguard been contacted by the police since their conversation? Was Jimmy one more loose end to handle? There was one way to find out. A call to his new buddy Carlson should do the trick.

# CHAPTER TWELVE

On a sunny Saturday morning many people in River Bend were surprised and delighted to receive a very formal e-vite to the wedding of Lee Stahlmeier and Sean Hennessey.

Piper came racing into Lynn's house screeching, "Look at this!" She clutched her laptop to her bosom. "Sean and Lee." She flipped her laptop onto the kitchen table, bobbling Dusty's coffee. She grabbed the computer before it got wet and snarled, "Clumsy."

Dusty snarled back, "This is my house. You knocked over the coffee. And why are you here. I thought I locked that door."

"Children." Lynn admonished as she placed a plate of scrambled eggs in front of Dusty. He got up to grab a cloth to wipe the coffee spill off the table. Piper sat at the table, moved her computer far away from Dusty and slid the breakfast plate in front of her. She salted the eggs and began to spread butter on the toast.

Lynn quickly got the remaining eggs in the skillet on a plate and grabbed more toast and placed it in front of Dusty as he returned to his seat. Jason came into the kitchen. "Any breakfast?"

Lynn started breaking more eggs into a bowl. Will walked in, looked around, found Piper, and asked, "Where did you go? I heard you scream." He sipped the cup of coffee Lynn had placed before Piper. "I'll take some of those." He eyed her eggs.

Bryce and Jeff walked in. "We heard Mom scream and run out the door." They both took seats at the table and caught Lynn's eye. Jeff said, "I'll get more eggs" and ran home. Bryce jumped up to get glasses for milk or juice, while Jason found more jelly and bread. Both boys acted like perfect kitchen helpers.

When everyone had finally eaten all the eggs in both Lynn's and Piper's refrigerator and finished all the sliced bread, coffee and juice, Lynn asked, "What was the emergency?"

Piper came out of her scrambled egg stupor and remembered. "This!" She grabbed her computer which had been placed on one of the stools at the kitchen bar. "Sean and Lee are getting married, and we're invited." She looked at Lynn. "Are you?"

Lynn ran to her home office and booted up her computer going quickly to email. She screeched. "Yes!" She dashed back into the kitchen. "I didn't even know they were seeing each other."

Dusty rolled his eyes. "You didn't know she's been spending nights there?"

"Where?"

"At Sean's."

"Oh yeah," offered Jeff, "I see her Prius there when I drive over to Ricky's." Piper scowled at him. "Should I have told you?"

"No," said Dusty. "Some people deserve privacy. Your mother doesn't have to butt into everyone's business."

Piper scowled at him and opened her mouth to reply. "Children," cautioned Will. He rubbed his hands. "This is great. Sean needed someone in his life. Someone to spend all that money."

"She's not marrying him for his money," declared Lynn and dared anyone to argue.

"We know that, honey," said Piper. "She's marrying him 'cause he can fix anything."

"Hey, babe," whined Will. "I can fix things."

"But do you ever?" challenged his wife.

Lynn sat back down at the table. "Here's a more important question." She looked closely at the e-vite. "What do you wear to a Zoom wedding?"

\* \* \*

As seemed to be a weekly routine, Dusty's staff brought their children to Lynn's mask-free zone to play. For a pandemic summer, the place was always filled with people. It was lunch time and Mars drove into the yard with his children, Brian and Holly. He waved, unbuckled them from car seats and let them loose. They ran first to the dog, then looked around for other youngsters. They spied Jason and Jeff going into the barn. They were off, streaming giggles behind them.

Mars flopped on a chair socially distant, under a dogwood. Lynn was certain that his sigh was so deep it fluttered the leaves of the tree. "What's wrong?" she asked.

He rolled his eyes. Sighed again. "It's my mother. If Dusty thinks Bergy is a problem, he should listen to her." He shifted in the chair. "She complains daily that her first grandchild is to be born and she can't get out of London. I keep explaining that no one can travel right now. Marshall, her husband, has promised her that she'll be bound for home as soon as the travel bans lift or adjust." He scowled. "I think Marshall would mail her here if he could figure out how to do it."

Lynn laughed. She had met Palmer Nolan at Mars' wedding. "She did enjoy Holly and Brian on her last visit. I can imagine that the thought of your new baby has her excited." She looked around. "Where's Trina?"

Mars said, "She said she needs at least two hours alone. She said that included me."

Lynn laughed again. "I hear that from so many of my friends with children." As she spoke, Lonzo, Tee's husband, pulled into the yard and his minivan ejected three children.

"Tee said she needs time alone." He carried a big bag from Uncle Chicken's carry out. He turned to Mars, "You got the drinks?" Mars hopped out of his chair and trotted to his car as the bakery delivery van came into the yard. Lonzo smiled, "Here comes dessert."

Danny waved as he helped his two children out of the van. "My wife wants time -

"Alone," shouted the other husbands.

Magically Jason and Jeff appeared and began giving agri-cart rides to the kids while the dads set out the food. Lynn ran into the house for paper plates, cups, and a few random beers. She sat at the table and asked Lonzo, "Are you EMTs busy with all this virus?"

He nodded. "We get calls from folks who are really sick. I think they denied and denied. They wait too long for care." He frowned. "We also have OD's. I think some folks feel isolated." He scanned the yard with all the children. "I don't know the answer. Have we frightened people so much that they have pulled away from everyone?"

Lynn tried to process his concerns. "I think Dad and Marianna are frightened. They stay to themselves."

"But they have each other," Lonzo pointed out. "Some folks have no one and they have even given up the daily normal interactions like shopping, taking walks." He hung his head. "We see a lot of lonely people." After a moment he added, "We do it ourselves. We keep the kids away from the grandparents because we worry. Is the risk of virus greater than the risk of mental and emotional health?"

"That's a tough question," she replied. "I've thought that the internet and our interconnectedness with phones and computers has kept us in touch, if not actually touching."

"Unless you don't have those things." He brought reality to the table. "There is TV, maybe radio, but they aren't interactive." He drank his beer. "These times have me thinking more than I used to. Life was pretty smooth - beautiful wife, healthy kids, great job." Another drink. "But now I worry. Will my great job bring the virus home? Will the kids lose something being locked down with me? They need to learn from the world, meet people, learn about opportunities."

Lynn softly smiled at this big man. "It's a burden being a parent in the best of times. I think the strength of friends and family is that we adapt to support one another. Like today, no one's alone, and everyone is smiling." She pointed to his own children racing and laughing with the others in the yard.

Lonzo smiled at her. "You are a bright star. Tee says you made Dusty a happy man when you married."

Dusty walked out of the house, looked around and found Lynn. He winked.

Lonzo chuckled. "I told you so."

* * *

By the time the dads took their children home it was late afternoon. Lynn collapsed on one of the socially distant loungers under a Japanese maple in the mask-free zone. "I'm exhausted. Those children have too much energy."

"That's why their mothers wanted a break." Dusty flopped on the other lounger. He rubbed his stomach. "With all that food, I don't remember eating."

Lynn laughed. "I don't think we did. I seem to remember Jason and the boys stopping by." By definition that meant you had to be quick or go hungry.

Dusty snapped his fingers. "That explains it. What's for dinner?"

"Yeah, dinner." Jason sprawled on the grass under another tree.

"You just ate all the food with those kids." Dusty would have snarled but he felt weak from having missed lunch.

"That was hours ago." He flipped on his back and stared up at the sky. "I could use some food from the Asian Market. Maybe one of those pepperoni rolls."

"River Dog!" Lynn and Dusty shouted together.

"What are the masking-eating-out rules?" Jason asked Dusty.

"The governor has some weird rules, but it allows bars to serve beverages under some scheme." He was quiet a moment. They thought he was reviewing the latest mandates. Or not. "I could go for a cold River Dog Amber and those pot thingies."

And that's how Lynn, Dusty and Jason had dinner in the extended outdoor dining area of River Dog brewery.

"Hey, Dusty," Zeke waved over the heads of the patrons seated at tables around the brewery back lot. "We almost have the same revenue as last summer." He scanned the crowd. "Folks like that they don't need masks to drink and eat. And we got two new food vendors." He pointed to two brightly painted vans. "Try them out. Darwin has their menus up on our website."

"How is everyone?" asked Lynn.

"You just take a table and I'm sure everyone will check in." Zeke grinned and waved his wife over. "Barbara hears all about you from her preacher brother and from Connie."

And Zeke was correct. All the River Dog partners stopped by the table to catch up on life and mandates. They were introduced to Lonnie and Dana, the young couple who moved to Portage to help the brewers after Eddie, Lonnie's brother, died of the virus. It was still a sad memory for the group, but Lonnie and his family were fitting in.

Lynn sat to catch up with Barbara. "Zeke says revenue is still good."

Barbara shrugged. "Sort of." She lowered her voice. "Granny has money, and she transfers funds to our account regularly. She's asked me not to tell the guys." Barbara looked around to make certain she and Lynn were not overheard. "She must have more money than any of us knows about."

Lynn nodded. "Mr. Hutch Dunn, her attorney, hinted that she had assets and they were to assist her family. I wasn't to ask for donations to the Philanthropies."

Barbara laughed and whispered. "She is really sharp. I think she owns most of the buildings here in Portage." She looked around again. "But the money she sends us comes from an off-shore account."

Lynn was puzzled. "Is that legal?"

"I don't know," shrugged Barbara. "She says it's an inheritance from that cousin, Yetta, who was murdered. It comes from a local bank account, but I can see where it originated. I just accept the money and keep us operating."

"What does Zeke say?"

"I haven't told anyone." She blushed. "Except you and I know you won't talk." Lynn nodded. "I'm in over my head. I ignore the origins of the funds and I book them as income. Granny told me 'no questions.' I abide by her rules. It's small enough amounts." She smiled. "We are doing reasonably well, but the extra income helps us stay even."

On the ride back to River Bend Dusty and Jason rehashed the new vendor menus that they had sampled that night. They measured the taste and quality of the tapas plate against the bratwurst platter. Dusty mourned the fact that he had not had the opportunity or the remaining apetite to order the pot thingies. Lynn, on the other hand, was silent, wondering about Granny Masterson and the offshore money. She finally concluded that Granny Masterson loved her grandsons and the families they were building. The old woman had a right to use her money to support her family. That's what you did for love.

# CHAPTER THIRTEEN

Although Dusty's family worked to protect his mother from the virus, it was still important to him and his brothers that they stay in touch.

Copying Lynn's mask-free zone idea, the Reid family collected for a mask-free summer cookout. The only rule was that anyone going into the house had to mask. No one wanted to be responsible for allowing strange germs to attack the matriarch, Flora Reid. For her part, Flora didn't care. She thought she had lived long enough and had seen her sons prosper.

The other rule was no hugs. Of course, Flora had her own rule. She would hug everyone under six years old. As she told the family, "They are too sweet to have germs." No one argued because the youngsters gathered around her like moths to a flame.

Lynn took the opportunity of the family gathering to check in with everyone. Her first discussion and exchange of gossip was with her sister-in-law Bonita. Bonita, a successful decorator, usually partnered with Carl to help his clients work through the contractor design demands - faucet finishes, appliance finishes, the perfect blue color for the bedroom and the right white for the hall. Of course, no one wanted to hear Carl harangue about the 'right white' or as he said, "It's white, right?"

Bonita shook her head. "We are swamped. Folks seem to be coming here to create new places to work. Everyone wants a house with a home office." She sipped her iced tea. "We keep Kevin busy designing the electronic schematics so we can organize efficient spaces."

"But you and Carl are really good at organizing efficient spaces." Lynn still got compliments on their efforts in her kitchen redesign.

"Oh, honey," Bonita sighed, "You were easy. Some of these folks are crazy. You wouldn't believe what they want. And they expect it to be done overnight."

Lynn thought about Carl's remodeling job and Emily Jacobs. She understood what Bonita was saying. "On the upside, you're busy and prosperous. And not sick."

Bonita almost sprawled across the picnic table. "We don't have time to be sick."

As everyone enjoyed the family afternoon, Lynn found herself sitting beside Allison Reid on a glider under a tree. They had been sitting without speaking for some time. "Are you ready to talk?" Lynn asked. She knew the younger woman wanted a shoulder to lean on. Allison had given her several nods and hints until they finally found this quiet spot. About a year ago Allison and Dusty's brother, Kent, had announced that they were separating. The family had been saddened but tried to keep the lines of communication open so that Allison and the children would always feel welcome at Reid gatherings. At that time Allison had begun a promising career as an actress in regional TV commercials working with agencies in Greenville, South Carolina and Charlotte, North Carolina.

Allison slumped into Lynn. "Thanks for sitting with me. The Reids are all walking on eggs around me. And Kent is a bastard."

Lynn was shocked. Allison never spoke this way. "Things are more difficult?"

"This virus has dried up my career for the time being. He thinks that means I'm hopeless and helpless and I should, in his words, 'straighten up.'" She sniffed trying to hold back both sorrow and anger.

"How are you getting on?" Lynn hadn't talked with Allison for months.

"Dad's got this virus." Her father owned a commercial nursery serving local farmers who owned orchards and with landscaping firms supplying shrubs and trees. "This virus is changing everything. There's no work in TV commercials right now. And it wouldn't matter. I've got to take over the nursery. The kids and I moved to Dad's place. It has plenty of room."

"I see," said Lynn. "With the nursery responsibility don't you have more contact with Kent? Does that make you uncomfortable?" She thought these were reasonable questions because Kent had always done the books for the nursery. He had a small business as a CPA helping local farmers with their finances and taxes.

That suggestion seemed to make Allison angry. "He thought we'd be together more. He had the gall to suggest he sell the house because of the hot market, and he could move into my place with the kids." She wiped a tear. "He is clueless. My father needs care." Her mother had died a few years ago. "My brother can't quit his job and move back here. I live in Dad's house and manage him, the business, and the kids."

"I guess you find the working arrangements stressful." Lynn was having trouble charting this conversation. Did Allison want to reconcile or end any relationship with Kent? She asked for clarification. "Do you want to work with him and get back together?"

"No and no!"

"That sounds final."

"Maybe with no virus and my career going forward, I would have thought about it. You know, able to support myself and the kids, and not be dependent on him. Kent thinks being dependent on him means giving up your mind and ideas and personal goals."

"But you still have the children and his connection through the business."

"No, we don't." Allison crossed her arms around her waist, sort of pulling in for self-defense. "He sold the house. The kids are with me. I wouldn't let him move in. He's staying with Flora." She glanced at the older woman sitting on the porch. "I found someone else to do our books." Lynn gasped. "A woman and her little girl moved into Doug Fiore's house in Verona. She came from New York or some place and wants to work from home. I don't know her story, but I think she left a worse marriage. Kent is just a jerk, but I think her husband was terrible." Allison shrugged. "I don't need to know, and she is very good at what she does."

This was a lot of information to absorb. Lynn finally said, "You know we all will do what we can for you. Is there anything I do for you now?"

"Nothing," said Allison. "The kids are doing well. They enjoy all the extra space at Dad's. Kent comes over regularly. I don't want to harm his relationship with the kids. I'm glad I always worked closely with Dad. This transition is working. Kent has to figure his own life out. Maybe when he does it will include me again. But for now, we're over."

"I'm sorry."

"Don't be." Allison smiled. "It's like this virus. Our divorce will force us to make changes. Some of the changes may be good."

Lynn held Allison's hand as they sat on the glider in silence. She thought that Allison had matured from the days they first met. The younger woman understood that sometimes life had to adjust to circumstances. Allison was stepping up, taking over her family's business, putting aside personal dreams. Lynn wondered if Kent had learned a similar lesson yet. He was the youngest of the Reid brothers and maybe the one the others had coddled for just a bit too long.

* * *

Over this strange summer, Beth and Bryce often sought each other out. Older than the college crowd and younger than everyone else, they talked about many things and were even comfortable enough to ask very personal questions. This evening they were in the river park sitting on a log alongside the abandoned roadway that paralleled the river. Years ago a flood had destroyed a bridge and road surface upstream. The road had never been repaired and now provided a running and walking trail along the river for about a half mile. They sat on a secluded log close to the roadway but sheltered.

"No relationships?" asked Bryce. "I can't be the only guy you talk to. No Mr. Pilot on the horizon?"

"You're the only guy I've talked with in three years who wasn't a client or classmate." He showed his surprise. She continued, "Remember there was a hundred pounds more of me. I stayed to myself and ate."

"Whoa," he gasped. "That sounds almost debilitating."

"It was. That's why I had to do something. I had to face who I was and decide who I wanted to be." She took his hand. Something she had never done before during their talks. "I know I'm on the road to success now. But I think I still have to keep looking for the right fit." She gave him a sidelong look. "What about your relationships?"

As Bryce opened his mouth to reply he was hit by a ball. It was followed by giggling children and Teniquia. The detective looked at the young couple. "Sorry to interrupt."

"Hey, Tee," Beth welcomed the harried mother. "We're just talking. Do you know Bryce, Piper's son?"

Bryce stood. "I'd shake hands but, you know." That was the virus in everyday life.

Tee smiled at him as her husband, Lonzo, and the children returned with the ball that had bounced off Bryce and rolled beyond the log. More introductions were made. Tee asked, "We've got some drinks and snacks if you'd like to join us." Both of her daughters had already snugged themselves up against Beth on the log.

"Sure," agreed Bryce. He had been uneasy about the direction of Beth's monologue and welcomed the interruption. She was trying to ask him something. And he was afraid he might admit more that he wanted to share with anyone. Joining Tee's family seemed safer. Lonzo and Bryce joined the kids in an impromptu kickball game while the two women set out snacks and talked.

"Have you had any more stunning court wins?" asked Tee. She enjoyed Beth's legal success, especially the help she gave Emily's great-grandchildren.

"Just routine," replied Beth, "but I have gotten my pilot's license and have been helping my instructor with some charters."

Tee was surprised. "I didn't know you were doing that. Do you like it?"

"I certainly do. That's why we hired Bryce to work at the recycling business. Dad wanted to stay retired, I wanted to fly, and Greg wanted help. It's working out well. What about you? More people trying to hide behind masks and commit crimes?"

Tee shook her head. "It's pretty quiet. I've met some women online and we're helping a lady in Des Moines with a cold case." Tee shook her head. "She's been interviewing old witnesses. I keep thinking one of those folks is the killer. I've done some research and two names pop up in places that make me uneasy. If these were normal times, I'd take off for Des Moines for a few days."

"I can fly you there." The words just popped out.

Tee looked at the new pilot as though she were speaking a foreign language. "Fly me?"

"I've been flying people all over the state. I haven't flown as far as Des Moines. You do mean Iowa?" Tee nodded. "I haven't flown that far but I have the knowledge and skill."

"How much would it cost?"

"I have no idea. I fly and the charter guy does all the bookkeeping." She thought about the flight. "We could use one of his planes and I can use my credit card instead of his to refuel and for hangar space if we need it."

"Hangar space?"

"We would have to stay over at least one night. We can't do a round trip in one day and get your business done." Beth gave the idea some thought. "We could plan one day to fly in. Give you one full day to get your business done. One day to fly out. We'd spend two nights in Des Moines." Beth sounded confident even though she knew that she had no idea about the specifics of such a long trip.

"I'm tempted," said Tee. "Lynn has a friend in Des Moines who would put us up. Let me talk it over with Lonzo. We'd have to co-ordinate babysitting."

"Just text me the date and I'll get ready." They exchanged numbers as the kickball skidded under the picnic table and the kids decided it was snack time.

* * *

True to his word, Janic called Lt. Carlson for a golfing date. He arranged for the match to be at a public course. No need to spend more than he had to on the source unless he thought Carlson would prove helpful.

"You're a pretty fair player," Janic observed of his new acquaintance.

"I grew up around a course," smiled Carlson. "My family had a sod farm and nursery. We had contracts with about three of the courses in the area for landscaping."

Janic gave him a friendly grin. "I see you're one of those guys who pretends to know nothing and sets up the competition."

Carlson chuckled. "Hey, who won this match?"

They walked toward the club bar with its visible sign that all who enter must be masked. "These damn masks," groused Janic. "How about I find us a beer at my place. We can sit on my patio." He thumbed his phone. "I just ordered a pizza."

"Sold!"

Once comfortable with beers and delivered pizza Janic finally got to his agenda. "Your rookie called me. Did she call others?"

Carlson looked across Janic's manicured lawn with a sod farmer's eye. "I told her to call folks, not meet them in person. I don't want us stirring up old memories and getting people upset. I don't know who else she called."

"She sounded young." He gave Carlson another beer.

"They all are. That's the definition of a rookie. But she's sharp."

"She also seems really dedicated to this case." Janic gripped his bottle tighter.

"She thinks her biological father was involved."

"She doesn't know?" Janic had a feeling things were moving out of his control. This rookie had a very personal interest in this case.

"He disappeared. But she's been talking to some out of state officers and she's waiting to hear from them."

"Other officers?"

"She talks with two other women cops who have an interest in this guy she thinks is her father." Carlson helped himself to another slice of the pizza. It was a pleasant evening.

"Interesting," offered Janic. "Do cases always go like this, involve other jurisdictions?"

"Sometimes." Carlson drank and put his bottle down. "I could tell you stories."

"Spare me," begged Janic. "At least this case is somewhat interesting because I was a bit player. Hey, we both were." He offered Carlson more pizza. "I know what. You keep me informed on the progress and we can write a book when she solves it, sort of the insiders' point of view."

"Or the fools who couldn't figure it out the first time." They laughed. Both men seemed to be enjoying the relaxing afternoon. Only one of them was. The other was working.

* * *

When Beth arrived home, she did her research about flying to Des Moines. Butch, her instructor had taught her a lot. She could, hypothetically, use Butch's Cessna 172. He insisted that this was the best airplane for a new pilot. It could hold 2-3 adults and would go the distances Tee needed. Diving into her laptop, Beth quickly plotted a course, found refueling sites and hangar space. She smiled to herself and went to bed hoping Tee was serious.

Across town Tee was speaking with her husband. "Beth says she can do this. I really want to get to Rose Marie. I just have a sense she's in danger, bringing up this old case."

Lonzo sat beside her with an arm pulling her snug. He whispered because the kids were finally asleep. "Babe, I know you want to do this. I can give you three days. My shift is rolling off duty tomorrow. I won't sign up for any overtime. What will Dusty say?"

"I don't think I'll tell him anything. I'll say I'm taking time off. Three days. I'll be back and he'll never know." She kissed him. "Thank you for understanding."

He chuckled and she felt the rumble in his chest. "I expect more than a kiss."

She nuzzled his ear. "Let me text Beth and I'll meet you."

In an apartment across town, Beth heard her phone ping. After reading the text she danced around the room in anticipation of an adventure.

* * *

Late night in The Heights and all visitors were home and hopefully snug in their beds. "I'm getting fat," Lynn announced. Earlier she had told Piper that working from home meant time in front of her computer and then a refrigerator break. Her day seemed to be more breaks than computer time. She hoped Dusty would be sympathetic because Piper had just ignored her.

"We're all working from home. Who will notice?" Dusty waited for a pillow in his face or a smart remark. Silence. He pulled her closer. "Something bothering you?"

She sighed into his arms. "I feel like I'm lost. Nothing is as I'm used to living. I've dealt with some horrible events in my life, and I've survived - mother's death, my husband's death, a life-threatening miscarriage. I survived. Those things happened to me. I found strength in my family and friends. But now although we aren't facing some of the family losses others are, we're still facing a strange new existence. And there's no one there for strength. Everyone is pulling from the same well and I feel it emptying."

"This is a pretty deep discussion to be having at bedtime."

"You asked," she huffed, disgruntled. "I spoke with Allison at the picnic."

"Yeah, I heard Kent lives with Mom now."

"She has taken on her father's business. She's growing into a strong woman, I think. But Kent doesn't seem to be doing anything. He's sort of stuck."

"He'll figure it out."

"Are you sure? He needs to find something to help himself." She snuggled closer. "He needs to respect her and let her grow."

"I think these days everyone has to learn new things and adjust." Dusty couldn't hold her any tighter, so he kissed her forehead. "I think what we have to learn is that we are our own strength. Those that give us strength are still around us. And in these times, they'll need us as much as we need them. After all when a crisis struck in the old days, it usually only hit one or two of us at a time. Now it's like someone dropped a blanket over the whole world and we have to figure our way out."

"That sounds sort of profound." She thought about kudzu again, hiding while alive.

"My work is done. But since we're under this worldly blanket," he nuzzled her ear.

"Sex? The world is coming to an end and all you can think of is sex?"

"You have a better idea?" His hands and lips found her favorite spots.

She sighed. "I guess I can worry about all this better in the morning when you're not distracting me."

# CHAPTER FOURTEEN

Monday morning Tee, masked, walked into the office. "Chief," she slipped off her mask as she closed the door. "Lonzo has some days off between shifts. Do you mind if I take some time?"

Dusty looked up from his screen. "What?" His eyes sort of focused. "Time off? Why not?" He motioned her to have a seat. "Have you reworked the training schedule?" She nodded. "Did you also get Danny's message recommending Sherri and Samson taking that online class?"

She laughed. "They are an odd couple. But they really work well together. They both want to become detectives. Samson finished his robbery training before lockdown. Sherri took the preliminary class in sexual assault." Tee was thoughtful. "She's tougher than I thought."

Dusty smiled at her. "She's like you - sweet on the outside but courageous inside."

Tee felt herself blush and her eyes tear. Why did he have to be kind when she was going to lie to him? "Next week I'll have a training review with each of them to make certain we've got them on the career path they want."

Dusty stared at her but seemed to be looking through her. "Now that Doug is in the department, review his training and see what more we can help him learn."

Tee was surprised to hear that. "Why? Has he asked for more training?"

"No, but a sheriff's department is different than Highway Patrol. It's more community oriented. Doug might appreciate some extra training opportunities with his new PR job."

"I'll look into it," she agreed. She stood, eager to leave the office before she spilled her guts and told Dusty her travel plans. "I left my kids at your place for a bit this morning. I'm still keeping them away from Mama. I'll be working from home the rest of the day." She had to run because she was certain he could read her mind.

"Enjoy your time off." He was back at his computer before she closed the door.

Shame on you, she thought to herself. She felt guilty. But she was certain Rose Marie needed her. When she got back home, she'd do some more research and maybe talk with Wanda. Walking out of the office she slid her mask up just in time. The sheriff rounded the corner. "Your boss in?"

Tee nodded. She glanced at Doug who was trailing the sheriff. He winked above his mask. She was glad her mask hid her smile and she moved on.

She returned to The Heights to get her children. Ricky Mitchell had met her there to babysit. It was great to have a roster of teens willing to help out. She waved as she drove into Lynn's yard. Her children ignored her. They were too busy playing with Ricky and the dog.

She plopped at the table in the mask-free zone and Lynn soon came out with a glass of iced tea. "This is unusual for you," remarked Lynn as she nodded toward Ricky and the children.

"I had to run in to the office." Tee sipped her tea. "I'm going to Des Moines tomorrow. I just gotta see Rose Marie face-to-face. Do you think Kennette would give me a bed?" She could hardly meet Lynn's eyes. Guilt!

"This must be an interesting case." Lynn looked at her speculatively. "What aren't you saying?" She knew the younger woman well enough that she could almost smell deceit.

"Lonzo has three days between shifts. He'll watch the kids. I'm not telling Dusty. I just asked him for some time off." There, she had confessed her sin!

"Why?" Lynn saw that the young detective was being pulled, loyalty to Dusty, and concern for her new friend. "Dusty would understand."

The detective shrugged. "I just have a feeling my friend in Des Moines might get herself into trouble. And I don't want to pull Dusty into this. He has enough to worry about with the sheriff always trying to catch him at some insubordination. Technically, I'm on vacation."

Lynn understood. Dusty's relationship with the sheriff had been deteriorating rapidly since this virus came into play. She thought the sheriff could function under familiar conditions - the way things always were. But he was having difficulty adapting to the ever-changing conditions dictated by CDC directives. Still, she was worried that Tee might cause Dusty and herself trouble. "Can't your friend's boss help and advise her?"

Tee grinned. "Not everyone is like Dusty. I think she works for a good guy, but I don't think they have paid attention to this case, nor have they done the research Wanda and I have." Another sip. "I don't want to rile everyone up. I think I can just go as a visiting professional interested in the case." But she did like the idea of flying with Beth. No one would be checking to see if she had a weapon. Because, for some reason, she wanted to have her weapon. Oh, Lordy, she thought as an ominous chill inched down her spine.

Lynn pulled her phone from her pocket. "Hey, Kennette, this is Lynn. I'm here with Tee. You're on speaker."

"You're coming!" Kennette cheered as her voice danced in the mask-free zone.

"I am," admitted Tee. "Can you put me up? I have to tell you I'm black if that's a problem for you."

"Not at all. I'm sorry you thought you should mention it." She chuckled. "But now I'll recognize you."

"And my pilot," Tee added. Lynn's eyes got big.

Kennette asked, "Anything distinguishing?"

"She's a lawyer in real life."

Kennette snorted, "And lawyers are all one color - sly. My ex was a lawyer."

Everyone laughed. "Kennette, can I text our arrival. Beth is filing her flight plan and didn't have all the details yet."

"Text when you know so I can meet you. See you tomorrow." The call ended.

Lynn was ready to burst. "Your pilot?"

"Beth Seymour." Tee looked over her shoulder making certain no one was listening. "She offered and I really want to get there."

"And I'm not to tell Dusty?" Lynn gave the younger woman a thoughtful look.

Tee nodded. "Please. I'll tell him when I get back. This isn't on my job time."

"No, it's freelance," Lynn reminded the detective.

"No, it's charity work. You understand charity work?"

Lynn smiled at her friend. "I won't say a word about your charity work."

\* \* \*

"Sir?" The shy rookie knocked on the office door frame.

Carlson looked up and motioned her in. "You solved it?" It was becoming his usual question.

"No, sir, but my friend is coming to visit from North Carolina. She'll be here late tomorrow. Can I bring her in to meet you Wednesday morning?"

"What have you ladies got planned?" Mel Carlson sensed this rookie would be a successful law enforcement officer in the coming years.

"Nothing." Rose Marie gave him a soft smile. "She sounds so cool and so professional. I just want to meet her and learn from her."

"Do you think your training is lacking here?" Carlson was serious.

Rose Marie gasped. "Oh, no, sir," she rushed to reply. "She's just my first friend in law enforcement besides everyone here."

"What do you think you'll learn from her?"

"Woman law enforcement stuff."

"Woman stuff?" He tried not to chuckle.

"Yes, sir," she nodded, "there are only three women in my class, and we're taught by men and sometimes the instructors say things that don't make sense to women."

"Don't make sense?" Carlson was very confused.

"Here's an example," she began. "You know Harvey, our trainer?" Carlson nodded. "Well at one of our classes he talked about making an arrest and watching that the perp didn't kick us in the balls." She looked at her boss with a very serious expression. "Sir, I don't have balls."

There was a beat. Then Carlson threw back his head and laughed. "Rookie, I want to know what your friend tells you. Let me know what she protects when making an arrest."

The rookie blushed crimson. "Yes, sir." Another beat. "So will you meet her on Wednesday?"

Carlson was still chuckling. "Yeah, now get outta here."

\* \* \*

After Tee left, Lynn sat in the mask-free zone and thought about going into her real office for a few hours. Then she looked down at her sweats. She'd have to dress for the office, put on make-up. And no one would be there. It was August, things were quiet. She was smug about being caught up with her work. And she understood why. When you don't have to plan fund raising events, you have time to get other work done. That made her think about not fund raising. Government loans and savvy donors were keeping nonprofit services running. But a time would come when fund raising would become vital to an agency's existence again. Would everyone be ready? Or were agencies becoming complacent? She nodded to herself. This was a perfect topic for one of her online chats with other agency heads.

She looked up from her spot in the mask-free zone to see one of her savvy donors coming through the stone wall and the fairy gate between her house and the old Cohen house. "Emily!" She waved and the older woman, followed by her grandchildren, came to the table.

"We're moving in," shouted Amy, the youngest. "Our beds are in that man's truck."

Emily smiled, a little out of breath. Sliding into an Adirondack chair at the edge of the zone, she explained, "Tee's cousins are moving us today. Carl says my suite is ready with the basics. Abe and Juan have gotten all of his mother's things out. The people who bought my house are so eager to move in they're taking the place as is."

Lynn smirked. "As is? Your place is lovely."

"It's old lady lovely," said realist Emily. "I'm certain they will make it their own over time. Their first priority is electronics. They have Kevin on contract to organize their home office space." Meg the oldest grandchild, brought Emily a cold drink. "Thank you, dear."

Lynn smiled at the youngster and noticed again how much Emily sparkled since she took responsibility for the children. "How can we help?"

"I'd like to supervise the movers," replied Emily. "Is someone here to entertain the children?"

"Ricky was here watching Tee's three. They just left. I'll text him." She worked her phone. Read a response, texted again. "He and Ryder are in the vineyard. They'll be right here." Lynn laughed at another text. "Ricky says the kids are more fun than the evil vineman. That's what they call Bri. He really works the boys hard."

Out of the corner of her eye, Lynn saw young Meg blush. The tween was in full crush mode over the older teen boys, Ricky, Ryder, and Jeff. Ah, the sweetness of adolescent love.

Soon life was organized for Emily and the children. Lynn realized that she would be needed at home today. The office would have to wait for another day. Working from home seemed to always turn into multitasking.

\* \* \*

"What shit!" Dusty jammed his thumb onto the 'off' button and Lynn was surprised that the remote didn't shatter. She had suggested they spend an educational evening watching political debates on TV.

"You didn't agree with the candidate?" They had been watching an interview with a Presidential candidate. Because in the greater scheme of life, the virus didn't seem to cause enough drama, there was also a political season and an election brewing.

"Do we make candidates into silly people? Or are they already silly and we just accept them?" He threw himself back on the sofa and tossed the remote to the floor.

"Both." She ran her hands along his arm. "You shouldn't take elections so seriously. You've lived through enough of them to know that there is campaign talk and then there is reality."

"Maybe it's not for me." He ran his fingers through his hair. "I don't think I can stand up and spout nonsense and expect people to believe me." He blew out his breath. "And if they believe me, I don't know if I want their support."

She laughed at his frustration, as she teased, "That doesn't sound like a fellow who plans to run a campaign in a few years." Dusty had confided in Lynn that he would challenge Sheriff Dunwoody in the next election.

"If there were another candidate I could support, I'd forget all about a campaign. But I know I have to do something to protect the good people in the department. Bergy worked hard to raise the caliber of deputies. Since he retired, my staff and I have done what we can to get them more training and opportunities. But some of the best have become frustrated and taken positions in neighboring counties."

"I'm sorry that the idea of a campaign disturbs you," said Lynn as she snuggled against him. "But you would make a great sheriff. You're already a great public servant."

"Hell, I serve twenty-four seven now," he sighed, "How much more would I have to give if I'm sheriff?" He sounded discouraged.

"I don't know what to say, Dusty. You have to decide if the additional responsibility is what you want and decide if it's the way for you to be an even better public servant."

"Maybe it's just this virus that makes the politicians sound crazier."

"No," she sighed, "I think crazier is the norm. The virus just keeps some of it masked."

He pulled her into his arms, and they sat together thinking about politics and viruses and public service until the dog let them know that he needed some personal attention.

# CHAPTER FIFTEEN

Tee had wanted to meet Bill's daughter, but COVID had everyone grounded. Today she was learning that all things were possible if you had clever friends. Beth showed up early to pick her up for the ride to the little airport in Henderson County, or as Beth called it, the FBO.

"When did you get you license?" Tee asked as they climbed into the small aircraft.

"I've had it two months," came the eager reply. Tee froze at the passenger door. Beth laughed. "Hey, all the instruction is fresh in my mind."

Tee said, "I go for experience."

"I've got some," bragged Beth. "I've been helping the charter company because so many folks are flying private these days."

"How many folks are we taking?" Tee asked as she scanned the inside of the plane which in her mind was growing smaller and smaller.

"I'm borrowing a four-seater because of the distance, and it will be more comfortable." She nodded to one of the back seats. "And it allows me to serve in-air meals." There were water and all sorts of healthy snacks to support Beth on her new thinner lifestyle.

"Whose plane is this?"

"Butch, my instructor." Beth sort of frowned. "He had an early morning charter, so I left a note on his desk. I told him we would return Thursday evening. Will that be enough time for you to do whatever?" Beth had a court case calendared for Friday. She had assumed this would be a quick turnaround flight.

"I don't know." Tee wasn't certain why she was going. There was just that nagging feeling of danger.

"Butch will be flexible." Beth helped Tee settled in, handed her headphones, straightened the seatbelt, and noticed a weapon clipped at the detective's waist. "You brought a gun?"

"Of course," replied the detective, "I'm not going to a party. Why did you think I wanted to get to Des Moines?"

"I guess you can't shoot anyone in only one day." Beth wondered what she had signed on for.

A member of the two-person ground crew, made some signals. Beth glanced out her window gave her own signal and taxied to the runway. Soon she revved the engine and began moving. Tee felt as though the plane was skipping down the concrete lane. Once in the air she let out her breath. Beth smiled over at her, "Easy-peasy."

Tee rolled her eyes. "When will we arrive?"

Beth handed her a clipboard. "We'll refuel in Evansville, Illinois. The flight should take about six hours. Weather is great for flying. What are you doing when we get there?"

"I'm meeting a rookie and want to help her interview some witnesses to a twenty-year-old crime."

"Will you get the crime solved by the time we have to leave?"

"You're learning to be a smart-ass just like Herbie." Tee was referring to Beth's brother-in-law, attorney H. Lawrence Grayson. "I just want to make sure Rose Marie doesn't walk into a wasps' nest. And I've got a place for us to stay. Lynn's friend Kennette is picking us up wherever we land. I can text her when we refuel."

"Sounds like a plan." Beth chatted with someone through her headphones, and they flew over the Great Smokies, charmed by the vibrant colors of the sky and the mountains.

"I won't have anything to do," said Beth, "I've never been to Des Moines and would like to meet folks who participate in the Iowa caucus. It's the early Presidential primary send off."

"I know what it is," said Tee. "Maybe Kennette can introduce you to some folks or show you things." Tee tried to stay out of politics. She was an at-will employee and wanted no part in campaigns. Dusty tried to protect his unit from the vagaries of local politics. Of course, if this jaunt turned ugly, Dusty couldn't save her from the fallout. She just hoped this didn't turn into a Thelma and Louise adventure. And she vowed right then to not think about how she had misled Dusty until she got back to River Bend.

\* \* \*

Managing a pandemic in a jail was a challenge for the most sophisticated of incarceration personal. So a county jail was probably a mind freeze for the managing local law enforcers. "This is a shit load of crap," groused Sheriff Dunwoody. "I don't care if these assholes get sick. We don't need all them rules and restrictions"

"Ah, sheriff," one of his minions offered, "if they get sick, we can be sued or something. Besides, our jailers might get sick, too."

"Who gives a shit?" barked the sheriff. "There's got to be better ways to do this." The two masked men were talking as they walked through the county jail, a facility that had been built about a decade ago with all the then-standards for well-planned facilities. "What's this?" the sheriff asked, distrust and suspicion in his voice.

"The infirmary."

"This place has an infirmary?" He looked around. "That asshole Bergman added all those bells and whistles. What happened to a few cells in the basement of the courthouse?"

"Sheriff," the minion almost moaned, "you remember that the state threatened big problems if the county didn't fix the jail about fifteen years ago. The county commissioners bit the bullet and built this place."

"And now we got to keep these folks healthy?"

"And our jailers," came the frustrated reminder.

Sheriff Dunwoody walked the aisle in the small six bed infirmary. There was only one occupant. "Who's he?"

In a low whisper the minion replied, "That's Dawson, the fellow who tried to kill those kids and that old lady."

"He killed Yetta, didn't he?" Yetta Masterson had been a sometime, very secret, hook up for the sheriff. "Why's he here?"

The minion nodded. "He got in a fight with another resident," the sheriff snorted, "and he had to be patched up."

"I got me an idea." The sheriff walked to Dawson's bedside. "Take us a picture with your phone. Me and this murderer that I caught." The minion opened his masked mouth. "My deputies catch someone it's my collar. Make a great campaign poster. His bruises will show up real good." Dunwoody pulled Dawson to a sitting position and removed both their masks. Dawson opened his mouth to protest but thought better of it. Listening to the sheriff and deputy talk might be useful.

"You can't use that if Dusty Reid is your opponent."

"I sure can." The sheriff got a mean look. "I ain't gonna lose this job to that asshole. He probably still has that old lady and those kids at his place, trying to look like some saint."

The two men walked out of the infirmary and Heath Dawson knew more than he had known a few minutes ago. The old lady and those kids were living with that detective. He'd figure a way out of this place because he had no confidence that the public defender could make any kind of defense to get him out of a murder charge.

\* \* \*

"How's our book coming?" Janic asked Mel Carlson as they met at Lake Red Rock, about an hour outside of Des Moines. Janic had invited the officer for an afternoon of fishing and an evening cookout - steak or fish depending on their luck.

Carlson threw his gear into the boat and cast off the line before jumping onto the deck. "It's still out there. The rookie hasn't had much time. We've had to beef up medical center security. She and all the other young officers are picking up overtime."

"She's giving up? We'll never get our story developed if she quits! I guess we could make it up." Janic captained his comfortable boat toward a quiet cove. They drifted close to the bank, and he cast out his anchor. They spent time getting lines ready, baiting hooks, and trying to become one with the fish. Once the lines were set, they talked infrequently about sports and the virus, the economy, and the virus, dating and the virus. Both men were currently single.

Finally, Janic said, "I got it. Our story goes something like this. Three women like the old Charlie's Angels go after a guy they think murdered someone years ago."

Carlson sipped his beer and thought. "Rose Marie is sort of neat and freckled looking but no beauty. The other woman from North Carolina, I haven't met her. Her name is Tee. And Wanda is the woman in Indiana. She's married and has a baby."

"Indiana?" Janic sounded disgusted. "Our story had to have a sexy place, like Lake Tahoe or Montreal or Vegas."

"I didn't know Lake Tahoe was sexy," opined Carlson. He was distracted. There seemed to be a fish on his line. He brought the catch aboard after reasonable play.

"That looks big enough for one of us to eat," said Janic. "Can you clean fish?"

"No, can't you?"

Janic took the fish and tossed it back in the lake. "Steak it is." Both men laughed and had another beer.

They pulled in their lines and packed their gear enjoying a quiet afternoon on the lake in a shady cove while Janic continued to build his story line. "Okay, it's Vegas and your friend Wanda is an undercover cop."

"She's got a baby."

"Ok, the undercover cop is this Tee person. You don't know her so she's really undercover." Janic was unreeling a story as fast as he could think. "All right this Tee is undercover. Rose Ann-

"Rose Marie."

"Rose Marie knows the murderer and follows him to Vegas. Wanda gets a babysitter and leaves the baby in..."

Carlson yawned in the warm afternoon air. "Huntington, Indiana. She's a cop in Huntington, Indiana. Her father might be Rose Marie's father, a guy we looked for in that cold case and never found."

"Indiana isn't sexy," chided Janic, "I don't think you're serious about our book."

Carlson laughed. "I'm enjoying the quiet. Something keeps buzzing. If I had my weapon, I'd shoot it."

"I can take a hint." Janic, pretending to slump in boredom, was excited about all the information he had gained.

"Besides," offered Carlson, "you got to follow procedure."

"That's why we write this story together, procedure." Janic was eager again. "What should be happening?"

"First, you have to have suspects to interview or research to follow."

"Suspects?"

"Rose Marie found your name in the file. She called to talk. Has she set up a face-to-face interview?" Janic shook his head. "She will. She's meeting that Jimmy somebody at the Botanical gardens early Thursday morning." He shrugged, "Masks and virus considerations means they're going to talk outside."

"She only found me and some Jimmy guy?"

"She's also trying to find some woman," said Carlson.

Janic thought to himself, that won't happen. Aloud he said, "That's a lot of writing and no action."

"That's police work," smirked Carlson, "research, follow-up and more research."

Janic was silent for a while, then he jumped. Carlson looked at him. "My phone." He scanned his screen. He gave the detective a sorrowful face. "Sorry, pal. Office emergency. I gotta get back to town."

Carlson straightened up. "No problem. You can owe me that steak. This has been a great afternoon."

"Any time." Janic seemed to agree with the analysis.

As Janic watched the police officer drive away, he got into his own car and returned to town. He had learned a few things and would spend some time on the internet tonight and tomorrow making plans. He would be at the Botanical Gardens Thursday morning.

\* \* \*

Beth landed at the general aviation operation at the Des Moines airport. Traffic was light these days with people staying home and the airlines still figuring out masking and sanitation for staff and passengers. She was struck by the fact that her limited number of charter flights had been a great preparation for interstate travel. She felt confident talking with the ground crew and understood their shorthand directions and could answer their questions and sound knowledgeable.

She and Tee walked into the building observing the mask requirements. They heard a screech and saw a woman waving from behind an improvised barrier. They waved back intuitively knowing that was their host, Kennette. Beth turned to Tee, "Go meet her. I have to do some paperwork."

Tee approached the barrier and slid her mask down for a quick smile.

"I know it's you," squealed Kennette. "You're the right color."

Tee laughed. "Beth says she has to do some paperwork. Let's go outside and wait." The two women walked through the building to the parking lot. "Are we on time? I've never flown private before." She looked around. "It's a lot less controlled and managed."

Kennette nodded. "I've never flown this way. It makes you two so mysterious and dashing. Have you eaten?" They stuffed masks in their pockets.

"That's the downside. Beth threw some water bottles and protein bars on the back bench if I got hungry."

"I've got dinner all planned," promised Kennette. "And your friend Rose Marie called. I invited her to join us."

"Thank you," said Tee as she waved to get Beth's attention. They threw their small bags in the car and enjoyed what Kennette called the scenic tour back to her place.

They arrived at Kennette's snug house in an older area in what their host described as the best neighborhood in town. Late summer blossoms scented the air. Someone was mowing a yard trying to beat dusk. Kids rode bicycles along the sidewalks and drifted in and out of parked cars.

"Just like home," Beth whispered to Tee.

"And so is that." Tee nodded to the patrol car parked on the street and a tall, slim young woman leaning against the door. She grinned and waved.

As Kennette parked in her driveway Rose Marie raced from the street. "I knew it was you. The car almost glowed." She hugged Tee, hugged Beth, hugged Kennette, then was appalled. "I could be giving you all a disease."

The women laughed. "Let's get inside," urged Kennette, "before the neighbors notice our un-virus behavior." She led the way through the door into the kitchen and directed everyone to their rooms. "Wash up and get back to the kitchen for dinner."

Rose Marie took a seat in the living room to wait. Kennette motioned to her. "You can help me set out dinner. You're staying, right?"

"Yes, ma'am." Rose Marie grinned. "I'm so excited. Tee came to help me work this case." She followed Kennette into the kitchen as she continued. "We met because she's interested in this case. She knows my father. My biological father. I've never met him. I hope I can."

Kennette handed her dishes and pointed to the table. She followed with glasses and a pitcher of iced tea. "How long have you known our guests?"

"I only know Tee. We've been talking online for a few months. We meet with Wanda. She's in Indiana." Rose Marie took a breath. "I should calm down and be more professional."

Kennette patted her arm. "Take a deep breath. I know you'll do Des Moines proud." She looked over her shoulder then whispered, "I can't wait to listen to you talk about this case. Your friend Tee has solved some cases with my friend Lynn. I have so many questions." They heard footsteps and exchanged conspiratorial grins.

Tee entered the kitchen. "Those rooms are lovely. I hope we aren't causing you too much inconvenience." She handed Kennette a small bag. "Some jellies from us. A lady makes these and sells them at the farmer's market."

Beth walked over to Rose Marie. "I'm Beth, the pilot." She turned to the other women. "I love saying that."

"She's also an attorney. I don't know whether that's bad or good." Tee thought a minute. "So far, it's good. She just helped three kids get away from their guardian. He tried to kill them."

Rose Marie opened her mouth to ask questions, but Kennette said, "Sit. We'll eat and talk. I want to know why you're here. Then we can listen to Beth brag about her court cases." And that was dinner. Kennette made certain that she had every morsel of information on the cold case. Her guests delighted her as they dissected each line of the cold case file.

As the evening drew to a close Tee was glad Beth had been in the discussion. She challenged Rose Marie's assumptions about information in the file, pointed out the need for facts not speculation. It was a good lesson for the rookie to learn.

Tee yawned. "I think I need to rest. I'm sure you have a busy day planned for us, rookie."

"We have an appointment with my boss tomorrow morning and one with Jimmy Knudsen Thursday morning. I would like to meet Mr. Janic and talk with Rhonda Knox who was his alibi for that old murder. I haven't scheduled those because I wasn't certain about your time here."

"I wanted to leave Thursday morning because my husband has to go back to work," said Tee.

"How late can you leave on Thursday? Mr. Knudsen's interview shouldn't take long, and he asked for it early in the morning."

"I told Butch we'd be back Thursday late. He trusts me," said Beth. "We can leave here by ten and even though there's a time change, we'll get home about seven. We only stop and refuel once."

"You are so cool." Rose Marie was in hero worship mode.

"I like to think so." Beth was in attorney mode.

The evening ended as it began with laughter and friendship.

\* \* \*

Lynn and Dusty snuggled on the couch in his home office watching TV. The talking heads were reporting that a virus vaccine was speeding its way through FDA approval. The projection, promise or prevarication was that frontline workers and those most vulnerable could be receiving inoculations as soon as December.

"That's what the emergency manager is reporting," confirmed Dusty. "The health department and the hospital are already planning vaccination sites."

"Wow!" Lynn sat forward to listen more closely to the reporters. She turned back to Dusty. "This sounds promising. I hope that means Dad will feel more comfortable and re-enter life." Lynn slumped into Dusty's arms.

"I know what you mean," gasped Dusty, trying to hold her up but he just sank back into the couch. "Have you gained weight?"

"Gained weight?" Eyes blazing, she almost leaped from his arms, scowled instead and then slumped into him again. "I don't have the energy to lose my temper. I won't eat tomorrow."

He laughed as he held her. "Maybe I've gotten older. You know, no quick reflexes, no strong arms."

She threw her arms around his neck. "You'll never get older because that would mean I'm getting older, too."

"I like your logic." He helped her to her feet. "Is there anything to eat? I could use the strength." He hugged her and moved her toward the kitchen.

"Whatever you can find you can eat, I'm starting my diet tonight."

# CHAPTER SIXTEEN

Meeting with Lt. Carlson was nerve wracking for Rose Marie. But Tee and the lieutenant had experience meeting colleagues. In fact, as they informally explored the other's credentials, they found they had both trained with the FBI at different times and attended a national meeting at the same time. Carlson teased, "I only pay attention to North Carolina during March Madness."

She liked this man. He was older than Dusty but seemed to have the same calm, professional personality as her boss. Tee grinned, "The ACC always gets everyone's attention then." The discussion dissolved into a lament about the future of college basketball in a pandemic. Rose Marie cleared her throat. And Tee said, "I think the rookie wants us to act like professionals."

The rookie blushed. Carlson asked, "Coffee?"

"No, thank you," replied Tee. "Our host made certain we were fed."

This led into another sidebar conversation as Carlson asked, "You have friends here?"

"My chief's wife has a friend here, Kennette Willoughby."

"I know of her," said Carlson, "She runs that nonprofit that packs grain for the world or something."

"She's the one," Tee nodded. "She's hosting me and my pilot."

Another sidebar. "Pilot?"

Tee grinned. "It's not what you think. My friend Beth is a pilot, so she borrowed her friend's plane. Beth's really an attorney."

"Hell," groaned Carlson, "at least if she's flying, she's not impeding law enforcement."

Rose Marie gasped. But Tee chuckled. "She's not so bad. But her boss! He gives new meaning to the term pompous ass." The two officers laughed. Rose Marie cleared her throat.

"The rookie wants us to be professional," said Carlson. He got serious. "You want me to okay your weapon?"

"I'd feel more comfortable if I could wear it while I'm here."

"You expecting trouble?" Carlson began to wonder about the cold case.

Tee looked at the man. "I've been involved with Bill, Wanda's nanny. We know he's not her father, but he watches the baby while Wanda works." Tee went on to relate the whole story including how she had met Rose Marie. "I've read the files, and I had time to do some detailed research. We all want to clear up Bill's name. I don't promise that we'll solve the case, but we'll at least determine Bill's role in the events."

Carlson was puzzled. "But why do you think you need to be armed?"

Tee shrugged. "My gut."

Carlson nodded his acceptance of that reply. He turned to Rose Marie. "What are you planning?"

"I want to schedule a face-to-face with Ms. Knox and Mr. Janic. We'll see Mr. Knudsen in the morning."

"What do you hope to learn?"

"I want to find out if these witnesses were at the scene that evening and if they saw Bill. Or saw him someplace else. Or know he was with someone else. Anything that would take him off our list." Was the rookie getting too personally involved in the investigation?

"Has Wanda asked this Bill any questions about the murder?" The lieutenant's curiosity was piqued. He started to outline the investigation steps in his head.

"Bill says he remembers the victim, but he says her murder occurred about the time he was assaulted. Someone did a number on him. When he woke up, he was in a shack someplace and Wanda's father was taking care of him. The two men traveled the road together for twenty years until Wanda's father died and Bill kept his promise to take care of Wayne's family."

"That's some story. I was a rookie investigator on that case. It went nowhere. The drug crowd clammed up. One of her guards was found dead a few months later. We all thought he was killed defending her. We wrote it off as some drug war for territory or something." He shrugged. "It never drew any interest."

Tee looked speculative. "Who took over her territory?"

Carlson sprang forward in his chair and put his arms on his desk. "Good question. Vice was involved, but I was a rookie and was moved to other things. I'll ask." He sat back in his chair. "Tee, I'll need some information for you to have a weapon. Let's get it done."

"I'll call Mr. Janic to see if we can meet," offered Rose Marie.

The two older officers left the office, and she placed her call. "Mr. Janic, this is Rose Marie Jaeger again. I've got another officer interested in Ms. Somerall's case. She's visiting from North Carolina. Do you have time to talk with us today?"

"How about tomorrow?" Janic asked.

"She has to leave tomorrow." Rose Marie thought, then asked, "We have a meeting at eight. Can you meet us at ten? Then she would only delay her flight an hour."

"That'll work, come to my office."

They hung up and Rose Marie again unsuccessfully tried to locate Ms. Knox.

\* \* \*

One thing about the pandemic, thought Lynn, it was allowing time for several agencies to reorganize or merge. Sadly, some, especially those not supporting direct services, were just melting away. The Arts Council was the best or worst example. So much of its income came from concerts and Little Theater productions. The income had vaporized. The board had announced yesterday that the last staff member had been let go. Rory! She was heartbroken. Rory Prentiss was a good friend and an energetic executive director who knew where to find grants and how to administer funds appropriately. She thought about his most ambitious effort - a prestigious grant that brought in a professional troupe to demonstrate to community college trades' students the type of jobs available backstage in the entertainment industry.

Sitting in her home office she was flooded with memories. That was the spring when she and Dusty married, when Jim met Marianna and when they all fell in love with Sonny Bosco. She took a minute to remember Sonny's courage through a devastating illness. In Lynn's opinion everyone who touched Sonny during her illness came out a better person.

Her cell buzzed; she checked caller ID. "Hey, Rory. I was just thinking of you."

"Sweetie," he moaned over the ether, "I woke up this morning and couldn't believe I have no job." She heard a sob. "I needed to hear a friendly voice."

"Rory, pick up some pastry and come over to my mask-free zone."

She ran to the kitchen to make another pot of coffee. Many of her friends swore by those little coffee pods. But in her kitchen people drank coffee by the gallon. She knew that this second pot would be gone by noon. The first pot had disappeared during Dusty's early morning meeting. The mask-free zone had hosted Dusty's unit for a quick briefing on some hospital security issues. People were trying to break in to visit elderly relatives suffering with this virus. She didn't know what the team decided but it had taken one pot of coffee to decide. The current pot would serve Bri Llewellyn on his vineyard break; Emily Jacobs on her daily visit trolling for junk food; and soon, Rory as he lamented his lack of employment.

Thud, bump, crinkle. Rory arrived with two bags of treats and a lot of noise. "Sweetie, I hope you like day old." He sighed. "I'm unemployed and watching for bargains."

"Two dozen cheese Danish?"

"Umberto said no one wanted them yesterday." He handed one to Lynn and took one for himself. Soon they were settled at the mask-free zone table, coffee and sweets in hand. "I know why the board had to let me go. I feel so hopeless, though. What can I do? Who wants an old gay former executive director of an arts agency?"

Lynn licked her finger. Umberto's cheese fillings were heavenly. "Did the board indicate that this was forever, or temporary?"

"I don't care what it is, I need to have a job now!" He hung his head. "Sweetie, there is no money, my cupboard is bare. I don't save for rainy days. I enjoy the sunny days."

122

"No savings? Not even retirement?"

"Of course I have a retirement plan. Michelle organized that for me years ago when she was on the board. But I have very little cash for now." He took another pastry. "Maybe I could work for Umberto or become a checkout clerk at the grocery store."

Lynn had heard similar laments from others as local small businesses downsized or closed. "What skills do you have? We can put your resume out on the network. Maybe someone needs your skills." Over the years Lynn had helped establish a network of local agencies where they could quickly share good and bad news. Recently she had created a job available, and job wanted section. She hated that there were more folks who wanted jobs than there were jobs available.

Rory looked miserable. "I have skills, but no one needs them."

"Tell me and I'll help you present yourself."

He sat up a little straighter. "What not many know is that I have a business background. When I was younger and looking to succeed in the world, I got my degree in accounting and business."

"Accounting?"

"I never sat for the CPA exam. I landed a job in managing accounts for an insurance company." He sighed dramatically. "I quit because I felt my artistic side was being stifled. I took a job with a gallery as business manager and once I found the Arts Council job it seemed to bring me all together." He nodded. "You know what I mean, both sides of me fit and I became one person."

Lynn smiled. That was a good description of the man. He had flare, but also a deft touch in managing grants and budgets. She cleared her throat. "You know my board budgeted two positions for my office before things went crazy in the world. One of those jobs involved grant administration and management."

He perked up. "Did I just hear angels sing?"

She laughed. "I don't know about that. But I'm willing to give you an opportunity to see if you fit. Let's go down to the office. When the office space was remodeled, the second floor was designed with several staff offices. One of those offices is for my imaginary grant person. Wanna see if it fits?"

Eager to see his new office, Rory hustled her out to his car. Over her shoulder Lynn noted that they were leaving well over a dozen

Danish. She knew that by the time she returned, the coffee and Danish would have disappeared. She wished Rory wasn't in such a hurry. She would have liked to stash two or three of those pastries for this afternoon.

\* \* \*

Janic smirked as he hung up his phone. He had rushed back to Des Moines last night. He had no problem setting a meeting with the rookie because he would be on his way out of town by ten tomorrow. There had been a lot to do - research the names he had gotten from Carlson, design his action and assault at the botanical gardens, and then plan for a few days travel. He had worked through the night on the internet and finally had a good idea of where the professor was and who this Wanda was. He finally crashed about three in the morning. Awakening mid-morning he began formulating his plan. First a quick email to his virtual office to let the working-from-home staff know he was "going into quarantine" because as he typed, "This bug finally found me. Resting in Red Rock for a few days."

He scrolled through the immediate responses of recommended healing potions, good wishes, and commiseration from those already suffering. With a final, "Ron's in charge until I get back," he went silent in the business world. He'd take care of Jimmy tomorrow and keep driving. After cruising around the parking lot of the botanical gardens he had a clear idea of what to do. He knew the time for Jimmy's meeting. Using all the police process information he had absorbed during his years of staying close to the law, he knew his first moves should be to get himself off the grid.

Preparations began. Slowly and methodically, he got all the cash he kept at hand, packed some old clothes, sorted through camping gear, food, and a few of his weapons. Once he had the Mercedes packed, he spent time securing the house. He left home by late afternoon to establish a bunker at his hideaway.

\* \* \*

After Tee had met with Carlson, she had joined Kennette for what the woman called her political tour of Des Moines. Beth loved it. They did an outside walk around of the beautiful state capitol building, then drove passed several diners and meeting spots that Kennette identified as 'must visits' for any Presidential wannabe. They also had time to visit Kennette's office and learn about the agency's mission and success.

As Kennette observed, "It doesn't make any difference who's President or dictator or king, people are always hungry."

"Amen."

Beth said, "You're singing to the choir. Lynn has us all tuned in to community need."

"Yes," chimed in Tee, "but I've never toured an agency like this that attacks world need." They looked around the warehouse with packages of grain ready to go out to the world. "You do great work." She gave Kennette a quick, unsanitary hug.

"Thank you," their host said through her mask. "But there are always more people in need. Thank God, we have our bountiful harvests." She pushed her friends out the door. "We better get home. Rose Marie will wonder where we are."

"You've entertained us all day," said Beth. "Let's grab some Chinese carryout. My treat." She looked at Kennette over her mask. "There is Chinese carryout in Des Moines?"

Kennette laughed, "And Thai, Vietnamese, Korean, Mexican and a few others I haven't tried yet."

\* \* \*

Some hideaway, Janic thought as he carried a late dinner from his Mercedes into the most undesirable room in his motel. Years ago, when he had purchased the place and spent heavily to update it, he had learned that one room, close to the back doors, on the main floor was too noisy for customers. It seemed to collect noise - the ice maker, the entry doors, the HVAC system humming and grumbling all night, and smells of detergent and bleach from the motel laundry across the hall. He had to admit it was a hellhole. But useful.

He had claimed the room as his, moved in some supplies, enhanced the electronics, and found uses for the place that had never entered his mind in those early years of ownership. In those days he had thought of it as his play pen - women, drinking, all night card games. As he grew his wealth and his holdings, he found the room useful as a place for his other business. He used it to meet folks who shouldn't be his friends, to keep information close that he didn't want at home or in his office, and today he was using it as a bunker - the jump off for his witness elimination program.

Over lunch he began to plan the next phase of his program. At the top of the list - he needed different wheels. A person didn't disappear in a Mercedes. It was a car that shouted, "Look at me!" Staring through the motel window sheers into the backside of the parking lot, he saw the bookkeeper, Scottie, pull up in a sound, and anonymous looking truck. He had an idea.

Slipping on his mask per company policy he ambled down to the motel business office. Popping his head into the office he said, "Scottie? How's it going?"

The young man jumped from his chair, slipped on his mask. "Mr. Janic, I saw your car. Can I help you with anything?"

"Yeah, I'm taking some gear that I keep here to my place in Red Rock. I'm packing it into my car hoping I won't hurt the leather seats." He tried to look repentant about puncturing the leather.

"Take my truck, sir," the eager bookkeeper offered.

Bingo! thought Janic. "That's a kind offer, son." Butter him up. "You wouldn't mind?"

"No, sir, we're shorthanded as you know. I promised the manager I'd help out as night clerk. I don't mean to speak against an employee, sir. But Rhonda hasn't been in for a few nights."

Janic shook his head in understanding, or sympathy, or the fact that he knew why Rhonda wasn't coming in. "I appreciate your help here. Now I feel bad about asking this favor."

"No, sir. Anything to help. You're a good employer."

He was? Janic never thought in HR terms. If you worked hard, he paid well. "Scottie," he began sounding reluctant to ask, "are you serious about that truck? If so, I won't have to worry about hurting the Mercedes upholstery."

"Of course, sir. Can I help you unload or pack or something?"

"Sure," Janice replied. "I'm taking camping and hunting gear out to my country place. It doesn't do me any good in town." The two men secured their masks as they walked through the lobby, waved to the desk clerk, and exited the building.

The pickup had one of those secure tops over the bed, so all the gear would be protected from weather and from pilfering. As they transferred the items Janic said, "Scottie, let me run into my storeroom here and get a few more things."

When he returned he stashed two bags and a briefcase into the truck. Turning to Scottie he said, "Take these." He handed over the keys to the Mercedes. Scottie's eyes bulged. "Now, I may get stuck in Red Rock. You'll need wheels to get home and back to work. You drive the Mercedes until I return." He pulled out his wallet. "And here's a credit card for gas." He winked. "You must have a girl you want to impress." And Janic thought, if anyone checks, my credit card will be here in town. He was impressed with his own farsightedness.

"Thank you, sir," Scottie finally spit out, almost too surprised and delighted for words.

With that Janic did some last-minute work, including leaving his cellphone turned off and locked in a file cabinet, secured the room, and drove off. His final act of anonymity was to spread mud over the license tags. All trucks were muddy. This truck now looked hardworking and unknown.

Once Janic's transportation problems were solved, he turned to his plan for Jimmy. He decided that the truck was a great weapon and an accident at the botanical garden might be just the ticket. His initial thinking had revolved around a sniper assault as his target walked through the gardens' parking lot. But a truck! He'd hit James and leave town.

He drove into one of the suburbs and found a grocery store parking lot to spend the night. He spread his sleeping bag in the covered truck bed and crawled in for a quiet rest. He was off the grid now and wanted to stay that way. Cash for food and fuel. And sleeping bag nights.

\* \* \*

Renee Kumor

Four women sat around Kennette's kitchen table for another evening of laughter and friendship. Rose Marie ran through a list of places to see. "I showed them everything," boasted Kennette.

"It's hard to believe we're heading toward a Presidential election in November," observed Rose Marie. "The caucuses are much more exciting."

"And focused on us," said Kennette. "It's our big tourist season!"

"You all have to come to River Bend," said Tee. "We're small but we've got things to see."

"Like what?" asked Beth, wondering if she had missed the exciting parts of River Bend. Tee scowled at her. "You know, the place where you and Lynn were chased by those drug guys. And the place in the Little Theater where Lynn found that dead body. And the place where Lynn was tied up by the terrorists."

"I thought that was in Boston," interrupted Beth.

"Oh, yeah," agreed Tee. "I guess that's another trip. And we can go to Raleigh and find the place where she crawled through the escape tunnel with that little dog to get away from an assassin."

"He wasn't after her, he was after that old man who owned the dog," Beth reminded her."

"Oh, yeah."

"I really want to meet this Lynn person," chortled Rose Marie. "She sounds like Wonder Woman."

"Her husband calls her something else," said Tee. "We just think of her as a crime magnet. She says she wasn't this way until she married Dusty."

"Sounds like a match made in heaven."

"Or in True Crime magazine." Everyone laughed.

"I need some sleep," yawned Tee. "Tomorrow will be here soon."

"I didn't realize how late it is," gasped Rose Marie. "I'll be here by seven-thirty." The rookie was out the door.

The other women said good-night, ready for early meetings and a mid-morning flight back to River Bend.

# CHAPTER SEVENTEEN

Tee and Rose Marie walked into the botanical gardens. It was early morning and a staff member waved to them. She was wearing her mask and greeted them. "Mr. Knudsen told me he was meeting police officers." She looked at Rose Marie in her patrol uniform and smiled. "It must be you two."

"Yes, ma'am," the rookie replied.

The woman led them toward an exit door and directed them along a pathway through a work area to a utility gate. "He's through there waiting for you."

Walking through the gate, they found themselves in a small garden. Mr. Knudsen, masked, waved indicating that they should follow him. And they did, walking past the Bonsai display, through the rose garden, down a path with small bright blossoming shrubs and flowers to the Reflection Garden or, as Tee thought, the back of beyond. It was as far from the center of activity as possible. "He's a member of the board of directors here," whispered Rose Marie behind her mask. "He's pretty important in town. I wonder how he got mixed up in a murder investigation?"

James Knudsen had set the meeting early and he was prepared for them. He had arranged three chairs around a small table. When they got to the table, he removed his mask. Mr. Knudsen was a big, fit, aging blond farm boy turned attorney. "Ladies." He gestured toward the chairs. Both officers removed their masks. Rose Marie was in her uniform and Tee was dressed in what she thought of as her detective disguise - badge clipped in waist band on one hip and holster with weapon secured on the other. She was wearing a soft yellow summer weight blazer to keep both under wraps.

Once seated Tee, as the experienced detective, in a prearranged plan of action with the rookie, took over the introductions. "Sir, thank you for seeing us today. I am Detective Teniquia LaMont from River Bend, North Carolina. A year or so ago I worked a lost child case and a hobo helped us locate the child. He expressed a desire to leave the road and be reunited with his family. I contacted his family and helped them reunite." She took a moment to enjoy the garden area before continuing. "The story became complex when the hobo's daughter, also a police officer, became suspicious that the man was not her father. She was correct; he wasn't. He had traveled on the road with her father for twenty years and cared for the man until his death. Bill, the hobo, promised his road partner to look after the family he had left behind in Huntington, Indiana decades ago. That's why my hobo, Bill, pretending to be his old partner, had us return him to that family to honor his friend's request."

James interrupted with a curious smile. "That's already quite a story. I can't wait to see where I fit in." He gave Tee a smile inviting her to continue, and she relaxed with this courteous, friendly man.

"Wanda, the daughter, confronted Bill and learned that her mother had convinced him to pretend to be Wanda's father." Tee smiled. "I might add that Bill and Wanda's mother seem to be an item these days." Rose Marie gasped, and James laughed. "But Wanda is a good detective and during this time was very pregnant, so I continued investigating to see who this man really was. I might add that in Huntington he is becoming a beloved member of the small family and is the eager substitute grandfather for Wanda's baby." Now she hung her head as she continued, "Over the months as I had time, I pursued Bill's history and finally found his origins here in Des Moines. I was very surprised to learn that he was a person of interest in an old murder case. When I contacted the local PD, I met Rose Marie who, as a rookie, had been assigned to review cold cases."

"Does the department expect rookies to solve cold cases?" James asked with a twinkle in his eye.

"No, sir," replied Rose Marie. "They use it as an exercise to learn procedure. But I had an ulterior motive. I knew that Bill, William Halstead a former professor at Drake, was my biological father. And I wanted to learn all that I could about him and why he was a person of interest in this case." She smiled at Tee. "Imagine my surprise when Ms. La Mont called to ask about my father and indirectly about the case."

Tee said, "Neither Wanda nor I can imagine Bill as a murderer." She now looked at James. "And we know from the files that you were also a person interviewed during this investigation." She was a skilled interrogator and knew when to pause.

The attorney gave the two women a rueful smile. He understood interrogations, too. But he could cooperate. "I'm glad he's alive. That fellow's been on my conscience for decades." He blew out his breath then settled back on his chair. "Let me tell you about that night. I went into the military right out of high school and did four years. I only served one hitch because it wasn't the career I wanted. I came home. My family owns a hardware store in a town south of Des Moines. I didn't want to work for Pop, so I got this job as a bodyguard for this woman, Darla Somerall, who was a mid-level drug dealer. Very successful. I worked with another guy, Ray, and we guarded her house.

"That night your friend Bill, he was called the professor, came by to beg for some credit. He was already into Darla for thousands. I don't know what they said, but she called me and told me to give him a train ride." He looked guilty. "That was her signal to beat the guy up and put him in a box car at the freight yard. Your Bill was my first guy. I had only been on the job a few weeks. I didn't want to beat him up. I was much bigger. I put him in my truck. Then I gave him a couple of pills and told him it would take the edge off. I gave him some liquor to wash it down. I drove around and waited for the pills and liquor to work. He finally slumped into the passenger seat of my truck. I was going too fast and got pulled." Here he laughed. "That was my alibi. I couldn't have gotten the ticket and killed Darla. Once the traffic officer released me with my ticket, I took Bill to the freight yard and dumped him in an empty car. I drove home to my family. The next day I told Pop I was going to college."

"Obviously, the police knew about you working for Darla," said Tee.

"I think they had an undercover guy watching her operation. They knew about me and Ray and Janic."

"What happened to Ray? We saw his name in the file. He was never interviewed."

"About two months later his body was found down river when someone was pulling old tires out." James shrugged. "I always thought that whoever killed Darla killed Ray, too."

"And the other fellow, Janic?" asked Tee.

"He's a big real estate developer here," said Rose Marie. "I talked with him, Tee. He said he wasn't there that night. We have an interview with him later this morning."

"But why was he in the file?" asked Tee.

"He was Darla's boyfriend," James explained. "We're all adults here." They nodded. "She kept him around for her entertainment." The attorney decided that was all he would say. If Janic told the officer he wasn't there; James had no interest refuting the man's claim and getting dragged into a rehash of this case. They were only interested in their friend anyway.

"Oh," Rose Marie blushed.

"Sir," Tee recapped, "You admit to being at the murder scene but according to the evidence timeline, you and Bill were away from the area, together, when she was murdered."

"Yes." James smiled. "He might not remember, but we do have my traffic violation on record."

"You also say that you had no other contact with Ray?"

"That night was the last I saw him. We never hung out unless we were working, and I was off to school within two weeks of the murder."

"Did you have contact with Mr. Janic during those days?"

"No, we never associated at that time and our paths don't cross these days. I'm counsel for the medical center. I know he's successful in his real estate ventures, but we don't move in the same circles." Something began to puzzle Knudsen. Why had Janic called him the other day? How did the man already know about the renewed interest in this case? Should he mention the call? That would lead back to informing the officers that Janic had been at the house the night of the murder. No, he told himself, stay out of this investigation. But he felt uneasy.

"Are you surprised by Mr. Janic's success?" asked Tee.

He laughed. "Look at me, from bodyguard for a drug lord to attorney for the hospital. I don't have the right to be surprised at anyone's reinvention."

The two women laughed. "Thank you for your time." They could feel the day already heating up. It was time to move on.

"I know a shortcut back to the parking area," he said. They all refitted their masks and followed him out of the gardens, taking time every so often to admire certain settings. In front of the admissions building, they waved to the gardens' staff and walked toward their cars. At the parking area Tee and Rose Marie stopped to plan their next appointment as James continued to the curb, mask removed, already talking on his phone. The officers were distracted by a revving engine. To their dismay they saw a truck careening along the parking lane, seeming to aim at Mr. Knudsen as he stood at the edge of the pavement focused on his phone discussion. Tee ran, flying through the greenery, seeming to grasp the man as the truck tossed him in the air. They tumbled backward into an evergreen planting. The truck continued to the gardens' exit and disappeared through the tunnel under the highway.

Rose Marie was talking on her radio and had activated her body cam as she raced to the two people sprawled in the dirt. "You grabbed him in mid-air like a spiral pass." Spoken like a true Hawkeye fan. Tee flopped onto her back gasping; James coughed as he tried to catch his breath. "Are you all right, sir?" The rookie was beside herself, trying to talk to the dispatcher and check on her victims while being professional and calm.

Knudsen coughed again, then spit out some blood and dirt. "I'm in one piece, I don't think anything is broken. Officer, what about you?" He rolled onto his side and looked at Tee.

"I tore my pants." Her summer blazer had protected her arms, or she was certain she would have had scrapes and bruises along her elbows and forearms. They heard sirens in the distance.

James crawled toward Tee. He spit more blood. "That was an attack."

"Yes, sir, it did seem personal." They could hear Rose Marie talking to the dispatcher.

Knudsen chuckled softly. "An understatement, officer." He winced as he tried to move. "I think I'll wait for the medics." Tee nodded as the man lowered his voice, "Before you ask, I didn't see the driver. But something has me uneasy. I wasn't going to say anything. But now." He seemed to do another physical inventory. "I think there is some damage. My shoulder and maybe a rib." He shuddered.

Rose Marie was beside them. "Please stay calm, sir, the crew will be here soon."

"I want to correct some information." The two officers gave Knudsen a steady look. James began, "Janic was there that night when I took your friend Bill for a ride. Ray was out front, and Janic was inside. He called me the other day to tell me that someone was reopening the investigation. He somehow knew the professor was alive. He seemed to have a lot of information. Once I heard the professor was alive, I cut him off. I said I had an alibi for that night and hung up." He spit more blood. The ambulance pulled up as paramedics catapulted from their truck to attend the victims. Knudsen summed up his concerns as the EMTs collected their gear. "I've been wondering why he is so interested in this case."

Tee nodded as she put pieces together. Interesting information, freely offered, prompted by a threatening incident.

* * *

Janic had been in such a hurry, he never looked back to see what happened to Jimmy. He had felt the truck hit something. He had one goal - get on the road and then stop somewhere in Illinois to make some plans. He drove the truck through the exit tunnel and made his way quickly out of town. No interstate for him just in case those detectives had time to notice the truck. He would make his way to Indiana by good old country roads.

Soon he was on the road, plenty of cash, good size vehicle, armed and ready. He was allowing himself four or five days to find the professor. That would give him enough time to return to Red Rock to wrap up his self-quarantine, be seen at the grocery or someplace obvious and return to Des Moines, ready to work. It never crossed his mind that Jimmy had lived or that he had become a suspect.

This virus was working in his favor on this trip. Every food vendor along the highway seemed to be drive-thru only. This made him wonder about sleep accommodations. It was fortunate that he had enough gear to sleep in the back of the truck, if necessary. He'd play it by ear once he got close to his target.

\* \* \*

As Rose Marie waited for Tee and James to be checked and prepped for transport, Tee said, "What time were we to see Mr. Janic?"

Rose Marie replied. "At ten." She gasped. "We'll be late." She quickly placed a call. After some conversation she turned to Tee. "His office says he left for his lake place to self-quarantine."

"I'm uneasy about this, Rose Marie," explained Tee. "We just had a potential witness attacked." She studied the rookie. "You do know this was intended?" The rookie nodded. Tee continued, "We have two folks on our list that you've talked with but haven't met. Ms. Knox and Mr. Janic." Rose Marie nodded.

Tee asked, "Would Janic or Ms. Knox know we were meeting with Mr. Knudsen today?" Rose Marie shrugged. "Did you tell someone in your department?"

"Only Lt. Carlson. Remember you told me about backup. I always try to make certain he knows my plans."

"Would he have told someone?" Tee winced as the EMT swabbed her knuckles.

The rookie shrugged again. "I don't know who he talks to. And anyone could have heard us talking in the office. Some of the guys from my class have been interested, especially once we heard from you." They were quiet with their thoughts. "Do you think either Knox or Janic might have a friend in the department interested in what I've found?" speculated the rookie.

Tee looked at her new friend and nodded. "Someone may have kept up friendships for all these years to make sure no one reopened the case." She stood. "Let's assume that Janic is the perp and that he has inside information. Who else would he go after?"

"That's a leap," said Rose Marie, remembering Beth's cautions. "Do we have any evidence?"

Tee thought about this. She couldn't say she was listening to her gut. This was a rookie who hadn't developed a gut sense yet. Going into trainer mode she said, "Let's think about what we know. Mr. Knudsen is attacked. He gives us information revealing Janic's interest and prior knowledge of the case reopening. We have no other information. And Mr. Janic is not available for a previously set interview." Tee flexed her finger, covered with antiseptic. "It is thin, but all we have. Or we try the last name in the files."

"The only one left in the file besides my father is Ms. Knox. I phoned her last week. She works at a motel as the night clerk. She remembered the murder and confirmed her alibi for Janic saying he had been an off and on customer and helped her get a job once."

Tee edged off the gurney. "Why do you think Janic bought sex when he has been referred to by Mr. Knudsen and in the file as Darla's sex partner?" She frowned trying to organize her thoughts better. She factored Knudsen's information about Janic into her thinking. "He didn't need to buy sex." Tee offered her conclusion to Rose Marie.

"Maybe he was a sex crazed person?" The rookie was beet red again.

Tee chuckled. "Maybe in novels. Besides this Darla probably kept tabs on her lover boy. She didn't want an STD."

They were distracted by the lead EMT issuing directives. Knudsen was being placed into an ambulance. "You can go, officer. Your gentleman friend needs further x-rays." The policewomen asked to stay with the victim, but the EMT said, "No dallying in the ER. It's this virus. Call the ER in an hour." The emergency vehicle raced away. Virus protocols would keep them from the ER and made it necessary for them to wait for a report on James. He had taken the brunt of the fall. The EMTs had speculated on injuries and wanted x-rays.

As they sat on a bench at the edge of the lot    Rose    Marie frowned, "You believe Knudsen, don't you? And you suspect Mr. Janic is important to this case?"

Tee was certain Janic was in the wind. "Sort of." Her gut was working overtime. "Let's ignore him for now. If you have the Knox woman's address, let's make a call, in person. We can check Mr. Janic later. We'll check on Mr. Knudsen later, too." She wanted Rose Marie to post a guard at the hospital but thought pandemic protocols would be sufficient for now. "Let's go find Ms. Knox."

\* \* \*

They left the botanical gardens and Rose Marie drove through Des Moines. "You have to tell me more about sex." Rose Marie recapped their earlier discussion. "You were explaining about Janic not buying sex. You're teaching me so much. The guys here would never talk to me like that or include me in this type of a discussion. They would all be blushing and find a reason to leave the room or send me for coffee."

Tee nodded at the rookie with the angelic, innocent face. "Once you start to learn more and have suggestions that add to solving crimes, they'll forget that you're a girl rookie." She gave an experienced nod. "It'll help if your partner is comfortable including you in any discussion of the dark side of a case."

"Dark side?"

"You know," Tee shrugged, "Rape, child assault, really messy murder scene. Those will be tests for you and your partner. You'll have to hold your emotions in check, be very professional. He will have to learn to not try to protect you from seeing these things."

"Wow, no one ever talked like this to me at the training."

"Aren't there other women on this force?"

"There are. And some of them command high regard and respect for the work they do."

"Why aren't they mentoring you?" Tee sounded angry.

"Calm down." Rose Marie smiled. "They are. But they told us new women rookies that we had to make our own way. They said they want to see if we can handle stuff before they work with us." She thought a moment. "I guess they want to see if we're tough enough, and they don't want to waste time on quitters." She respected the older women in the department and hoped she had expressed herself well.

During their discussion Rose Marie had driven them through the city into a small, derelict area. "Rhonda lives somewhere around here," she said as she drove slowly through the aging neighborhood. "It should be on the right after the next cross street." They came to a stop before a small faded yellow house with an old Kia in the driveway. The house on the left looked vacant and there was only an empty lot, overgrown and desolate looking even in the summer, on the right.

As they stepped over broken pavement and clumps of weeds, Rose Marie said, "Ick, what's that smell?"

Tee put out a hand and stopped the rookie. She did a quick visual of the front of the house noting the open window beside the front door. Determining that the odor was coming from the house, she pulled out her weapon as she said, "Call for back-up."

"What? Why?"

"That smell means there's a dead body in that house." The seasoned detective walked slowly toward the house. Rose Marie tiptoed behind whispering into her shoulder radio. "Have them notify your supervisor. He'll want to be here, too." The radio whispering continued.

After surveying the front of the house, Tee said to Rose Marie, "I know you've never done this before. And by the smell I know the body is going to be ugly. I'm going to look around the back of the property. You wait here for the troops." Rose Marie nodded as they both slipped on masks, mostly because of the smell. Tee disappeared behind a scraggly hedge toward the rear.

When she returned to the front of the house Rose Marie was explaining things to her supervisor. Tee joined the conversation, "Lieutenant," she nodded to the man, "Officer Jaeger and I came here to interview Ms. Knox. Your officer smelled the body as we got close and while she notified you, I did a survey of the property."

"Anything?"

"No, sir." Tee secured her weapon back on her hip. "It's an overgrown area and it doesn't seem that anyone has passed through to the alley recently."

"So, our perp came and went through the front," Lt. Carlson stated. He turned to speak to the assembled crew. "We think we have a dead body inside." He turned to Rose Marie. "Rookie, outline our operation."

Rose Marie was shocked at being told to run the search of the property, but she remembered Tee's instructions to be very professional. "Yes, sir." She turned to two patrolmen and said, "You fellows secure the back of the property." They trotted off. Turning back to Lt. Carlson, she said, "Sir, I'd like you to take the lead going in, but I'd like to be second. And Sgt. Reyes, could you please be our backup here on the porch?" The man nodded. She nodded to Lt. Carlson, and he signaled her to follow.

He stopped at the door as he smelled the unmistakable odor. "You'll appreciate your mask." They slipped on latex gloves and made certain their virus required masks were in place, then Carlson tried the door. It opened as he turned the knob. A cat came racing out. He gave Rose Marie instructions as they entered the house and began the search. It was a small house, and the body was found on the floor in the bedroom. He stepped to the side and allowed Rose Marie to inspect the scene briefly. "That's all you need," he said kindly, "the crime scene folks will take care of everything else. Let's look over the rest of the place."

Her eyes were watering with shock, odor, and sadness as she kept repeating to herself, "Be professional." They finished a quick walk-through, opening the back door for Rose Marie to tell the patrolmen to begin to search the bedraggled lot for any items of interest.

Returning to the front, Lt. Carlson nodded to her, "Still your operation."

She took a deep breath. "Sgt. Reyes, thank you. Please organize a canvas of the neighbors." The man nodded. The crime team, the ME and photographer were waiting. She said, "All yours," and stepped aside.

* * *

Tee stood along the property line watching the practiced chaos of a crime scene. She called Beth. "We're not going anywhere today."

"What? Kennette and I are waiting at the house." Beth had already filed her flight plan.

"We've got a murder and an attempted murder."

"Are you guys all right?" She had not expected to hear a crime report.

"Yeah, but Rose Marie caught the case."

"Kennette wants to know where you are." Tee gave the address. "We'll be right there," said Beth. "It seems this is what Kennette has been waiting for - true crime."

Beth heard Tee groan as the call ended.

# CHAPTER EIGHTEEN

Lt. Carlson lowered his mask and found Tee in the crowd. With a slight nod she understood the man wanted to talk. Tee moved toward him trailed by Beth and Kennette. "Can I do anything, Lieutenant?" She tried to be very professional though her pants were torn, her jacket dirty and her knuckles bandaged.

"Who are they?" He nodded to the other women.

Tee lowered her mask. "My pilot and our host."

"What are they doing here?"

"I was supposed to be leaving town this morning." She nodded at Carlson's scowl. "I know, I'm here for a while longer."

He noted how interested and eager Beth and Kennette were. Tilting his head, he said, "Let's all step aside. I need some information." The two women were thrilled to be included in the invitation. They all huddled around Carlson, no one concerned about social distancing. "You better tell me why we're at a murder site. You were going to an interview this morning. This isn't the interview." He scowled, daring her to explain all.

Tee took a deep breath and thought she felt Beth and Kennette move even closer. "We had a conference with Mr. Knudsen this morning and someone attempted to run him down with a truck." Kennette and Beth gasped. Tee gave them a threatening look. They lowered their eyes, but she knew their ears were on alert for any information. She went on to explain the truck at the botanical gardens. "Because of the attempted assault we wondered who might have known about the meeting? Or was someone following us or was someone after Mr. Knudsen? We had an appointment with Mr. Janic later in the morning. When Rose Marie called him to say we would be late she couldn't reach him."

Tee looked over her shoulder and moved closer. "Mr. Knudsen then told us that Mr. Janic had called him several days ago to warn him about this case reopening. Mr. Knudsen thought Mr. Janic was very well informed on current police activity." Carlson paled. Tee continued, "We decided to visit Ms. Knox while the hospital deals with Mr. Knudsen's injuries." She took a deep breath. "I'd like him under guard."

As Carlson nodded and placed a call, they watched Rose Marie walking toward them holding the frightened cat in her arms, rubbing its ears. "Shit," said the man as he ended his call, "she'll never be tough enough for this job."

Tee laughed. "You know she will. She just saw her first body and helped you organize the scene. And I haven't seen her retching or crying."

He was quiet for a moment, and finally said, "Please send your friends home. I want to talk to you and Rose Marie back at the office." He turned on his heel and walked to his car.

After a quick exchange and a hand off of the cat to Kennette, the officers drove back to headquarters.

* * *

"That bastard!" Mel Carlson bellowed as Tee and Rose Marie sat silently in his office. "He's been milking me for information for weeks and made it seem like a friendship." Carlson picked up a pencil and threw it across the room. Rose Marie and Tee sat bug-eyed. "I'm your leak," he admitted. "He calls and asks about goings on here. Janic wined and dined the old captain for years. He retired a few weeks ago. I guess he tapped me as his next insider. Once you," he pointed to Rose Marie, "started on that cold case, Janic heard it from the captain. When he retired, Janic friended me, and he's been checking in almost every day. Golfing, BBQ lunches, fishing. Anything to learn more. I was such a fool. I should have wondered why a guy that rich wanted to be with me."

They were all silent for a few minutes while Carlson leafed through some papers. "And this fucking report is the icing on the cake." He tossed the report to Rose Marie.

She scanned the front page and gasped. "Janic was the dealer after Somerall. Vice says he seemed to slip into her role, but never got too interesting. He seemed to retire after a few years and began his real estate business." She flipped the pages for the conclusion. "They could never get to him, but they think he used his drug money to make himself legit."

Carlson continued to swear and blame himself.

Tee listened to the tirade but stopped as a scary thought crossed her mind. "We can't find him. His secretary said he thought he had this virus and was self-quarantining at his place in . . . .?" She looked at Rose Marie.

"Red Rock." The rookie explained, "It's an Army Corps of Engineers project and lots of folks have vacation places in the area."

"I've been to Red Rock," said the lieutenant. He was not happy. He grabbed his phone and placed a call. "Sammy? . . . . Mel Carlson. Can you do me a favor and check an address? See if anyone is there and if the house is secure?" He rattled off an address. "Thanks."

While they waited for Sammy to return the call, he explained, "Janic has been my friend," he used finger quotes, "since he learned Rose Marie was working on this case." He squinted at the two women. "He seems to be top of your list now."

"The attack on Mr. Knudsen was personal. He was with us when it happened." Tee nodded. "Thanks for putting that guard on him."

"Guard?" gasped Rose Marie.

Tee nodded. "With one person on our list attacked and another dead, we had to get serious. Lt. Carlson put a guard at the hospital and let it be known that the accident was fatal."

Carlson frowned. "I'm not always stupid. Knudsen's working with us on a relocation plan." He was angry at himself for being fooled by Janic's interest. The phone rang. "Yeah? It's me. . . . Yeah? . . .. Okay, thanks. I'll call you in a few days and explain. Just keep an eye on the place. See anyone, call me." He looked at the two women and sighed. "He's not in Red Rock. Now what do you ladies want me to do?" He flopped back in his chair, looking like he wanted to spit nails. Tee had seen that look on Dusty's face a time or two.

She nodded her head. "I think he's on his way to find Bill Halstead. Bill's the only person left still alive or unharmed."

"And I told him where to look," snarled Carlson. "I want us to stop that bastard."

Tee thought of James all bruised and sore. "Janic will think he killed Knudsen. Thanks for spreading false info. Maybe we should concentrate on Bill?"

"Why is Janic doing this?" Rose Marie was puzzled. "He could have just let us keep spinning our wheels. My father doesn't even know any of this."

"Janic doesn't know that," explained her boss. "I think he's been worried about being charged with Darla's murder for decades." He looked thoughtfully at Tee and offered, "Do you think there's something in his current operation that wouldn't survive an investigation?"

The experienced officer nodded. "I think you may have something," agreed Tee. "We have Janic pegged for the two murders." She gave a side glance at Rose Marie and saw her nod. "He did Darla and Ms. Knox. And probably that guard, Ray. But you're adding a whole new level for this investigation."

"I think he's overplayed his hand, but I also think something must have happened to scare him. That Knox woman or Knudsen might have indicated they wouldn't go along with his story." Carlson grimaced. "And now we know Knudsen had the information to place him at that old murder scene." He looked at Rose Marie.

"Mr. Knudsen told us he told Janic to go away because he had an alibi for that night and didn't care if they brought the case back up." The rookie stared out the window collecting her thoughts.

"That shouldn't have gotten Janic armed for murder," said Tee. She flexed her fingers as she thought through the case.

"I had a phone conversation with Ms. Knox a few days ago. Maybe she told Janic we were checking, and she might have asked for money to keep quiet if the original alibi was false." Rose Marie gave the thoughtful summation. Because through Knudsen's cooperation they now knew Janic's alibi was false.

"The alibi was false." Tee stated everyone's conclusion. "Mr. Knudsen told us Janic was with Darla that night," said Tee. "Once he was attacked, Mr. Knudsen admitted to some uneasy feelings about

Janic's interest in the case. That's why he told us everything while we waited for the EMTs."

"Did he think Janic drove the truck?" Carlson asked.

"No," said Rose Marie, "I think lying in the dirt, aching and puzzled, made him want to be honest about that night, made him rethink his truthfulness about the case." She gave them a slow smile.

"You're okay, rookie," Carlson praised her. "I think you ladies might be on to something. The ME sets the Knox death about thirteen hours after your file says you talked with her. All we need are her phone records to see if she talked to Janic during that time." He turned to Tee. "I agree, he's on his way to find the final witness."

Tee pulled out her phone. "In that case, I'll alert Wanda. Do you have a photo of Janic that we can send?" Carlson nodded. He did some taps on his computer and soon Tee had the image on her phone. After informing Wanda she announced, "We have to get to Huntington. We can ID him and Wanda will need us."

Carlson opened his mouth to object, then closed it. Finally, he said, "Rookie, you'll be in a different jurisdiction. Make sure they know why you're there. Like Tee stepped aside and let the locals handle the crime scene. You do the same. I don't want to be embarrassed." He made some notes. "I'll get a team looking into Janic's current activities."

Rose Marie smiled at him. "Will you watch the cat while I'm gone?" The cat from the Knox murder scene had found a new home. "She's with Kennette."

"I'll stop at your friend's place and check on the litter box." He scribbled Kennette's address in his notebook along with a list of things a cat needs that Rose Marie rattled off.

Tee looked up from her phone. "Beth is making her flight plan. Wanda says she'll meet us at the county airport. We leave here in the morning." She rattled off their itinerary. "We'll stop at your place, get your things. Go to the hospital to check Knudsen. Stay at Kennette's tonight with your cat and Kennette will drive us to the FBO. Beth says to remind you. One change of clothes. There's not much space and you already will add extra weight."

"Weight?"

Tee shrugged. "It's all about weight and fuel ratio, or something. More than I want to know."

Rose Marie's eyes sparkled. Her life in law enforcement was on the fast track. Flying to intercept a murderer and maybe meeting her father.

* * *

Tee and Rose Marie stopped to visit James as best they could in a lockdown hospital even with flashing their badges. It was a hectic visit. Tee had insisted James be placed under guard. The hospital admin wanted James and virus magnet police guards out of the hospital.

The officers found him being placed in an ambulance in one of the bays of the ER. He had solved everyone's problem by having himself discharged to his parents. "They told me they're bored. My sister won't let them work in the store. They're happy to take care of me." He processed what Tee reported about Ms. Knox. "His alibi is dead?" James was bandaged and bruised, but alive. "You're certain Janic murdered Somerall and is now after the rest of us?" Tee nodded. "I guess that guy is serious about no witnesses."

"Yes, sir," said Tee, "You were lucky. We think he might be on his way to Indiana for the last witness. We can't be certain, so we've let it out that your accident was fatal."

James smiled gratefully at the detective. "I heard Rose Marie tell you that you tackled me, and we slid into the end zone. Thank you, detective."

"After that great touchdown, I want you safe," teased Tee. "Are you sure living with the family will work?"

James rolled his eyes at her. "You're from a small town. My brother and brother-in-law will be close-by. My cousin is a deputy, and his brothers already plan on spending nights at my family's place. My wife and kids are moving to another town to stay with her brother." He winced as the EMT pushed the gurney into the ambulance. "I'm supposed to stay calm and let this rotator cuff heal so I won't need surgery."

Tee laughed. "I hear ya. My chief always uses his house as a safe place to hide people." And that was how they dealt with James before going off to find Janic.

\* \* \*

There were not many cars on the roads. Janic decided to stay on country roads; with so few cars on the interstate, his truck might draw attention. Stopping in a small town for gas, he slipped on his mask, reluctant to be caught on security tapes. As he filled his gas tank the man at the next pump said, "We don't wear that shit around here. We're real Americans."

Janic thought he must mean the face mask. He turned his back to the security camera he had spotted, pulled down his mask and said, "I just buried my father because of this virus. He tried to breathe for a week. I ain't taking chances, asshole." He slipped his mask back up.

After he paid the clerk for his fuel and returned to his truck, he noticed that the outspoken anti-masker had slipped a kerchief over his face. It made him look like an old-time stagecoach robber. Janic climbed into his truck and was back on the road before he removed his mask and allowed himself to have a good laugh.

\* \* \*

Rose Marie was spending the night with Kennette who had plenty of rooms for visitors. They had just filled her in on the murder investigation. "This is so exciting. I thought Lynn was making it all up when she told us about her crime solving."

Tee rolled her eyes. "She doesn't solve crimes. She just has a knack for being in the wrong place at the right time." She then went on to relate several more Lynn crime stories to Rose Marie and Kennette. Beth just shook her head.

"I've always worried she would drag my sisters into her life of crime. That's why I moved back to River Bend. I'm sure they'll need a lawyer sometime." Everyone laughed.

"Have you solved this crime?" Kennette asked the detective.

Tee shrugged. "This isn't my jurisdiction. You should ask the rookie."

Rose Marie blushed. "Lt. Carlson gave me a lot of responsibility today."

"How did the rookie handle the crime scene?" asked Beth as she smiled at Rose Marie.

Tee teased. "She didn't faint or throw up." Then she added, "Lt. Carlson is a fair man and he allowed her to take a lot of the peripheral responsibility at the scene."

Kennette hugged Rose Marie. "I'm so proud of you. When our guests leave, we'll have to stay in touch," Kennette wiggled her brows, "just in case you need help solving more crimes."

Rose Marie gasped. "Kennette, my job is to keep you safe, not endanger you!"

"No worries," explained Kennette, "I'll always let you enter a building first." Everyone laughed.

Beth was eager to get in the air as early as possible because of the time change. Taking on last drink, she announced, "Bed, ladies, the plane takes off at 5:37 a.m.!"

* * *

Tee eyed her bed but thought she better call Lonzo before she settled in for the night. "Hey, babe," came his comforting greeting. "You okay?" She had been sending him quick texts throughout the day once she understood she would be delayed.

"We found a dead body today and kept one guy from being killed."

"A normal day for my wife," he chuckled.

She sighed into the phone. "I want to be home. But I think we'll be delayed another day or two. How are the kids?"

"We're good. I asked for vacation. You take your time getting back."

"Has Dusty asked about me?"

"Why? Aren't you reporting to him about all those troubles?"

"We-l-l-l."

"Babe?" Lonzo was aghast. "He's not in this loop? I know about the dead body, and he doesn't?"

Tee yawned into the phone. "It's late. I'll call him tomorrow. Kiss the kids. I love you." She sat in the dark room wondering how she would explain all this to Dusty. Maybe just a quick text. Something like, *I haven't really been on vacation. All well, only one dead body.* She frowned at that thought. Yawned again and decided she would think better in the morning.

# CHAPTER NINETEEN

"Hey, Rookie Reid?" shouted Captain Swain of the Henderson County Sheriff's office. Way Reid was not yet a full rookie, but more of an intern as he worked to complete his law enforcement certification. His Uncle Dusty had helped get him the position in a neighboring county. Law enforcement was something genetic in the Reid family. He admired his uncle and wanted to follow in his footsteps. But did the captain always have to shout for the rookie?

"Sir?" Way was working at controlling the paperwork and electronic data that officers amassed daily or used for research.

"You know someone in James County named Elizabeth Seymour?"

The young man nodded. "Do you mean Beth? She's an attorney. A pretty good one."

"Well, seems she's stolen an airplane."

"What?" Way looked at the man standing behind the captain.

Captain Swain waved at the man. "This here is Butch Blackburn. He teaches flight instruction. It seems your friend, Elizabeth Seymour, took a plane out Tuesday and never brought it back." Way walked over, slipping on his mask making certain it covered his nose, then greeted the complainant. The captain handed him the paperwork. "See what you can find out. Butch helps this department out a lot. We want to help him."

One look at Butch and Way knew that he was not a happy fly boy. "I'll get right on it."

\* \* \*

When Tee and Rose Marie arrived in Huntington, Tee insisted that they meet with Wanda's supervisor. Last evening after receiving Tee's call, the Huntington PD had secured Bill's home. This morning Tee wanted to make certain they were fully briefed. Once the captain had heard their report he asked, "What else do you need?"

Tee knew then that all the good things Wanda had said about the man were true. "Captain Whitacre, we need eyes around town. We've given you the man's photo. I don't know what he's driving. We got here as fast as we could. I suspect he may arrive today, scouting, looking for Bill."

Captain Whitacre said, "I got a couple of fellows who have extensive military experience. They've been antsy with these masks and things."

Wanda said, "Isaacs and Brown. They moved into Mom's place last night."

The captain explained, "We're going to do a Teams meeting. I don't want them visible to the neighbors. He clicked his computer and two men, whom he introduced as Isaacs and Brown, popped onto the screen. Tee blinked. They looked as formidable as her partner, Mars, but not as handsome.

"Gentlemen," she nodded. Smiles all around.

The captain introduced the project briefly concluding with, "I'll let Detective LaMont lay out her concerns. I picked you two because of your military training."

"Please call me Tee," she began. "You know Wanda, and this is our third member, Rose Marie Jaeger from Des Moines PD." Tee pulled Rose Marie in front of the screen. "We're hunting a man we believe committed a murder twenty years ago, has recently murdered one witness from that time and tried to murder a second. He is here, we believe, to assassinate Wanda's father, Bill. Bill may also have testimony from that time to implicate our shooter, Michael Janic. Here is his photo." Janic appeared on the screen.

"You don't know if he's here?" asked Brown. Tee knew he was Brown because he was brown, or as the census bureau defined, African American. She knew she was profiling or something, but it was an easy memory tool.

"I just feel he's here. He spent time, years in fact, mining the Des Moines PD for information. We think he got enough to find his mark." She raised her hand to silence them. "Before you ask, he would have gotten information because he is a very wealthy citizen who contributes to various police activities and fund raisers."

"They thought he was a friend." Isaacs nodded. "I know the type. They think money will get them favors."

Tee looked at Rose Marie who blushed as she heard the distain for the Des Moines officers. Tee said, "To be fair, no one except Rose Marie who was investigating the cold case even suspected he had other motives. Once her colleagues learned his motive, they were on board."

"Fellows, you have the experience. These officers appreciate your help with this protection detail." The captain summed things up. The work began.

\* \* \*

"She what?" Dusty had been sitting in his home office wondering how bored he could get. The budget had been adopted by the commissioners, the virus was rumored to be all over the jail, and his staff seemed to be happy to work from home and fight crime on one of the many apps that allowed people to communicate face-to-face electronically.

"She took a plane and never returned it. I looked into her flight plan, and she ended up in Des Moines." Way was glad he was speaking to his uncle from a distance.

Des Moines? That triggered something in Dusty's stagnant brain. He quickly ran through his email from this morning. And there it was. A cryptic message from Teniquia, something about a murder in Des Moines and her friend that hobo. His mind was so numb from inaction, a murder hadn't even registered. After a short conversation with his nephew, Dusty decided to get down to his real office. He began to suspect that Beth's crime wasn't something to float around a home office. And he knew his officer was the instigator. Tee abetting a crime. The Great Plane Robbery! What would the sheriff say?

\* \* \*

Way ended the call to Dusty and walked to the captain's office where Mr. Blackburn was waiting. "Sir, she flew a detective to Des Moines."

"Iowa?" The instructor jumped out of his seat.

"Yes, sir." Way gulped. "Her passenger, a detective, is looking into a murder."

"Do you know how much this is costing?" shouted Blackburn. "Is James County paying for this?"

"I don't know, sir. I can give you the contact information." Way was really glad he was in another county.

"I have other folks waiting for charters. She's losing me money. By God, they're going to pay for this if I got to rent another plane to fulfill these booked charters." Butch Blackburn was furious. "Give me that contact. I'm going over there and raise hell."

Captain Swain lowered his mask as he watched Blackburn race from the department. "You better warn Dusty." He chuckled and went back to his office.

Way returned to his desk and called his uncle.

\* \* \*

Dusty got into his office and called Tee. "Where are you?"

"I told you I have been in Des Moines." She hesitated then decided not to mention that she was now in Indiana. "Didn't you get my email?"

"Have been? How did you get there?"

"Well."

"Someone wants me to arrest Elizabeth Seymour for stealing an airplane. Is she with you?"

"Wel-lll-l."

"You want to call me back when you got some answers?"

"Give me about five minutes." Tee ended the call.

Dusty's phone rang almost immediately. "That was fast."

"What was fast, Uncle Dusty?"

"I thought you were Teniquia with an explanation about that airplane."

"She better have a good explanation because the owner is on his way to your office to demand to know who is paying for the use of the plane. He's spitting mad and loud. Everyone in your office is going to hear him when he gets there."

Dusty growled into the phone. "Thanks for the heads up." He ended the call and contacted Mars, "I need you and your checkbook in the office. Now!"

As he ended that call his phone buzzed. This time it was Tee. "Chief, I don't have any answers. We got to Des Moines and there was a murder and an attempted murder."

"Where are you staying?"

"One of Lynn's friends was putting us up. There are no hotel charges. I won't file for my meals, okay?" He didn't remind her that office policy required his approval before she could travel and expect to be reimbursed.

"It's not the meals," he cautioned her, "It's the cost of plane rental, hangar fees, fuel." He'd give some thought later to how his wife got involved with plane theft.

Tee sucked in her breath. "Beth didn't say anything about that."

"Maybe she doesn't realize what it will cost."

"She just hands everyone her credit card. Or maybe it's Hank's credit card. Everyone just smiles and she signs the receipt."

"It's costing a bundle and her instructor wants to charge her with stealing the plane. That's a felony, you know."

"Ah, chief," moaned Tee, "I didn't mean this to be such a mess. I just wanted to clear Bill."

"I thought he was in Indiana."

"We-l-l-l."

"Dammit, Tee, where are you?"

She sighed into the phone. "We're watching Bill's house -

"In Indiana?" She didn't know Dusty's voice could reach that decibel.

"In Indiana with Wanda and her guys because we think a murderer is after Bill. I'll explain it all when it's over." He heard the plea in her voice.

Dusty looked up as Mars entered the office. Into the phone he said, "We got you covered. Just keep me informed." He listened to her grateful thanks and ended the call.

Mars threw his checkbook on the desk. "This is one of your stranger requests."

"Let me fill you in." Dusty explained what he knew about the airplane, Des Moines, Indiana, and the angry flight instructor. The desk phone buzzed as he finished. "Yeah…I was expecting him…. Put him in the conference room." He turned to Mars. "Get your checkbook." Together they pulled on their masks and went to meet the angry pilot.

They found Mr. Blackburn fuming in the conference room. He had no patience with a mask so the scowl on his face looked fierce. Before they could speak the man began his harangue. He was angry, abused, misused, and wanted his plane or some money.

Dusty motioned him to a seat. "Thank you for coming in," he began, hoping the man was finished speaking, "we appreciate your cooperation in the case. Detective LaMont had to get to Des Moines quickly in an ongoing murder investigation."

"No one told me anything," Butch grumbled. "Beth Seymour just acted like she was doing a quick hop for someone. I got other charters. I'm losing money."

"How much?" asked Mars.

"How long's she going to use the plane?" He became cagey, sensing his favorable negotiating position.

Mars opened his checkbook, scrawled something, tore the small page, and handed it to Blackburn. "Does that cover it so far? We'll square up when they return."

The pilot's eyebrows jumped to his hairline. "That'll do for now," he gulped.

Dusty stood. "Please email us a receipt." He handed the man his card. "Thank you for your help on this case. We'll let you know when they plan to return."

Blackburn stood, nodded, because no one shook hands anymore, and left the office.

Dusty looked at Mars. "How much?"

He grinned. "We'll square up when they return. Besides, I think this is going to become an entertaining adventure. Sort of worth the price of admission." Mars gave him another grin. "Maybe we better warn Hank."

* * *

"I don't know why we have to stay here," groused Beth. Wanda's husband Greg was pacing the living room with the baby on his shoulder. He, Beth, and the baby had been assigned to stay at home and out of sight and out of any possible danger.

"They wanted us safe so we could tell the story, if it all goes wrong." He smirked. He didn't know why he was baby daddy, and his wife was killer-hunter mommy. Beth's phone rang.

"Greg ?"

"What?" asked baby daddy.

"Not you," said Beth as she looked at her phone screen. "My Greg." Baby daddy nodded and continued his pacing. "Greg, yes, those are my charges . . . . Don't worry . . . .. What do you mean, Dad is threatening Dusty? . . . . Yes, Tee is with me. . . .. Just pay the charges," she screamed into the phone. She listened while her blood pressure climbed. Although how could it get any higher when her charter passenger was out stalking a killer? She nodded with the phone to her ear and finally said, "Dusty knows. Just pay and calm Dad down. I'm safe away from the scary stuff. Tee wouldn't let me go where there might be shooting." The baby began to cry. "Yes, that's a baby. See how safe I am. Me and baby and her daddy are safe . . . no it's not some love nest. It's not my baby!" She pulled the phone away from her ear again, then put it back and shouted. "I hear Bryce laughing. Did he tell you to ask about a love nest? . . . Both of you are on shaky ground . . . remember who's the boss . . . . No, it's not Hank. . . No one is going to arrest me. . . .. Just pay the bills!" She flung the phone across the room. It landed softly on the baby's blankets.

"Trouble?" asked Daddy Greg. "I'm an attorney; maybe I can help."

"I'm an attorney, too," groused Beth.

"I thought you were a charter pilot." He squinted at her. "A charter pilot about to be arrested for something?"

Beth couldn't believe Greg hadn't heard the whole story. Maybe Wanda kept things close so he wouldn't worry. She said, "Let me fill you in. I'm an attorney with a pilot's license who helped my friend and detective, Tee LaMont fly to Des Moines to help PD rookie Rose Marie interview some witnesses in an old cold case because she thought it involved her father."

"Bill?" Greg was happy to have that tidbit to offer.

"Right, Bill." Beth shook her head. "I haven't even met him yet." She continued, "I thought we would only be gone for a short hop. But we've been gone four days. I borrowed the plane from my instructor. I'd been helping him with charters because he has gotten so busy." She looked very guilty. "When I didn't return the plane, he wanted me arrested. Tee's boss, Dusty, paid for all our charter costs to keep him quiet and not swear out a warrant. I've been putting my fuel and hangar charges on my company credit card."

"Your law office?" Greg knew that wouldn't be done at his firm.

"No, my family company," explained Beth. "Besides being an attorney in my brother-in-law's firm, I'm CEO for the family industrial recycling business. My dad wanted to retire." She gathered her thoughts. "Now my story gets confusing."

"Now?" he smirked.

"You just heard one side of the phone conversation," she said, "I'll explain. My Greg, not you, is our chief environmental engineer. Business is great. Bryce just started working for us because he lost his job as a Broadway chorus guy and came back to River Bend to live with his family. Dad, also known as Hank, likes him so we hired him for his Broadway experience to work for us."

"He sings to your trash?" Greg had an image of an Astaire-like dance sequence across trash cans.

"No, he had some experience backstage in admin stuff which is what we needed - someone to handle paperwork - because Greg was busy handling all this virus trash."

"Which one do you date, Greg or Bryce?"

"Greg dates Kew. They're both Chinese." She sputtered, "not that I wouldn't date someone Chinese. Kew is a physics professor at our community college and they both make dumplings for her father for the family's carry out restaurant. Greg hopes that Mr. Lee will accept him if he can make dumplings. Mr. Lee is very old school and Greg's parents are very well-known, successful West Coast physicians."

"And Bryce?" Baby daddy was entertained by River Bend relationships.

"He'll go back to Broadway when this is over."

The baby had fallen asleep, and Greg sat on the sofa. "You stole an airplane? Really?"

Beth looked ready to explode. "I left a note." She hung her head. "I guess he didn't see it. Or maybe I shoudda called?"

"You know, I was in River Bend once when we met Bill. I guess I missed all the drama."

"I should have guessed you're an attorney. Smart-ass."

* * *

"What do you know about Tee going to Des Moines?" Dusty stomped into the kitchen.

Lynn didn't like the sound of his voice - or the stomping! "Tee and Beth were flying there and needed a place to stay. I have a friend."

"Have you ever been to Des Moines?"

"No."

"But you have a friend there?"

"Yes." She didn't want to give details until she understood the direction of this discussion.

"Well, I got a detective who flew to Des Moines with a woman accused of stealing an airplane and using her father's credit card to charge aviation fuel and plane parking or whatever they call leaving your plane at some airfield overnight."

"Stealing?"

"The plane's owner was vague on what he knew, or what Beth said. I think she just stayed too long, and he had paying customers waiting. Mars had to give the man a check for fees so he wouldn't press charges. We told him Tee was on the trail of a murderer."

Lynn started to laugh. The more she thought about the situation the harder she laughed. It was contagious. Dusty started to laugh, too. "And I had to call Hank Seymour to warn him to cover the charges Beth was putting on his credit card." He continued to laugh. "You should have heard him swear. Your friend Greg," Hank's plant manager, "had just called to ask him about these strange charges. They were getting ready to cancel the card."

Lynn stopped laughing. "Is she in danger?"

Dusty turned to face her. "I don't know. She talked about an attempted murder and finding a body." He paused. "I thought she was investigating a cold case. But she's now involved in some current investigation. And she's now in Indiana. I don't know what she's up to." He put his arms around Lynn as he worried about his officer, away from home and away from her team.

Jason burst into the kitchen. "Way said Beth stole a airplane!" He rolled his eyes at Dusty and Lynn embracing. "And Bryce said she's organizing a manhunt and doing fly-overs in Indiana."

Lynn laughed. "Talk about how gossip can evolve." She stepped back from Dusty's embrace. "I think you better explain."

He got a beer from the refrigerator. "I like his story better. Then no one will know my detective is involved."

"Danny? Mars?"

"Tee," said Lynn.

"But she's on vacation or something."

"Or something," growled Dusty. They both looked at him. He said, "Tee is involved with some law enforcement activity in Iowa and Indiana." He shrugged. "Beth is her pilot, and she swears she's keeping Beth safe."

Jason looked so excited he could hardly contain his glee. "Wait'll I tell the guys. Does Lonzo know? Will Beth be in the shoot-out?"

"We're hoping there is no shoot-out," cautioned Lynn.

Jason frowned. "Yeah, we don't need a shoot-out." Then he brightened. "Maybe Beth called Patti Ann." He ran out the door.

Lynn went back into Dusty's arms. "I think Tee's secret is already all over town. Is she in trouble? Are you?"

She felt him shrug in her arms. "I don't know. I guess it depends on whether she succeeds in catching this guy and on how skilled the other officers are. And a million other things." He chuckled. "Who would have thought I'd be happy to spend the weekend at Piper's party? It will at least be a distraction."

Lynn agreed. "A small group of friends celebrating an anniversary. It'll be a quiet weekend and you'll have time to prepare a story to cover Tee's exploits."

"Beth stole an airplane?" Piper came rushing into the kitchen followed by Will.

Dusty walked over to the drinks' refrigerator pulled out four beers and passed them out. "Have a seat. It's a long story."

# CHAPTER TWENTY

Two Huntington, Indiana police officers had volunteered to take the night shift in Bill's house. They wanted the women to slip into the house just before sunrise Saturday morning and they could do a little recon then slip back into the house to set up a command post.

And that's what happened. Three officers snuck in during the night with Bill and Nora while Isaacs did a little neighborhood recon. "Nothing," he said as he returned to the cottage wet with dew.

While he was out Brown made certain all outside doors and all windows were secure. "You need to paint the house trim," he told Bill. "I have a cousin who would do a good job."

"Is that part of the security service?" Bill teased the officer.

"No, sir," Brown grinned. "I just try to keep him employed so he stays out of trouble."

Bill winked. "Send him out when this is over."

The old hobo had refused to hide. No matter the reasoning, the pleading or finally an outright order, he had been steadfast. "I am the target. I will be the target." Wanda's mother had had no problem leaving. As nursing director of a long-term care facility, she was up to her armpits in virus. It had been easy to convince her to stay at one of the facilities for a few days. Staffing was becoming an issue anyway.

Although he wondered if sending her to a virus raging nursing home was safe, early Saturday morning Bill packed Nora off to a more secure location. He walked back into the house and cooked breakfast for the five people who were hiding throughout the small house, staying away from windows. Then lunch for five, and finally dinner. "I think I'm running out of food," he announced to the house.

"Don't worry," came a reply. "We'll arrange a delivery. Just make a list."

Bill chuckled. "Who's paying?"

Isaacs answered. "Our captain. He doesn't want Wanda to starve."

\* \* \*

Janic spent as much time on the internet as he could at rest spots while he drove to Huntington. After that fishing trip with Carlson, he knew several things. He was able to search the police department in Huntington and find an officer named Wanda. Assuming she was using her married name he googled the officer and finally found an article with her maiden name. Pulling up the tax maps for that county he was able to pinpoint several pieces of property with that name - Hansen.

He searched for the name of Wanda's father and for her mother's name. Using Wayne and Nora Hansen he refined his search to a residential address. In addition, he located Wanda's address, reasoning that if she was at home tomorrow, or going to work, she, and by extension the police in Des Moines, were not aware of his activity.

Doing Saturday morning recon Janic located Wanda's place but did nothing more than drive by. As he passed the house, he noticed a man walk out for the morning paper and a woman standing in the window holding a baby. Wanda was home! He did the same with the place he suspected Halstead lived - Nora and Wayne's address. As he checked at the Hansen home, he was gifted with a view of an older man helping a woman into a car with an overnight bag. The man gave her a peck on the cheek and watched her drive off. Well, well, thought Janic, a man alone.

He drove around the neighborhood one more time. The house was next to what looked like an older elementary school. Between the house and the school was a playground and grassy area. The road passed the house and did a sharp turn because on the other side of the house a stream ran along the property line with a farm field across the stream. The road continued to curve and connect with the next street running parallel. It made the house almost isolated.

Secluded. A man alone. Just before dawn would be perfect for an assault. Tonight Janic would walk the neighborhood and get a lay of the land. After considering his options he would decide on which weapon to use.

* * *

Everyone had shown up for Piper's end-of-summer party. It was a small pandemic-regulated gathering. Piper decided to only count the adults as a safe number of attendees - her and Will's wedding party and her parents. The college and high school crowd didn't count because they never sat still, taking turns on the old motorcycle and the agri-cart to race around the property.

"Where's your computer?" Miguel asked Lynn as he came into her kitchen in midafternoon. The party cookout was in Lynn's yard in the designated mask-free zone. "I told Lori we would do our weekly chat from your place. I thought we could all gather around your screen and say hi."

"That sounds like fun," replied Lynn. "I haven't seen her in ages. School has kept her so busy. The computer is on the dining room table." She put a tray of sliced vegetables on the counter and set out several dips and assorted crackers. "We can all snack and talk." She looked out the window to make certain Dusty was heating up the grill.

Miguel walked into the dining room to set up the online chat. Lori was in her chair in front of her screen as he connected. "How's my girl?"

"Hi, Daddy, I'm fine. I work a lot. With registration for the fall and all these classes online, students and professors need tech support." Lori, a dark eyed beauty, was trying to explain to her protective father that she was living a quiet pandemic directed life in Raleigh. Although other students had been sent home, Lori, a computer science major, had been offered a job as tech support for all the online services the university would be providing to staff and students.

"But you're all alone," moaned the protective father.

"That means I'm not getting any germs," she grinned into her screen on the weekly Zoom call.

Miguel's eyes seemed to search into the edges of her screen. "You have enough to eat? Do you need anything?"

"Daddy, I'm fine." Her eyes roamed the screen. "Where are you? I don't recognize the background."

"Piper is having her usual anniversary celebration, but only with the wedding party." He looked at his surroundings. "I'm in Lynn's dining room." He winked. "She calls it her home office. And she's got this big monitor so we can all see you."

"Piper's there?" Lori seemed to panic as her father nodded.

"You stay there," instructed her father, "I'm going to get everyone." Rushing through the kitchen, he raced out onto the porch and called to his wife and the others, "I've got her connected, come say hi."

While he was gone from the screen Lori sent a quick text message. It said, *Now's the time.*

Miguel returned to the dining room and settled himself before the screen and found himself looking at her empty chair and a portion of the suite entry. He saw her open the door to a visitor. He couldn't identify the caller because the light from the hall was behind the mystery person. Miguel squinted. It was a mystery man! Lori's silhouetted head tilted up and the mystery man bent his head to meet her lips. Was he seeing things? Was it some strange electronic static? Was someone actually kissing his daughter? His eyes almost popped out of his head. The outraged, protective father started to shout, trying to get her attention. He saw her turn back to her screen. She turned back to 'someone' and said something. Soon, two people were walking toward the screen. Miguel couldn't see much because the light was behind them and before they were seated, he only saw torsos.

Lori and a young man sat in front of the screen. "Daddy, you know Doyle." Miguel's eyes seemed to spin in his head.

"Hey, Mr. Santiago," said the very uncomfortable young man. "How are you and Mrs. Santiago?"

"Don't 'how-are-you' me!" Miguel shouted from the computer. He must have really been yelling because the sound coming from Lori's computer filled her whole apartment. "Why are you kissing my daughter?" Doyle hung his head and Lori grinned. After some silent exchange between the two young people, Doyle stepped away from the screen, texted on his phone and returned to the computer.

"Did I hear you shouting?" Justine asked her husband as she rushed into the dining room. She glanced at the computer screen. "Hi, Doyle, I'll get your mother." The two young people were silent, watching the activity in the dining room as folks gathered.

"Doyle?" Piper smiled at her son. "What a great idea that you both called together!"

"That's not all they did," growled Miguel. He was beside himself. "They were kissing!"

"Kissing?" At least five pairs of eyes stared out from the screen into Lori's place. When had all those people joined the conversation?

"We've got a problem," Miguel growled in an ominous voice eyeing the group huddled around the screen.

"Daddy," Lori jumped in, "no we haven't." She looked at Doyle. "We weren't going to say anything yet."

"Anything?" Piper sounded sort of shrill. "Someone's sick. It's this virus."

Jason came into the dining room and pushed Piper aside. "Hey, pal, I got your SOS."

Piper wormed in front of Jason and almost screamed into the screen. "You're sick and didn't tell me?" By this time Will, Lynn and Dusty had edged closer to the monitor while the rest of the college crowd huddled in the doorway.

"Mom!" interrupted Doyle, "please calm down. What Lori means," he put his arm around her and they smiled at one another. Justine, Piper, and Lynn sighed at the obvious warmth. "We plan to marry after graduation." Four parents, Dusty, Lynn, and members of the college crowd sputtered. "We don't know how long this pandemic will last, but we're making plans." Doyle nodded. "Right after graduation. Sort of a year from now."

Justine was crying and laughing. "I am so pleased." Miguel was still scowling. She elbowed him and everyone laughed.

He cleared his throat. "When were you going to tell us?"

Lori shrugged. "We were trying to figure that out since no one is traveling now."

Doyle grinned. "This worked out. We didn't even plan it." He meant the online family chat, but it was possible he meant the opportunity for him and Lori to spend time together during the pandemic.

"Where do you live?" asked Lori's curious father.

They could see Doyle swallow. "Lori needs a lot of quiet when she's working. We have quarters in the senior dorm. The school provides quarantine space for campus workers. I work at a lab on campus."

"And he helps me," offered Lori. "He runs errands and shops, so I don't have to go to the stores. The school provides meals. We manage." Everyone noted that Lori never answered the question.

"I think this is just great!" said Will. "A wedding next summer!" He had been listening and decided the kids needed a change of subject. It was no one's business if they chose to do more than share meals. "Will the wedding be at the lake?" Miguel had become the general contractor for his brother-in-law Zachary Rawling's lake-front development project. Justine and the kids had enjoyed moving to the upscale resort community. As her boys always said, "Who wouldn't want to spend their days learning to fish and sail and water ski?"

Will's question started a flood of other questions. The parents were talking among themselves, allowing Jason and Patti Ann to stick their heads in front of the monitor's camera and give the young lovebirds a smiling thumbs up. Then Justine and Piper reclaimed the screen with ideas and questions about the wedding, such as menu and dresses and shopping and invitations. They could see Doyle hugging Lori closer as both youngsters became dazed and confused by the minutia of weddings.

The call finally ended with Lori promising to have a "girls only" discussion with Piper and Justine at a later date.

The wedding was all that anyone talked about at dinner. On this lovely summer evening Lynn and Piper had called to share the news with Piper's parents, better known as the delighted grandparents of the groom, and Lynn's father and Marianna. Most of the kids - Patti Ann, Ricky Mitchell, Jason, Piper's two sons, and Miguel's three sons had witnessed the event and enjoyed reviewing Miguel's almost hysteric response.

"What did Miguel say?" asked Way who had arrived late.

"Apoplectic," said Jason. Everyone laughed.

"His little girl," laughed Patti Ann. She turned to Piper. "I bet all you parents are pleased."

"We are." Piper wiped a tear from her eye. "It was lovely. Even on the computer screen you could see how cute they look together. Doyle was hugging her like he was protecting her from some fierce animal."

"Her father," offered Jason.

"He calmed down," said Piper. "Justine had to swat him. But he calmed down."

Piper scanned the mask-free zone and declared, "They're so cute together!" The engagement announcement had raised a range of responses. Gasps. Cheers. Stunned surprise. But everyone seemed to think it was a good idea the more they thought about it, until Piper screeched, "Next year! A wedding!" She was thinking of all the planning but everyone else cheered at the idea.

It was the perfect family gathering.

* * *

When Piper's party broke up, Way offered Patti Ann a ride home. They had been friends for a long time. The two young people had been fast friends through the years of Patti Ann's frightening childhood as she survived shared custody weekend visits with her drunken mother until the later years when her father, Hank Seymour, had attained full custody. In was through Way Reid that Patti Ann had been welcomed into life in The Heights when Way's Uncle Dusty had married Lynn Powers. Those years were a source of calm and warm memories of friendship and security for Patti Ann.

Now she and Way were college graduates. He was following a career path in law enforcement, and she was preparing to enter medical school, a curious experience with the world mesmerized by a virus. As they rode along in the summer evening, she was in deep thought. An engagement in their group. Life was changing. She was drawn out of her reverie when Way pulled the truck into the field where they had watched meteor showers so often with Jason and Ricky Mitchell. Instead of parking out on the knoll to see the sky, he coasted under the trees at the edge of the field. The truck stopped. "Is there a meteor shower tonight?"

"You know, Patti Ann," said Way as he cut the engine and turned out the headlights, "Tonight some folks asked me if we were going to be announcing our engagement soon." He looked at her out of the corner of his eye.

Patti Ann sighed. "They asked me too."

"What do you think?" the young man asked.

"We've never even done much kissing or stuff," replied Patti Ann.

"You think maybe we need a test run? Sort of to see stuff?" Way gripped the steering wheel, not certain what answer he wanted.

"If you want," came the unenthusiastic reply from the young woman.

He turned to her, "I do like you, Patti Ann." He pulled her to him and gave her a kiss. When they parted, she looked at him with sad eyes and ran her fingers along his lips.

"You don't love me," she whispered. He opened his mouth to protest as he tried to pull her back to him. "I don't love you either," she confessed.

"What?" Way was confused. He and Patti Ann had been together for years. It was true they had never had much interest in an intimate relationship, but years of friendship and fun should mean something. Shouldn't it?

Patti Ann thought about the young man. She remembered years of joy. He had saved her from her sad family circumstances. They had met in elementary school because he always seemed to need help with a lesson, and she had been delighted when their friendship blossomed. There had never been any urgency on her part to be more than they were. For his part Way had never demanded more.

Way patted the console between them. "Can we get out and talk?" Patti Ann opened her door and climbed out of the truck. When Way came around to her, he embraced her and kissed her with the awakening passion of a young man. They weren't teenagers anymore and his kiss reflected his maturity.

Patti Ann pushed him away. "You kiss pretty good."

He chuckled. "I guess I had plenty of practice in college." He stopped and looked at her, the moon making her hair silver. "How do you know what a good kiss is?"

"I go to college, too," she laughed. He moved closer focused on her lips and she pulled back. "I've known you a long time." He nodded. "Who's the girl you wish I was?"

"I've known you a long time, too," whispered Way, "And I can ask you the same question." She put her head on his shoulder and they stood in the moonlight wondering what was happening.

Finally, she whispered, "Let me guess." Way dropped his arms as she stepped back to see his shadowed face. "There was a girl you talked about a lot who was in that elective Lit class you took." Way gasped.

"How? I didn't know I talked about her a lot." He looked up and sighed toward the night sky. "I don't know what it is, but I have to know her better." He stared at the trees overhead as a soft wind moved the limbs allowing stars to peek through the branches. "How did you know?"

She tilted her head. "How long have you known me?"

"Right." he conceded. "You have ESP or something." Way watched her as the breeze touched her face and danced through her hair. "Who's your guy? Some wannabe doctor?"

"Who what?" asked Patti Ann.

"You know who what." Way knew her as well as she knew him.

She put her head back on his shoulder and he held her, feeling her deep, sad, sigh. After a moment she whispered, "Jason."

"Good grief, Patti Ann," protested Way in shock, "he's clueless." He felt her tears on his neck. "I'm sorry. I don't mean that he's a bad choice. I just think he's not ready for you." At that statement she began to sob. "I mean, well, I don't know what I mean, but I'll do anything you want." Patti Ann held on to him and cried. She finally used his T-shirt sleeve to dry her eyes.

"I think you're right," she admitted. "He's doesn't know. He also doesn't have a girlfriend. He never brought anyone back for us to meet. He won't be surprising us with an engagement like Doyle did." She half smiled, "Besides, I've got too much schooling to get through before I'm ready to settle down."

"You mean to date him?" Way stared at her, not understanding. Settle down sounded to him like marriage.

"I'm not talking about dating. He's it. I just hope he agrees." Way hugged her again and marveled at how life twisted and turned.

# CHAPTER TWENTY-ONE

All through Piper's party Dusty had communicated with Tee. *Snuck into house last night.*

*How big is this operation?* He had felt helpless being so far away. *Small town; everyone engaged; These folks well trained. Don't worry.*

Don't worry, he thought, of course I'll worry! *What's happening? Another boring wait.*

Piper's party was over, but spirits were still high. Dusty hugged Lynn as they walked into the bedroom. "That was quite a surprise, Doyle and Lori." He kissed Lynn. "We should celebrate."

She kissed him back. "You should also thank me. I promised you a quiet weekend, a distraction from Tee."

He pulled away and began undressing. "I wasn't distracted. She's been texting me all day. Nothing has happened." He chuckled. "She's been locked in that guy's house with four other officers." He pulled out his phone and scanned her texts. "Read these," he handed the phone to Lynn.

She read the pithy comments and laughed. "These observations are really funny. I like the one about Beth babysitting Wanda's baby."

"I kept telling her to keep Beth safe. She says Beth has been arguing that dirty diapers and the baby's father are dangerous duty."

As they spoke one more text came in. *No action yet - we expect late night attack.*

Lynn read the message. "Will she be okay?"

Dusty shrugged. "She tells me that the other officers are well-trained. She says the two men remind her of Mars, but with no money. I have to trust my staff."

Lynn hugged him again. All the distractions hadn't made him worry less about Tee. "She'll be fine. You know she's kept her head in many threatening situations."

"I know." He walked into the bathroom to wash up for bed. After brushing his teeth, he returned and waited for Lynn to apply nightly lotions. He was never in a hurry. He liked the way she smelled when they cuddled each night.

Lynn flopped into bed, smelling great. "Piper will be going crazy with this wedding."

"It's a year away." Dusty pulled her close. "Besides, she's the groom's mother."

"Do you think that will stop Piper?"

"No." He kissed her temple. "But I think Justine is a force and will keep Piper contained."

"It sounds like you're talking about a tornado or something."

He kissed her. "It's not my problem." He pulled back. "And don't let it be yours. I know how folks pull you into weddings."

She kissed him to distract him because she didn't want to tell him that Piper had already dragged her into the wedding plans.

\* \* \*

The tension was increasing Saturday night in Huntington. A report had come in from patrol. They found a pickup truck with Iowa plates parked on a quiet street behind some small factories, close to Bill's neighborhood.

"We checked the tag. The truck belongs to some guy in Des Moines. Des Moines PD checked him out. He says his boss, Michael Janic borrowed his truck to move some gear to his summer place."

When everyone heard the report, Rose Marie smiled. "My guys are doing their job."

"That means he's here," Brown reminded them. "Isaacs is going to move outside and watch." With that plan, Brown called for a little neighborhood distraction so Isaacs could slip out. Tee smiled at the distraction. An old-fashioned ice cream truck parked in the road near Bill's house. The neighbors streamed into the street lured by the music and promise of treats.

All evening Bill behaved like a man at home alone. He watched TV, read a little and tried to stay calm. He had closed all the drapes and blinds early in the evening to allow him to move with some amount of safety. He finally turned out the lights and went to bed. He had no illusion that he would sleep. Even though there were four people hidden in the house, it was eerily quiet. Bill thought he could hear everyone breathing.

Isaacs, perched on top of the elementary school building next door, had a commanding view of Bill's house and surrounding area. He had equipped everyone with mouth pieces and ear buds. He clicked into his mouthpiece. That was the signal that someone was approaching the house. A double click, the person was moving to the back of the property. That suggested that he would try entry through the kitchen. Small shuffling sounds came at the back door. Everyone got into place.

Using a small penknife, Janic worked the door open, then moved through the kitchen into the dining room. He carried a small light that swept the rooms as he moved about the house, and he swore when the light shone on Rose Marie holding a weapon. He leveled his weapon at her as he said, "Well, well, the rookie, if I'm not mistaken. You guarding the old man? You here all alone? Or did you bring your other girlfriends with you?"

There was a click as another weapon was aimed. Janic felt the barrel at his temple. "I'm not a girlfriend or a rookie," snarled Brown.

Tee flipped on a light. "I'm not a rookie either." She retrieved Janic's weapon, spun him around, and very quickly had his hands bound with plastic ties.

"Code," Brown said into his mouthpiece and the neighborhood became alive with police cars as armed officers came through the front and the back doors.

Bill pushed his way out of his bedroom. He looked Janic over. "Who the hell are you?"

"You don't know him?" Wanda stood beside Bill. She had been assigned to keep him in his room until things were settled.

"You don't know him?" asked Rose Marie. She looked over the intruder. "Let's see. Suspicion of murder, Ms. Somerall and Ms. Knox, maybe Ray the guard. Attempted murder, Mr. Knudsen." She stopped then offered an explanation for Janic. "Mr. Knudsen says you were at

Ms. Somerall's house that night and we suspect you tried to run him down the other day with that truck you borrowed from that young man who works at the motel. Those are the Des Moines charges." She smiled. "Wanda, this is your jurisdiction."

"Breaking into a house, armed, with suspicious intent." Wanda stepped forward and did the prescribed Miranda recitation. Brown grabbed Janic and led him from the house. Soon it was just Bill and the ladies.

He smiled at what he thought of as Bill's angels. "I'm exhausted. Be here for breakfast. Tell Isaacs and Brown to join us." He winked at Rose Marie, "We have a spare room here, if you want to stay."

She gave her father a shy smile.

* * *

Dusty went to bed but placed his cell, as usual, close by. He knew how he and his staff would handle the operation in Indiana. But could he trust some strangers to watch out for one of his detectives? He knew he would have a restless night, so when the text came in, he was already alert.

*Sorry to txt so early. Wild night. We got him.*

A cell buzzed in Indiana. "Morning, chief." Four-thirty was morning, wasn't it?

Dusty could tell by the sparkle in her voice that the stakeout had been successful. "Don't chief me. What happened? Are you okay?"

She laughed into the phone. "We're all fine. My new friends got the job done." She went on to relate the play-by-play to appease Dusty. "We were a real team. Three different jurisdictions, three different states and we jelled."

He chuckled, "I hear ya. Just don't decide to become a mercenary force. We want you back safe and sound." He heard her yawn. "What's next?"

"We'll all get some rest and then we're meeting at Bill's for breakfast."

"What about Beth? Hank's been worried that she would be shot or something."

173

Tee laughed again. "She spent the weekend with Wanda's husband and the baby. They were safe, but Beth and Greg, the husband, are both attorneys so she's complained that he's a smart-ass and he says she should stick to piloting. They hit it off."

Dusty was silent a moment. Finally he said, "I'm glad it worked out for your friends. I'm proud of you. Just get home safe."

"Love you, too, chief."

# CHAPTER TWENTY-TWO

French toast stayed warm in the oven while bacon sizzled on the stove top. Bill's kitchen was jumping. He took another look at the dining room table. He wasn't certain he had enough dishes. But Wanda had bragged about his cooking and everyone showed up to eat. Wanda, Tee, and Rose Marie were acting as hostesses. Isaacs and Brown had places of honor. Scattered around the other chairs were that pilot, Beth, Wanda's husband, Greg, balancing the baby on his knee, and Wanda's boss Whitacre. Nora was still at the nursing home. She had called earlier to get an update and inform Bill that she might have to stay a few days because of staff shortages. He was philosophical. He was certain it would take him that long to clean up after all the action.

The food was ready. He piled stacks of French toast on a platter that Wanda carried into the dining room, followed by Rose Marie with a plate of crisp bacon. Tee brought up the end of the parade with Bill's special breakfast fruit compote - blueberries, peaches and watermelon with chopped walnuts and coconut added. He smiled to himself as he listened to the complements fly.

Walking into the room with the coffee pot he asked, "Everyone have what they need?" The baby gurgled because everyone else was too busy eating.

"Sir, this is great!" sang out Brown. Nods around the table.

"I'm happy to feed you folks after all the trouble I caused." Bill put down the coffee pot and picked up the baby. "Is everything settled?"

Nods. Wanda finally spoke, "We have a little more paperwork to do. And the guys need to prepare their gear for the next event."

Isaacs agreed as he grabbed the plate of bacon. "Janic has lawyered up. Des Moines PD and our office are negotiating priority of charges. You know, who prosecutes and when?" He studied the ceiling. "I think he might go back to Iowa first. The charges are bigger."

Wanda's boss chimed in. "Yeah. He didn't kill anyone here."

"When do you leave?" Bill asked Tee. She looked at Beth.

"I'll file a flight plan for tomorrow afternoon," replied the pilot. "In case you guys find some loose ends."

The only loose end was a cookout planned at Wanda's for the evening and breakfast at Bill's as a sendoff Monday morning.

\* \* \*

In River Bend it seemed as though the virus came to the county jail on jet propelled wings and infected everyone, jailers and detainees. Heath Dawson had missed contracting anything because he had made an effort to fake his pain and stay in the infirmary. He had noticed a secure entry for emergency personnel and had decided the door might open one day because of all the illness and he could scamper out. And it seemed the day had come.

The jail was short-staffed and one of the detainees had taken a turn from that virus. He was wheeled into the infirmary. The three jailers worked to don protective covering, and one staffer tossed a blue package to Heath. "Put that on. You don't want to catch this shit."

Sirens screamed and EMTs rushed in through the emergency door. Two jailers returned to the general population leaving one behind to assist the EMTs. Everyone focused on preparing the sick man for transport to the hospital. Heath knew opportunity when he saw it. He slid from the bed, ripped open his protective gown package, and slipped into it as he slithered out the door. The EMTs worked on the patient and soon had him ready to transport. The remaining jailer held the door. Once the gurney was aboard the ambulance the jailer closed and secured the door as his radio alerted him to another jail crisis. He rushed from the infirmary. It was three hours before he got back to the infirmary, carrying a late lunch tray for the patient.

\* \* \*

When Heath slipped out the infirmary door, he dashed barefoot for some distant trees. The jail was behind the courthouse and sat on a small promontory above the river. It occupied a location overlooking the end of the river park and the old shipping docks at South End where in times past small river barges had carried produce downstream to packing houses to be readied for market. These days, the docks were in decay, the packing houses had moved out toward the interstate, and another old way of life had disappeared.

Of course, Dawson didn't care about the history of river commerce. He was grateful that the area was abandoned. He quickly got rid of the blue paper protective gear but realized that he was only in a hospital gown and his underwear. Not even shoes! He found a spot to sit hidden in the thicket near the riverbank. He watched the activity and thought about his options. He was confident he could think his way through this mess. He was also confident he would find that old lady and get even.

\* \* \*

Sunday morning was clean up time in Lynn's yard. If the party prep was organized, it dimmed in comparison to Piper's cleanup organization. By Sunday evening, the house and yard would be back to normal and anyone helping would get to finish the leftovers. Dusty and Jason were doing their annual litter basketball, seeing who could get the most paper plates in the big trash bags on first toss. Will and the other kids were folding chairs and tables, returning borrowed lawn furniture.

Lynn was on vacuuming duty in the living room and dining room. She picked up trash, carried empty glasses and dishes to trash bags, and in general got the room back to its usual state. Miguel came through collecting the bulging trash bag. "I'll leave you a new one and take this." He looked around, then whispered, "The general is a little distracted today, or we'd be repainting your kitchen."

"You're just as distracted," Lynn teased. "You didn't expect the big engagement announcement, either."

"I sure didn't." Miguel flopped on the couch and stretched his legs out in front of him. "But I can't think of a better choice, for either of them." He stared into space.

"You'll be a handsome father of the bride," said Lynn as she dumped more trash into the fresh bag.

"I was thinking of all the things that will happen," he blushed. "They're talking about grandchildren."

"Do you think you're too young to be a grandfather?" She tweaked his ear.

"No, I just never thought that my daughter would be a mother."

"Or a wife?" Lynn laughed at him. "Come on, Miguel, this is life. We've all married and made someone a grandparent."

He stood and gave her a hug. "I know, but she's my little girl."

Piper walked in as Miguel finished speaking. "Save that maudlin speech for the wedding," said the general. "We've got our calendars in the kitchen, trying to set a date."

"So soon?" moaned Miguel. He followed Piper into the kitchen.

Lynn smiled as she listened to the great date debate.

\* \* \*

It was late afternoon and the shadows allowed Heath to move closer to the old docks and the seedy South End street life. He watched street people walk along the dock and exchange money for drugs. He watched patrol cars drive through the area slowly. He watched fishermen put small boats in the river prepared for some fishing. Bingo! The plan came together.

He slipped into the river and worked his way toward the community boat dock. Diving under the planks of the pier he bobbed up near a pair of fishermen. "Hey," he called. "My boat tipped over. Can you help me?"

The older of the two men looked up. "You get caught by that snag over by Smiley's hole?"

"Yeah," lied Heath. "I had to swim here. Lost my clothes."

The other man looked up. "You must be a powerful swimmer. That hole has an eddy."

"That's how I lost my shoes." He pulled himself up on the dock. "I lost everything. Can you help me?" He threw his arm out to show his wet muddy boxers.

The older man shrugged his shoulder. "Go down the next street. There's a rescue mission. They'll have clothes and food."

"I can't walk the streets like this." He was getting angry. What ever happened to human kindness?

"Wait," said the other men. "I maybe got some junk." He ran to his car and returned with a dirty pair of shorts and an oil-stained t-shirt. "Take these. I don't have any shoes."

Heath pulled himself to a standing position, slipped on the shorts that were baggy and the t-shirt that was tight. He glanced down. "This'll do. Where's this place?" The men gave him directions and he was on his way.

At the rescue mission he was greeted by a masked volunteer who invited him to use the hand sanitizer, don a mask and go in for a meal. The volunteer directed, "Go into the dining room; someone will bring you a plate. We ask that you only unmask to eat." That suited Heath. He didn't want to be recognized.

As he sat eating his meal, another masked person came with a clipboard. "What services do you need this evening? We can't help with everything because of the pandemic, but we'll try."

Heath put his spoon down and slipped his mask on. "I just need clothing." He chuckled. "I was fishing and hit a snag. Boat sank."

"Oh, my, did you have to swim back to the dock?"

He nodded. "I feel like a fool. Lost my wallet and car keys. But I can call my wife if you let me use the phone. And I could use some shoes and clothes. Another fisherman gave me these." He displayed the stained t-shirt.

"I understand. Certainly we can help. Please follow me." In the musty smelling room, the man found a pair of slacks and pull-over shirt that fit and almost looked okay. It took some time, but he found a pair of shoes and some socks. "You look almost decent," teased the man.

"I appreciate your help." Heath looked down at his outfit. "Now a phone," he prompted.

"Certainly. Is your wife close by?"

"She's visiting our old friend Dusty Reid."

"Lovely man and his wife. They aren't too far from here."

"Could I walk? Then I wouldn't have to disturb anyone's evening."

The man chuckled. "If you walk, you're closer than by car." Heath's eyes skimmed along his mask edge, eager for the information. The man continued. "If you walk into river park," he pointed, "and take that old roadway along the river. It doesn't go anywhere, but when it ends you climb the hill to his backyard."

"Thank you, very much. I think I'll surprise them." Before the man could say much more, Heath hurried from the clothing storeroom and dashed out the door. He made his way slowly and cautiously into the park and onto the old roadway. Once there he knew no patrol car would find him. It didn't look as though a car had been on this road for decades. He tossed his mask in a trash barrel as he began walking along the old roadbed.

* * *

Sunday evening found everyone settling down. Miguel and his family had finally returned to their home after agreeing to consider several wedding date options. Tee had checked in several times, easing Dusty's angst. She had managed to solve all Wanda's problems and Rose Marie was getting to know her father. It was time, in Dusty's opinion, for a beer or three. Listening to Tee and the Indiana crew chase down a killer on his phone had been nerve wracking. She had made him proud with her intelligent support for those guys in Huntington. He was glad his staff was so well trained and capable.

Everything was quiet. The sun was creating long shadows, the beer tasted great. Lynn joined him in the mask-free zone and took a sip of his beer. A car spun gravel as it entered the yard. Lynn looked over at him. "That can't be good," she observed. As they watched, five small children were ejected from the car.

Mars' head popped out of the driver's side. "Lonzo's taking Trina to the hospital. Nowhere else to put these kids." Mars' two children and Lonzo's three stood in the grass as the car disappeared.

Lynn waved to the kids and sent a quick text to Piper. "C'mon kids, let's get inside for a snack." They all grinned and trotted toward the kitchen porch as the dog danced in ecstasy.

"Miss Trina's sick," reported Moses, Tee's son. "Daddy helped her to the hospital."

Brian, Mars' son, agreed. "Mommy gots sick." The three little girls nodded in agreement.

Piper rushed in from the front of the house. "What?" In a voice that was not happy. She had planned a Sunday evening meltdown after the surprise engagement announcement at her party. Oh, and the setting the date tussle she had with Miguel. But before she could get into a whining drama, she noticed the five children in the kitchen and looked at Lynn for an explanation.

"Mars dropped everyone off and said Lonzo was taking Trina to the hospital." Five children nodded.

Children were Piper's weakness and joy, and she immediately morphed into her good fairy imitation. "Did everyone have dinner?" Five heads gave her a negative answer. "How about hot dogs and chips?" Five heads agreed. The two women organized dinner while the dog twirled in delight to have so many of his favorite visitors at the house.

Outside, Dusty finished his beer and thought that he should go inside to help with the guests. His phone screamed. It was an emergency override. Was something happening? He thumbed his phone. "Yeah?" He listened. Stood. Spun around. "Got it."

Jason had just arrived home and was climbing out of his car. "Was that your phone? Is something wrong?" He had even heard the loud alarm.

"Get over to Emily Jacobs' place. I'll get someone else there, too. That Heath guy escaped from the jail." Heath Dawson had tried to murder Emily and the children a few months ago. He had succeeded in killing Yetta Masterson at that time and was being held at the county jail in anticipation of his trial within a few months. Emily and her great-grandchildren had been living at their new place next door to Dusty for only a week.

Jason paled. He had helped Dusty's team catch the murderer several months ago. He nodded and dashed from the yard, hustling to the neighboring house.

Dusty was running through his roster of available people. Tee was in Indiana. Mars was in the hospital. Danny! He called the detective. "Heath Dawson escaped from jail. Get over to Emily's. I just sent Jason."

Danny sputtered into his phone. "How?"

"Something about moving prisoners because of this virus."

"I'm on my way."

Next Dusty texted Will. *You and the boys my place ASAP.* He collected his beer bottles from the table. He had only enjoyed one. Walking into the kitchen he was happy to see Will, Jeff and Bryce had arrived. He motioned them back into the living room so that the five children would not hear. "Heath Dawson, the guy who tried to kill Emily and the kids escaped." Anticipating the next question he added, "They were moving some prisoners who are real sick and trying to keep others from catching this thing. I guess he slipped out when no one was looking. They think he's on foot. We don't know if he knows where she lives." He rubbed his eyes. "And we got five kids here because Tee is out of town and Mars and Lonzo have taken Trina to the hospital."

"When it rains, it pours," muttered Will. "What do you want us to do?"

"Doug called me," replied Dusty. He tried not to remember how he had shouted at Doug. Heath had been unaccounted for for several hours before Dusty had been alerted. "He's organizing the manhunt. Jason is at Emily's and Danny is on the way. When Doug can, he'll get to Emily's, too. We're not calling out a lot of cars. That would call attention to her new place."

"Does that bastard know she's moved?"

Dusty shrugged. "I have no idea. In fact, he may think they're here. Remember we kept them here after we rescued them from that cabin."

"If he's on foot," observed Jeff, "this is closer than Mrs. Jacobs' old place."

Dusty thumbed his phone contacts' list and paced in thought. Finally, returning to his makeshift crew he said, "I told Samson to park a patrol car at the old place. The new buyers haven't moved in yet. Jeff and Bryce, I want you fellows in the house to help Lynn and Piper with those kids. Nobody goes outside to play! Will, you help me patrol outside." Security was in place.

Dusty had a brief conversation with Lynn and Piper while the boys entertained the children. He concluded by saying, "Sherri Steiner will be coming. I'll text you when she arrives. Will, Sherri and I are security detail outside. Keep the dog in here." With that, the two men slipped out into the night.

# CHAPTER TWENTY-THREE

Jason pounded on Emily's kitchen door. Lucia answered, looking confused. "Is something wrong?"

"That Heath guy escaped from jail," Jason spoke hurriedly. "I'm here for security. Danny is on his way."

"What?" Emily had come into the kitchen. The children followed. "I will call Juan," said Lucia.

Jason nodded. "The more help, the better."

Juan appeared quickly since he lived above the garage. Jason explained the situation and advised, "I think the kids and Lucia should go upstairs. Ms. Jacobs, can you climb those stairs?"

"Tonight I can." She would stay with her grandchildren at all cost. Danny knocked at the door, calling out to identify himself.

With Danny there, Jason felt more confident. Danny said, "Good idea to get them out of the way." He explained to the family, "Stay away from the windows, close all shades and curtains. We don't think he knows where you live." Lucia helped Emily up the stairs.

In the kitchen Danny said, "Let's turn out the lights so he can't see inside. Dusty's patrolling the grounds here and at your place."

"What happened with Mars?" asked Jason. "I just got home, and his kids are with Mom."

"Trina is in the hospital. Lonzo had taken his kids over there for dinner, and she started to have contractions."

"It's too early." Even Jason knew the pregnancy basics.

"That's why she's in the hospital. It's you and me, fellas, since Tee is shooting up Indiana." They proceeded to secure the house, anticipating a long night.

* * *

Sunday evening in Indiana, Wanda hosted a cook-out for her visiting friends and most of the local PD. Tee was having a wonderful time. She talked with Captain Whitacre and exchanged ideas about training and learned of some regional workshop opportunities as he said, "You Tarheels would be welcome."

She had a little share of the baby's time, cuddling her until someone else needed baby magic. She noticed that Bill seemed to need the most of baby's time. Tee thought that in the future he would build a relationship with Rose Marie that reflected the same affection he lavished on his Indiana family.

As she thought about Rose Marie, she looked for the rookie and was immediately concerned. Under a bright umbrella the rookie was gesturing and talking to the only two attorneys invited - Beth and Greg.

Tee stepped over to eavesdrop. "Yes," said Greg, "but you have to draw a line connecting them now, not over twenty years ago."

The rookie wrinkled her nose at the lawyer. She was developing the standard attorney-police bias. "I have a request in for her phone records. I hope to find that she had been speaking with Janic before her death."

"You need more than that," Beth growled. She had her own biases. Defense attorneys had to be on the lookout for prosecution tricks and lax attitudes in securing evidence.

Rose Marie scowled. "The crime scene techs haven't had time to analyze everything they found at the murder site. My boss says I'll work with the DA and learn how to build a case."

Tee interrupted. "Neither one of you high-priced attorneys is going to defend this guy, so why are you hassling Rose Marie?"

"It's our duty to help her become a great investigator." Greg smirked at the detective.

"We have to help her understand what sort of things a great defense attorney will challenge." Beth added her smug response.

Rose Marie gave them a confused smile. "You were helping me?"

Tee dared the attorneys to burst her bubble. Beth said, "We want you to be prepared for things the defense will challenge. Your murderer has the resources to hire an expensive defense team. Is your DA up to facing that kind of talent? Have you been trained to testify?"

Greg added, "We're taught to go after you young investigators, try to make you look nervous and unsure."

Tee scowled in agreement, "Trust me, I've faced those kinds of attorneys."

The rookie paled. "I trust our team in Des Moines." She looked at Tee. "Won't my DA bring you to town to testify, too? You heard Janic carry on when we arrested him."

Tee thought about that. "It's possible. My pilot and I can be subpoenaed." She grinned at Beth.

Beth laughed. "I think it's against my law license to help the prosecution."

Greg walked over and put an arm around Rose Marie. "We'll do anything to help Bill's daughter." He kissed her cheek. "Another beer, everyone?"

* * *

Dusty organized his limited security detail so that Sherri would be nestled among the hostas and azaleas in the flower garden Lynn had created on the cul de sac. "You can see back to the barn with that yard light," said Dusty as they both studied the light and shadows created by the big outdoor light.

"Yes, sir," she agreed, adjusting her vest, and pulling her blond hair into a tight ponytail. "I can see this whole side of the house."

"Will and I are going to be walking along the stone wall between our house and Mrs. Jacobs. Danny is in the Jacobs' house."

"I guess we have eyes on both houses." Sherri tried to hide a yawn. She had been working overtime all day on paperwork to cover for Tee. She trotted off to settle in her lookout spot in the shrubbery.

By midnight everyone was in place. Lynn and Piper had the children bedded down. Danny had sent word from Emily Jacobs' place that all was well. Samson was in Emily's backyard because he had assigned another patrol car at Emily's old place.

By 2 a.m. all lights were out in both houses. No word from the patrols around town of anything unusual.

* * *

186

When Heath got to the end of the river park roadbed, it was dark. There was no moon and the hillside, in the shadows of the night, looked like a mountain. He slowly began making his way to the top, working around trees and tangled briers. But finally he was there, standing at a tree line looking at a big old house. He watched for some time and saw nothing that looked like police security. After studying the situation, he worked his way through the trees to get behind the barn and closer to the house. There was one of those yard lights high on a pole. It lit the area close to the back porch, but created a lot of deep shadowed areas, helping him work closer to his goal.

Inside the house young Moses stretched, awakened by the dog. He liked to visit Miss Lynn because her dog liked him best. Chips had chosen Moses as a bedmate this evening. The dog snorted and became alert. Moses sat up as the dog jumped off the bed. Chips looked at his young friend and moved to the bedroom door. He looked back at Moses, who understood. "You gotta go pee-pee?" The youngster found his shoes, opened the door, and followed his friend.

Downstairs, Lynn had decided to spend the evening on the living room couch. She had too much to worry about. She was just dozing when she heard the dog's nails clicking on the wood floor. She struggled to sit up because she thought he would come to wake her to let him out. He didn't come. He went directly to the front door, and she twisted, looking over the back of the sofa just in time to see young Moses closing the door as he followed the dog outside. She sprang to her feet, searched for shoes, and woke Piper who was sleeping in Dusty's office. But it wasn't Piper, it was Bryce. "What are you doing here?"

He yawned. "Mom said she needed a bed."

"Get your shoes on and follow me." Lynn raced for the door as Bryce wondered what he was to do outside with Lynn. But he found his shoes and did as he was told. When he got to the porch Lynn was gone. Because he knew things were not normal tonight, he was cautious as he left the front porch and moved toward the backyard, staying in the shadows. The night was warm and moonless, the usual night insects singing. Bryce stooped beside a hydrangea and stared into the shadows looking for movement.

A hand came down on his shoulder. Someone whispered, "Don't move. This is mine." It was Sherri Steiner. Bryce knelt in the shrubbery and watched Officer Sherri creep forward.

Moses followed the dog toward the old barn. The dog stopped sniffed, growled, and ran into the darkness on the barn side away from the house. Moses dashed after Chips and barreled into a solid object. Harsh hands grabbed him and swore. Moses struggled. Heath moved them into the light.

He looked at the small black youngster and asked, "Who are you?"

"The Black Panther," announced the boy and bit Dawson's wrist. Heath released him but quickly grabbed his arm as Moses tried to run off. The dog began to bark.

As he gripped the youngster and shook him demanding an answer, Lynn stood in front of him with a pitchfork. "Put him down," she ordered. Even the dog froze at the command in her voice.

"Who are you? Fucking Wonder Woman?" Heath threw Moses at her. They went sprawling in the grass lit by the yard light. As Heath picked up the pitchfork and stood above them, raising the implement, ready to plunge it into his victims, Lynn scrambled to protect the little boy. The dog danced and snarled. Heath kicked out at the dog sending the animal whimpering in a painful sprawl. Dawson turned back to the bodies on the ground and raised the pitchfork again.

"Stop! Police!"

He turned to face Sherri Steiner. The blond, petite officer held her weapon ready. "Who are you, Tinkerbell?" he snarled. Holding the pitchfork as a charging weapon he lunged at her. She fired.

"I'm the Black Widow, you asshole." She moved to protect Lynn and Moses.

Dusty and Bryce came racing to the backyard. The dog stood on three legs also hovering over Lynn and Moses. The animal was going to need a vet visit in the morning. Sherri held her weapon ready, covering Dawson. Bryce helped Lynn take Moses to the back porch where they all watched as the dog limped to the bottom of the stairs. Will and Samson came rounding the corner of the house ready to fight. Jeff and Little Brian as well as the three little girls dashed from the house, crowding together on the kitchen porch. Everyone yawning and confused.

Soon the yard was swarming with activity and emergency equipment. Dawson was transported to the hospital. It was almost dawn before it was all sorted out. Dusty reorganized everyone now that the threat was gone. Jason and Juan would stay at Emily's just in case the kids had nightmares. Jason smirked at that suggestion. Only he and Juan had even awakened. Jeff and Lynn got the kids back to bed, though both Moses and Brian wanted to sleep with Jeff. Will and Bryce went home. Danny and Sherri went to the office to deal with the paperwork. No word yet from Mars.

"I found Piper," said Lynn as she met Dusty in the upstairs hall. "She's in our bed sound asleep."

He took a bed inventory. The boys were snuggled against Jeff in Jim's old room. Three little girls were asleep in the guest room. The two twin beds in Jason's room were vacant. He and Lynn shrugged, kissed and each tumbled onto a bed.

# CHAPTER TWENTY-FOUR

Yesterday had been a success. They had stopped Janic in Indiana. He was in jail awaiting a hearing and transport back to Des Moines. Bill had no memory of the man. "Honestly," he shook his head, "I never saw the guy. Maybe when I was in a drug haze, I may have seen him. But I have no memory." That was when he had taken Rose Marie's hand. "I do remember your mother. She tried to get me to reform. But I was a professor, and I knew everything. She was just a sweet farm girl."

"She still is," Rose Marie said. They had spent Sunday evening talking, with Wanda sitting close to make sure Bill was safe, because she didn't want Rose Marie to take him back to Des Moines.

So here it was Monday morning. Bill was cooking pecan pancakes and sausages for everyone. And that included the team from the Huntington Police Department. Isaacs and Brown finished their second servings as Tee's phone pinged. "My son," she said. She scanned the message. "He sent a video." She held out her phone for all to see.

"Mama," the little boy sparkled out of the phone, "I was the Black Panther. I bit the man and Miss Lynn caught me and Miss Sherri shot him 'cause he called her Tinkerbell."

"What?" Tee screeched across Bill's dining room. She quickly dialed Dusty. "What is Moses saying?" She put the phone on speaker because everyone wanted an explanation.

"Hell," came a growl over the phone. "I was going to call you."

"Why are my kids with you? Where is my husband?"

"He had to take Trina to the hospital."

"Chief," Tee's voice was commanding, "begin at the beginning." And he did.

He concluded, "Trina is fine. No problem with the baby. Still on track for a November delivery. Dawson died. Sherri will go through that review. And all your kids are still at our house because Lonzo had to go back on his shift today. When are you coming home?"

"Beth is filing our flight plan. We'll be home this evening if they don't need me for any more paperwork."

When Dusty ended the call Isaacs asked, "Who did the kill?"

Tee rolled through the photos on her phone and showed him a photo of Sherri at her swearing in. "She saved my son's life."

"Is she married?" he asked. Tee rolled her eyes at him. "I mean if I came for a visit could I take her out?"

"Just be careful and don't call her Tinkerbell." Everyone guffawed.

Things wrapped up nicely in Indiana with Bill taking a few minutes to have a quiet chat with Tee. "Thank you for everything. Since I met you, I've gained two daughters and a granddaughter and soon," he winked, "I might even have a wife. We'll invite you and your family for the celebration." Wanda and Rose Marie had bonded, happy in their relationship with Bill. Or as Wanda said, "We're almost sisters." Rose Marie was staying for another few days to tie up all the loose ends of an investigation that went from Iowa to Indiana.

"We'll come for the wedding," Tee promised. "Enjoy your daughters. They're both good officers and now they're my good friends." She and Bill hugged. After a shootout no one worried about a virus.

"Ahem," said Beth. "We do have to get going. Wanda is taking us to the airport."

After more hugs and goodbyes, the ladies were finally in the air. Beth laughed out loud once they leveled off. "We've had this plane a week. I don't know who's paying and I don't care because I had a blast."

"I think Mars paid," said Tee. "The sheriff won't okay the expense. And you can be arrested if no one pays."

"My dad would find the money," she chuckled, "he likes me best!" She laughed again as they soared over farms and rivers, touching the sky.

* * *

191

Piper was in Lynn's kitchen cooking breakfast for all the children and her family. She was just saying good-bye to Bryce and Will as they left for work when Dusty ambled into the room. "Where's the coffee?" He had just finished bringing Tee up to date.

"Morning," sang the cheerful principal. "I heard you were busy last night."

"With no help from you." He took the cup of coffee and a plate of pancakes.

Mars pushed through the door. "Daddy," shouted his children.

"Sorry to miss the fun, chief." He scooped up his kids and kissed them. "Mommy is at home waiting to see you. Finish your breakfast." The kids sat back at the table. Mars turned to the adults. "Trina is fine. It was something that didn't put the baby at risk. She must rest for a few days. I've rented a hospital bed for the house. Lucia has a friend who's going to help us for the time being." He dropped a kiss on each of Tee's children. "How's Tee?"

"She's coming home. I was the Black Panther," bragged Moses.

"I heard." He smiled then turned to Dusty. "How's Sherri?"

"She's all right. She'll be going through the regular reviews for firing a weapon." He chuckled, "I talked Doug into working for the sheriff. He's got to handle the media on this one. Word has gotten out about Tee and her exploits. He may be sorry he left the Highway Patrol."

Lynn walked into the kitchen showered and ready to have breakfast. She looked tired and stiff. Dusty could see bruises on her arms from the assault last night. He had seen her curl her body around little Moses when Dawson threatened them with the pitchfork. The memory still gave him chills. He got up and gave her a hug and kiss. "Coffee?"

"Please." She noticed Mars. "How's Trina?"

"Everything's fine. I was just telling Dusty that Mrs. Jacobs' lady Lucia has found a friend willing to work for us and take the pressure off Trina."

"I thought you were moving into a new house," said Piper as she handed him a plate of pancakes.

Mars looked at her. "Did you really sleep through all the action here last night?" She scowled at him. "It's all over town."

"How can it be all over town," snapped Piper, "we're in lockdown."

Mars shrugged. "Social media. That's how we're all staying sane." He poured a cup of coffee and offered, "They're saying if Sherri was Tinkerbell, you must be Sleeping Beauty."

"I'd argue the beauty part," snarled Dusty as he held his plate for more pancakes.

Piper filled his plate then popped him on the head with the spatula. The kids giggled and Lynn yawned. "All back to normal here."

\* \* \*

Sprawled on his bed, enjoying a quiet time as dusk settled, Jason replayed the weekend. Things were finally calming at the house. He had never been asked by Dusty to be part of a security detail. He had been so scared at Mrs. Jacobs' place. The safety of her and those kids had been on his shoulders. He had been so happy to see Danny arrive, and to have Juan come in bleary- eyed from his apartment over the garage. But everyone was safe.

As much as he sometimes wondered about what adulthood would be like, he was pleased to find that he carried off maturity when needed. He felt good about the whole thing. And Dusty had even included him in the debriefing at the office this morning.

Wait! Adulthood! He smacked his forehead. Doyle! Things had been so crazy he hadn't even had a chance to talk with his best friend. Or as the family now thought of him - the groom. He grabbed his phone and texted, *So?*

His phoned chirped. Thumbing the FaceTime icon, he saw Doyle's blue eyes. "Are you mad?" asked Jason's best friend.

"No. Is that why you didn't tell me?" Jason stared into the little screen.

"Sort of," admitted Doyle. "But Lori said you wouldn't care."

"But married?" Jason thought over the idea, then asked, "Don't you want to be a bachelor for a while? Maybe date other women, or travel, or buy a new car?"

Doyle was silent for a moment. His eyes rolled around the screen. "I've hardly dated before Lori. If I were a bachelor, I'd just sit around wishing I had the nerve to ask someone out." He admitted to what his college life had been like before Lori. "Besides, she's perfect. She thinks I'm sweet and kind and I'll make a great dad.

"Dad?" Jason jumped off his bed forgetting to hold the phone steady. "You got her pregnant?" he challenged in a hoarse whisper as he settled the screen back in front of him.

"No. We...." Doyle sighed into the phone.

"I'm sorry." Jason interrupted. "It's none of my business." They stared at one another across the ether. "You just surprise me, marriage, kids. You're an adult."

"That's what's supposed to happen. We can't stay doofus kids for the rest of our lives."

Jason got back onto his bed. "I guess we all become adults in different ways."

"What does that mean?" Doyle looked really confused.

Jason looked over his shoulder making certain he was still alone in his bedroom. "Let me tell you about this weekend."

When Jason finished Doyle was aghast. He finally found words. "You did security for Dusty?" He processed all the information. "Sherri Steiner shot somebody? She's a cheerleader."

Jason rolled his eyes. "She's a police officer. You gotta talk to Bryce. She knocked him into some shrubs to protect him as she ran to the guy who was going to hurt Mom."

Doyle heaved a big sigh into the phone. "I guess we're both becoming adults." He grinned at his best friend. "I kinda like my way better."

\* \* \*

Piper flopped on a lounger in the mask-free zone and yawned. "This weekend was exhausting." Yawn.

"How can you be tired?" screeched Lynn. "You slept though my assault."

"But I cooked breakfast this morning." True. "And you know I helped with all those cute kids. Little kids love me." True.

Lynn was sitting at the picnic table scanning her phone. "My friend, Kennette, has been texting all weekend. She wanted to know what was happening in Indiana. I told her to check with Rose Marie's supervisor." Lynn waved her phone. "Guess what? They're going out for a beer tonight."

"The wedding planner strikes again." Piper teased.

"I don't think a beer is a proposal. But Kennette may have gotten the crime fighting bug we nonprofit folks seem to cultivate."

Piper snorted. "You just cultivated it so Dusty would notice you."

Lynn threw back her head and laughed. "And what did you cultivate so Will would notice you?" Piper gave her a sly grin.

"Hey, Sleep," called Will from the kitchen porch, "Can I bring you anything?"

"Don't call me Sleep."

Will bounced down the stairs with three beers. "It's all over town."

"Social media," chanted Lynn, grinning.

Piper jumped to her feet. "It's that Mars! And I was so nice to his kids." She stopped. "He never answered me about his house."

Will and Lynn blinked trying to follow Piper's change of topic. "Oh, his house," Lynn finally said. "He had Carl working on that old house his father lived in, but Emily needed to move sooner. That put things on hold. And the new house has stairs. Mars wants Trina to stay in the little rental house with no second floor until the baby comes."

Dusty came from the kitchen and joined the talk, dropping bags of chips and cookies on the table. "Carl says that Mars' house is ready, but Mars won't move yet. So, under orders from Mars, he keeps telling Trina it'll be a few more weeks." Everyone laughed. Dusty chuckled himself. "Mars is one tough guy, but fatherhood may break him. He worries about everything."

"Dr. Rita told me that after Trina's hospital stay, she wanted to prescribe Valium for him."

Will frowned. "I thought Doc Noah was Trina's doctor."

Dusty rolled his eyes. "Mars wanted a second opinion about Trina's condition. Doc Noah says in his opinion he would double the Valium dose."

"Poor Mars," grinned Lynn. "We shouldn't be enjoying his condition."

"What condition?"

"Pending fatherhood. It's more serious in some men."

Lynn shook her head. "Pending fatherhood may be hard on some man. I think pending father of the bride is more difficult for others."

"Miguel!" hooted Will. "We may have to get him some Valium, too."

Dusty joined the laughter adding, "And what do you think he'll do about grandfatherhood?"

"Grandfather?" screeched Piper. "That means I'll be a grandmother." She paled. "I'm too young!"

"Or too crazy," offered Dusty. Will and Lynn scowled at him. He grinned.

# CHAPTER TWENTY-FIVE

Doug walked into the Unit's office. The detectives all raised their face masks, but Doug was alone. He closed the door, and everyone slipped their masks off. "I've only been at this job two weeks and you give me this?" He scowled at Tee.

She smiled. "I'm so glad you're working with us. I think I got all the news articles and other information from those departments that you asked for." She handed him a folder. "I printed it all out and also included a list of the online sites for reference."

He rolled his eyes at her. "I need a story that I can put out for Jasmine Fuller. I know she's your friend, but the sheriff's new policy is that I do the talking."

"She'll understand," said Tee. "We told her you were a good guy. Besides, she'll only ask the questions you can answer."

"What's that mean?" He was suspicious now.

"She sort of knows the story because she contacted all the reporters in Des Moines and Huntington."

He laughed. "You guys are always one step ahead, aren't you?"

"We just make sure we cover our asses," drawled Mars.

"Does that mean writing a check to cover the airplane charges?" Doug showed them that he had his own network for information. They didn't have to know that Butch Blackburn was his sister-in-law's brother.

Dusty cleared his throat. "I think we should reimagine that check. Like maybe, Herbie and Hank Seymour covered the costs because of Beth. If you know Butch, maybe you can help him reimagine things our way."

Doug laughed out loud. They did know his relationship to Butch. "He'd be happy to. He made more money on this jaunt than any of his regular charters." He gave the detectives a conspiratorial look. "And with all the publicity Beth is getting for her piloting exploits, he's getting more calls for charters. She's in demand." Everyone laughed.

"How can we help you?" asked Dusty.

Doug shook his head. "I'll write up a release. I'll talk to Jasmine. Butch will reimagine the check. And we'll let the sheriff take credit for helping keep America safe."

The detectives all moaned but knew that's what had to happen.

* * *

"Tim!" Lynn rushed to hug the man who had just walked into her kitchen. She sputtered because she had so many questions.

Her brother-in-law from her first marriage grinned at her as she tried to ask all her questions at once. "I love the greeting. Quarantine has made you lose your ability to talk coherently?"

She hugged him again. "Oh, maybe we shouldn't touch." She looked around her kitchen for a mask or hand sanitizer or something.

He gave her an enthusiastic embrace. "If you say so." He looked around. "This kitchen is new. It looks great." Tim and his wife and children had been in Japan for the last three years.

"You can look over my kitchen later. Tell me about the move." Lynn hadn't changed even if her kitchen had. She liked getting to the heart of a matter.

"I'll be resigning from the Navy, but through Janet's business, I'll be available as a consultant for the work I've been doing," Tim explained as they each took a chair at the kitchen table.

"Will you have a job besides consulting?" Lynn was worried. "Things are a bit different under all these restrictions. How will you find a job?"

Tim frowned as he thought how to explain his decision. "For years the Navy was my life, my very exciting life. But Janet and two kids and Polly changed things." He looked around the new kitchen as he framed his next answer. "Janet needs a business manager. Do you know how much money she makes? She needs me to manage her business and share baby stuff." Janet, an IT developer and designer, consulted for secret government projects. He grinned. "All of a sudden, married life is more exciting than the Navy. Besides, her consulting contracts will keep me involved with the work I've been doing in that combined services IT task force. We're the perfect work-from-home model."

"How is the transition going? When will you all be here?" Lynn wanted all the news about his wife, their children and their adopted daughter, Polly. During the time of his visits to River Bend Tim had met and married Janet Bergman, daughter of the retired sheriff. They had also stepped in to adopt Polly Carmichael.

Tim began his explanation. "Janet and the kids are fine. She's worried about her parents here in River Bend and she's worried about her inability to be close to her parents at this stressful time. Bergy's antics weigh on her."

Lynn frowned. "You know that the management of the retirement community where her parents live maintains a very restrictive quarantine. Life on their campus is limited and visitors are not allowed. And he fights every regulation." It was an ugly truth of the times.

"We know," Tim nodded. "But I think Janet would be happier closer to them. Once any restrictions lift, she wants to be the first one through the gate, not have to travel from another country and deal with quarantine rules. As it is now, just to get back here I had to be quarantined for two weeks." He smiled. "We'll manage."

"When will the family get here?"

He laughed out loud. "She's already stateside. You have no idea how valuable Janet is to the military. They have her and the kids at an installation in San Diego. I'm here to get Bergy's old house ready. Some guys are coming to put secure tech lines in the house. They worry about hackers and ransomware stuff and want Janet on as secure a network as possible." He looked around as though searching for spies. "And you don't know about the network. It's all hush-hush."

Lynn laughed. "I can see why your new life is more interesting. What about Polly?"

Tim sighed. "She's a quiet kid. And a very talented artist. She's not happy about coming back to River Bend and its memories. I think going to school online will suit her. She's also asked about the early college program at the community college as an option." He shrugged. "We'll figure it out. Right now, I'm glad she's with Janet, helping with the kids while I get things settled here."

"Do Bergy and Thel know when you're coming back?"

"You didn't hear them shout for joy?" He grinned. "Bergy got rid of his tenants at the house and got his guys cleaning it." The old sheriff had a posse of retired deputies who always responded to his calls for help.

"I think it's great that you'll be around permanently." Lynn took his hand. "You can stay here while you're in town working on the move."

"Where else?" He grinned at her. "I'm looking forward to spending time with Jason and Dusty." Lynn remembered how the three men liked to spend Sunday afternoons in disreputable sweats watching some sporting event and eating.

* * *

Beth had been back in town for two whole days and Herbie was texting her for the third time. *Where's the file on the medical practice merger?*

*On your desk beside the last file you asked about!*

He finally gave up. *Get down here!*

Beth lived in the apartment above the law offices. It was very convenient to work from home. If she needed something she ran downstairs, masked up and retrieved the info. Today, Herbie, H. Lawrence Grayson to most of River Bend, was being a pain in the ass. She dug up a mask and clumped down the stairs to the office.

"What?" she growled, slipping her mask off because they were alone.

"Pre-nup?" He raised an eyebrow. "Sean's wedding is in a few days, and you told me you were representing Lee in this thing."

"Why do they need a pre-nup?" Even though Beth had explained things to Lee, she still wasn't certain.

Herbie nodded. "I've gone over this with Michelle. It's just best for both of them. They can rewrite or dissolve it when they chose. It will give them time to allow Lee to become familiar with Sean's wealth and then allow her to have some say in their finances."

"Oh." Beth gave Herbie a soft smile. "You are a romantic. Lee thought it was your goal to protect Sean from her clutches."

"What do you mean romantic?" He tried to look evil and sly.

She kissed his cheek. "You want Lee to become a partner in Sean's financial plans, not just an observer."

"Well, yeah." He tried to project attorney attitude.

"I'll get it done today."

Later that day, Michelle, Lee, Herbie, and Sean received a text of Beth's first pre-nup draft.

> *Sean Hennessey,*
> *I will love you to the day I die. In the meantime, I will work with you to plan our future of    sharing our wealth with each other and with as many folks who need our care and money       as we can find.*
> *With all my heart,*
> *Lee Stahlmeier*

Beth added her comment, *Edit at will.*

Sean replied with emojis of clapping hands. Lee sent hearts. Michelle called to tell her sister it was a beautiful pre-nup. And Herbie sent a text, *Have her come in and sign it!*

* * *

Abe Cohen parked his car in Lynn's drive. She watched him grip a folder and his iPad before marching toward her mask-free zone. She was, again, reminded that she hated when people marched in her direction. Abe, like all the past marchers, was on a mission. Yolanda pulled up behind him and climbed from her car balancing two bakery boxes. Lynn's conclusion, Abe's marching was related to his ancestor search. She shouted to her oncoming guests, "Drinks?"

Yolanda shouted, "Apple pie and biscotti. Got any sangria?"

"Any hard cider?" requested Abe.

What do they think this is, a bar? Lynn, of course, had both. Miguel had left about a gallon of sangria from Piper's party. She wasn't certain how the hard cider arrived, but it was cold and in the drinks' refrigerator under the counter. She raced into the house for drinks, plates, and utensils.

As the women set out the food and drinks, Abe plopped at the table. "I need advice. That's why I asked Yolo to join us." He popped the top off the bottle of hard cider, took a cool drink, and studied the pies - yes, she brought two. It was the mask-free zone with more people than Times Square these pandemic days.

Once settled, both women looked at Abe. He put down his drink and said, "I heard from someone. I think it might be a daughter of my mother's sister."

"Your first cousin," said Yolanda, the genealogy expert. "Does she want to meet?"

"I guess." He opened his iPad and showed them a photo. "She looks like my sister."

"Did you send photos?"

"Yeah," another drink. "I sent my photo, my sister, and my mother. I also sent Mom's obit." He sighed. "She said she showed the stuff to her mother, and she cried."

"Who the mother or the cousin?"

Abe rolled his eyes at the genealogy expert. "My cousin is Suzanne. Her mother is Terry, I think for Teresa. Terry cried. Suzanne said that she had gotten on the ancestry site to find my mother because Terry is old and wanted to see Mom one more time before she died."

"So, now what?" Lynn was curious.

"That's what I want to know?" He looked around the yard then opened the file he had carried from his car. "Suzanne wants me to come visit. She says her mother needs this closure. I don't know how I feel. They abandoned my mother. Now I'm supposed to please *her* mother?"

Yolanda studied him. "Do you remember when we started this and you said you hadn't a grudge against anyone, you just wanted to learn your parents' history?"

He thought about that remark. "I remember, but now I want to protect my mother."

"From what?"

He shrugged, then he chuckled, "I guess she doesn't need any protection now."

"Where do these relatives live?"

"Des Moines."

Lynn gasped, then laughed and pulled out her phone. "Hello, Kennette? You're on speaker."

"Another crime to solve?" came the excited reply.

"No, this is a little different. No dead bodies." Yolanda and Abe stared at Lynn, bug-eyed. She made a calming gesture and continued talking. "Kennette, I'm with my friends Yolo and Abe. They have been doing some research into Abe's family and found relatives in Des Moines. We called to see if you know them."

"Sure, it's still sleuthing. I think I've got the bug."

"Sleuthing?" asked Abe.

"When Beth and Tee came and found that dead body and arrested that Janic fellow," explained Kennette. "Didn't Lynn tell you?"

"*That* dead body!" said Yolo, as though it explained everything. "My son is Tee's partner."

"Oh, she told me about her colleagues. They were shooting someone there while she was here." Kennette sounded in awe of folks in River Bend. "You must all lead exciting lives."

"I haven't shot anyone," said Abe, "Can we talk about my problem?"

"Sure, sweetie," came the Des Moines reply.

Abe rolled his eyes at the women in the mask-free zone. "Let me explain," he began, "Yolo helped me do some ancestor research and I found a cousin. She and her mother live in Des Moines and want to meet me. I want to know who they are before I go any further. Are they legit? Will I be sorry I connected with them?"

"Who are they?"

"Suzanne Troxler and her mother Teresa O'Connor."

Kennette squealed into the phone. "I love Suzanne. I don't know her mother. She's ill and has been in a care facility. You're her cousin?"

"Teresa was my mother's sister. They had a falling out years ago."

"What about your mother?"

"She died from this virus. I found all these family notes when I cleaned out her place."

"How exciting!" Kennette was ready to join the investigation. "Suzanne is a high school guidance counselor, and her husband owns a plumbing business. They are lovely people. Mrs. O'Connor had a hard life. She was widowed early and raised Suzanne and two sons. They take good care of her. You should come meet them. Stay with me. My house already has River Bend germs."

Abe looked helplessly at Lynn who said, "Kennette, that's a generous offer. Abe will think about it. He has a job. He also wants to correspond with Suzanne a bit before making any decision."

"I understand, sweetie," replied Kennette. "I'm here to help."

They ended the call and stared at one another. "It sounds like your mother had a more secure life," stated Yolo. "Maybe that's why her sister never got back in touch. You know, she might have been ashamed of her poor circumstances." Abe shrugged as Lynn's cell rang.

She looked at caller ID. "Troxler?" She glanced at Abe as she put the phone on speaker. "This is Lynn."

"Is Abe coming?"

"Suzanne? This is Lynn, you're on speaker. I guess you spoke with Kennette."

"Yes. Are you there, Cousin Abe?"

Yolanda and Lynn looked at him. He heaved a sigh. "Yes, I'm here, Suzanne."

"Please come, Abe. Mother needs to see you. She had missed her sister all her life and has blamed herself for the breakup of the family. Kennette says Beth could bring you."

Abe looked at Lynn, puzzled. "Beth Seymour is a pilot," she explained.

"Yes," came Suzanne. "Kennette will house you all."

"Suzanne," interrupted Abe, "here's my cell." He rattled off the number. "Let's you and me talk and let me talk with my wife."

"You're not saying no?"

"I'm not saying no."

"That's good. I'll talk to you later." She ended the call.

They all looked at one another. "You have to go," said Yolo. "Families are important."

"I've got to think about this." He looked at Lynn. "What does Beth charge?" The two women smiled. They turned as Piper walked out of the house carrying a carton of ice cream.

"Did I hear Yolo brought apple pie?" And as usual people appeared to dine in the mask- free zone.

\* \* \*

"Well, well, well," grinned Bryce, "the girl pilot hot off another adventure." He threw an arm around Beth as they walked along the old river roadway. "I want every detail. It sounded as exciting as a Broadway opening night!"

"It was." She looked at him and squealed. "I couldn't believe it. Shootings, dead bodies, racing to Indiana. More guns. And then Bill made us stay over so he could bake us pies and bread before we left."

"Are you going to make a career change to crime fighting?"

"No," she blushed. "I wasn't really in the shootings. I stayed with Wanda's husband and her baby while the police chased the bad guy."

"I can't see you as a nanny while the shooting was going on."

"Maybe that's because you're the only one who knows who I really am." Her demeanor changed. Bryce knew her well enough to know this had suddenly become a serious talk. "I'm thinking of applying for a job with the state Attorney General. Penny Rawlings has been working for them. She's been doing online work before anyone knew it was the way to work."

"So you would stay in town and work for Raleigh?"

"I'm not sure how it would be organized. But I want more than traffic citations and divorce work. And going to work for the AG gets into some interesting areas like white collar crime, SBI investigations, prosecuting cases in higher courts."

"Wow, I didn't know you had those ambitions." He was thoughtful as they walked. "What about your family?"

She nodded. "You and I both value our families. But we both feel that we don't fit in River Bend. We've talked about this before."

"Sometimes I don't know what to do with my family. You seem to have come to some truce in your feelings. They just support you - fat, skinny, crazy." Laughing and teasing he pulled her along the path.

"Gay or straight," she said, giving him a pensive look as she stopped them on the shaded trail.

He gasped in surprise. "Are you talking about you?"

"No, you," she whispered.

She stared at him. "You're making me uncomfortable," said Bryce.

"Families have a great capacity to love us, as we are. When I finally admitted to the therapist that I had been molested and threatened, I didn't want my family to know. I knew it would hurt my dad because he would think he had failed me. And my sisters would be frightened. And maybe shun me or something. But when I told everyone. They loved me more." She held his hand in both of hers. "When will you tell your family that you're gay?" Beth studied his face.

Bryce was angry. "Who are you, the homosexual police?" He stared at her for a long time. She didn't seem to even blink as she returned his stare. Sighing, he finally said, "I was going to do it during this summer, but I ran into my brother's engagement announcement. I think I'll wait a bit longer."

"You and I are like those trees all covered in kudzu vines. All people see are leaves shrouding stifled, stunted trees. We have to escape from those vines and let folks, our families especially, see who we really are."

"Maybe I'm not ready for them to see the real me?"

"Your mother probably knows."

"Why do you say that?"

"I've heard mothers have a sense about who their children are. Not that my mother knew anything about us." Beth sighed. "Your mother would sense something. My mother was always drunk. Sorry. I try to avoid self-pity."

"I'll have to think about it," he hedged. "I'm not in a relationship now. When this virus happened, we just went our separate ways. I guess he wasn't as committed as I thought."

"Maybe you weren't either," she challenged him.

"Hmmm. I never thought about it like that." He gave her a shy smile. "Maybe I need this quarantine time to build a life that fits me. When this settles, I can decide if my life fits me here or someplace else." He squeezed her hand. "You know, like you."

"Tell your mother first," she advised, "then you won't worry about being found out and you can concentrate on making your life fit." She kissed his cheek.

He gave her a hug. "I have to think about this." He took her hand as they walked. "Let's go find Greg and hustle up some Chinese carry-out. I've exposed enough of my soul tonight."

# CHAPTER TWENTY-SIX

Lynn and Piper huddled around Lynn's big computer monitor. Since life was now demanding so many online meetings, Lynn was glad she had invested in a screen that allowed her to see meeting participants bigger than postage stamps. "Look," Piper pointed at the screen. "Lee is standing next to a tractor." They were settled in chairs in front of the monitor having decided that an online wedding was still a wedding and they had dressed in summer, wedding worthy frocks. Will and Dusty on the other hand had combed their respective hairs but were dressed for a lazy summer afternoon.

Lynn squinted. "I think she's standing in the back of the gathering getting ready to walk down the aisle."

"Or the corn row," chuckled Will as he watched the wedding preparations.

"Who's streaming this video?" grumbled Dusty. He needed to be at his family farm helping this afternoon.

The camera person moved to a position behind the preacher. Strains of music came through the computer speakers. Lee began her walk down the aisle. The outdoor venue seemed to be her brother's flower garden, abutting his corn field. It was a lovely setting. Lee seemed to walk out of the summer high corn with the hills of the national forest standing behind as guardians. She walked past three rows of hay bales on the bride's side, accommodating her family - brother, sister-in-law, nieces, and nephews.

And on Sean's side several of his friends socially distanced on the bales - Meyer Levine, H. Lawrence Grayson and his lovely wife, Michelle. Lynn pointed at the scene. "Nathan is the best man. Look how pleased he is."

"And Beth is the maid of honor?" Piper was puzzled by the choice. She looked to Lynn for an explanation.

Lynn shrugged. "I think Lee wanted some legal advice. And Michelle sent her to Beth." Beth and Lee were a strange pair of friends in Lynn's opinion. "Beth looks great after all that weight she lost."

Dusty snorted. "You mean after all the laws she broke. She and Tee should go to jail for all that flying and shooting and stuff."

Will stabbed at the screen. "Look how many folks are tuned in. Sean invited everyone at the plant." Sean was maintenance supervisor at Will's plant.

"And all my teachers," added Piper. Sean was a dedicated volunteer at Piper's elementary school.

There was a knock at the door. Dusty answered while the others watched the ceremony. Andy from Will's factory handed him a basket. "Sean sent gifts to all his friends watching his wedding." Dusty took a small basket. Will walked up behind Dusty. "You here, too, Mr. Zubov? I got a basket for you, too." He ran back to his truck and came back with another basket.

"What's this for?" asked Will.

Andy grinned. "Mr. Sean was sorry folks couldn't join him and Miss Lee so everyone that registered for the online wedding is getting a gift basket. Me and a couple of the guys from work are delivering." The young man smiled, "Gotta go. More baskets." He dashed back to his truck and left the neighborhood.

The guys carried the baskets back to the dining room. "Sean sent wedding baskets," announced Will. Dusty was already opening his.

"We got a small bottle of champagne, little wedding cake cupcakes, some candy and a little container of cheese and crackers." He handed Lynn the bow from the basket handle with its note tag.

Lynn unfurled the little scroll of thick paper and read, *"Dear friends, thank you for enjoying our day with us. Sean and Lee Hennessey."* She dashed a tear from her eye. "That's so sweet."

Piper blew her nose into a wrinkled tissue. "He does everything with flare."

"Yeah," grouched Will, "he's got enough money to out flare all of us."

"Father Nick is there," Lynn called everyone's attention back to the screen. She looked closer. "And that's Rev. Lundy. He's the pastor at Hanging Oak Presbyterian Church."

"How do you know all the preachers?" asked Will.

Lynn shrugged. "His church just offered two small apartments for the Sharing Shelter program. He has a young family of his own and learned that one of his daughter's kindergarten friends was homeless."

"Look, look," squealed Piper. "They're exchanging vows." Lynn and Piper sighed. "And both preachers are blessing them." Music came from the speakers again. Sean and Lee kissed. Then Sean signaled to the videographer who, in a clumsy but charming way, focused in on Sean and Lee as Sean took a mic clip from Father Nick.

He looked into the camera. "Friends, thank you for joining us. Lee and I want to share our story with you." He shared the story of meeting Sonny and receiving her tape. Lee shared her story of Sonny and receiving the earrings. The camera showed a close-up of Lee's earrings. Then Sean told the story of Lee seeing the earrings and his mother's blessing. Even on Zoom the audience was spellbound.

Finally Sean turned to Lee and said, "I told you once before Lee, now I'll say it for our friends to hear. My mother sent you for me to love."

At that statement the camera turned to Nathan who was holding a champagne flute. He raised his glass, "Please raise your glasses with me in a toast to Sean and Lee." Around River Bend and in Lynn's home office/dining room friends raised glasses in celebration. The screen dissolved into a prepared slide that read, "*Thank you for sharing this time with us,*

*Mr. and Mrs. Hennessey.*"

Sniffs, throat clearing. Piper wiped her nose on a Post-it note that had been attached to Lynn's computer. "That was beautiful." She crumpled the note and tossed it to the floor.

"I know." Lynn used a dish towel that she found hanging on the back of a chair to grab a tear. "They are perfect together."

"That's quite a story about his mother," said Will. "I wish I had those kinds of memories of my mother." He hung his head. Piper hugged him. It was rare for Will to mention his past.

"She's still with you," Piper said, "She found me to take care of you. Just like Sean's mother."

Will hugged her in return. "I think you're right, babe."

A silent warmth that filled the room. Lynn gave them both a quick hug and said, "We have to celebrate this day for Sean and Lee."

"And for mothers," said Piper, still clinging to Will.

\* \* \*

Jason came in for dinner. "Mom, Uncle Tim has a moving van at Janet's house today." He had a mask hanging from one ear. It distracted him and he tossed it on the table. "Gramps looked better today."

"Better?"

Jason nodded. "He seems to be less skittish." He thought about the word. "You know what I mean. He lets me in the house these days as long as I keep my mask on. He doesn't wear his. I saw him smile and he looked good. Marianna saw me and she winked. I think she's keeping him normal."

Lynn gave him a hug. "Thanks for the update. I was worrying after our last conversation."

Jason's eyes sparkled. "I think this shoot-out and stuff did it." Lynn looked puzzled. Jason explained, "All this action. I think he decided that the world is still going on and he didn't want to miss the action. But he'll still be cautious." Jason brightened. "I explained everything. He got the details about our shoot-out and Tee's adventure."

Lynn wondered how exaggerated the stories were, but said, "I think that's a good thing. He's decided to stay in life."

"Yeah," agreed Jason as he pulled a drink from the refrigerator. "But what about Uncle Tim?"

"The furniture is here, and Janet and the children arrive in a few days. Or I should say Tim is bringing them home as soon as he has the house ready."

"What about Sheriff Bergy?" Jason had enjoyed hearing about the old man's antics.

"Dusty says that Bergy isn't the only resident at the retirement community anxious to see family. They came up with a good option."

Lynn sat at the kitchen table and used her hands to sketch on the tabletop. "The management replaced the chain-link fence along the greenway with a lovely wrought iron fence. It's high. They created little seating spots with shrubs so that families could sit on one side of the fence and residents on the other. They planted low shrubs." Her hands flitted around the table. "That way everyone can see but people keep their distance." She shrugged and laughed. "I'm sure people will try to reach through the fencing. But the management has warned that if people start to get sick, they'll put up another fence to keep residents further away from the greenway."

"I guess it's hard for folks to give up their freedom."

Lynn nodded. "I hear that a lot. But I'm also hearing on the news that a vaccine is close to being ready. Piper is as crazy as Bergy to get back to normal. Starting this new school year will be a challenge. Online or in person, no one seems happy with any option."

"I'm in my college senior year working from home," he reminded her. "They say we'll be back on campus for sure for our last semester maybe sooner. Right now, they want to concentrate on freshmen." He frowned, then chuckled. "I think I miss learning in classrooms."

* * *

Janet and her family had only been in town one day and she knew that she had to get to the greenway before her father did something horrible. With two babies in a stroller, she and Tim walked along the greenway toward the fancy fencing. She smiled as she noted two of the old deputies standing guard at a small seating area. Bergy was taking no chances. He had his friends secure the area early in the morning to be certain he would see his family.

And there they were. Bergy and his wife Thel were seated on their side of the fence waiting. "Hi, Mom. Hi, Daddy," Janet greeted them. She lifted Little Bergy from the stroller and allowed him to toddle toward the shrubs. The boy was interested in the bugs and leaves within his grasp until a beachball bounced off his head. The boy giggled.

Thel waved with her latex gloves. Soon she and Tim were playing a version of beach volleyball to the delight of Big and Little Bergy. Janet lifted the new baby from the stroller and got close enough to the fence so that her grandparents could see the cute sleeping face. "She'll be awake the next time," promised Janet. "I think she's still on Japan time."

Tim noticed an attendant coming through the garden and stuffed the ball in the stroller. One of the old deputies slid over to place his body as a screen. They all tried to look innocent as the CNA smiled on her way along fence patrol.

Little Bergy started to fuss. Tim lifted him and whispered in his ear. The youngster blew a kiss to Bergy and Thel. Tim said, "We have to go. Janet has to get to work."

"That damn Navy," growled Bergy.

"They made it possible for us to return, Daddy, so you be kind." Janet snuggled the sleeping baby in her arms because the beachball was in the stroller. Tim let Little Bergy ride on his shoulders and one of the old deputies pushed the stroller. With waves and blown kisses they moved down the greenway.

"Damn," said Bergy as he wiped a tear from his eyes. "They're really home."

\* \* \*

Penny Rawlings had agreed to welcome the Bar Association members to the Philanthropies online presentation. She joined the meeting from her office because online meetings from home had become a challenge. Her toddler daughter, Olivia, liked to sneak into Penny's office and try to see herself on the screen. Then Cook usually tried to sneak in to grab the little vixen but always managed to bump something or say something to distract the meeting attendees even more than Olivia and her antics. Penny didn't even want to think about Olivia's kitten and the newest baby in the house who always managed to crawl into the fray to chew on wires - the kitten and the baby. So today she sat in her professional office, quiet all around smiling at the small faces as others joined the meeting.

Darlene Porterfield began the meeting. "Thank you all for coming today. My co-chair Beth Seymour and I have organized this community education series because many of you are new to River Bend and James County. Lynn Powers, executive Director of the Philanthropies, and her board chair, Penny Rawlings, are with us to present information for you to share with clients who want to include charitable giving in their estate planning. Beth and I ask that you send your questions through the chat option and Lynn or Penny will answer them once the formal presentation is complete. Penny, it's all yours."

Penny smiled and began her brief introduction. "Thank you for the invitation, Darlene and Beth. I want to say that as you young attorneys grow your practices, please consider finding time to serve in some capacity in local nonprofits. Today I want to introduce the Philanthropies director, Lynn Powers. Again, thank you for your attention and interest." It was a brief introduction because Penny had to be prepared for an online judicial hearing in thirty minutes and they had planned on Lynn's talk only taking about twenty. Everyone knew that the attention span of attorneys was about three nanoseconds.

As Lynn began to speak the chat box exploded with questions. She glanced at the questions and panicked. Everyone had questions about Beth's role in the hunt and arrest of that murderer. Lynn's digital eyes rolled to Penny who sent a private chat, *I've got court.* Her face disappeared from the screen.

Darlene jumped in as emcee of the presentation, "I see we have a lot of interest in crime instead of financial planning." She stared into her screen. "Here's the deal. Listen to Lynn for ten minutes while Beth prepares answers to your questions." Then she gave the young attorneys a taunting look. "Then if you behave, I'll ask Lynn to talk about her crimefighting." All the heads on the screen looked alert. They were ready to listen to a crimefighter disguised as the Philanthropies director.

Lynn sent Beth a private chat, *I won't mention your mother's death.*

*Thanks,* replied Beth, *now talk estate planning for ten minutes.*

It was two hours before the online presentation ended. Even Darlene was asked to talk about her role in helping little Cooper get his inheritance after almost being murdered by his father. But the story everyone seemed to like best was Beth and Lynn's adventure on a snowmobile as they sped over farm fields getting away from drug dealers.

* * *

"I think I'm going to take Penny's advice," Beth announced to her sisters. They were having a girls' night with Rita. Hank was helping Kevin babysit. The girls were sitting around Rita's table, finishing a great evening with something chocolate. "I'm applying for that job in the state attorney general's office. Penny said that I have a lot of business experience for the white-collar crime division. She's even made some phone calls." Her sisters cheered.

"You'll be closer to me at medical school," offered Patti Ann. Beth had flown her home for the weekend. It was great to have a pilot sister.

"You'll only be four hours away," Ronnie calculated. "You can still come back to babysit on weekends. Or Daddy can get you a plane to get here quicker."

The other girls moaned. "Is that all you think of?" asked Michelle.

Ronnie smiled. "I was just letting her know I'll miss her." Ronnie grabbed Beth and gave her a kiss on her cheek.

Rita loved these evenings with her stepdaughters. "Tell us again about your snowmobile adventure with Lynn."

Beth blushed. "You've all heard it a dozen times. But I will say, it was one of those life changing events. After that scare, I felt brave enough to do anything."

"Like get your pilot's license!" They all cheered. All through dinner Beth had shared the Des Moines story.

"When will you know about the Raleigh job?" asked Patti Ann.

"I guess the call from Penny did it because they're just waiting for my application. It seems I'm hired." Everyone toasted the new attorney in the AG's office.

\* \* \*

Piper and her son, Bryce, sat in the back garden, holding hands as the sun set. "You're my son, Bryce. I don't require anything else from you. You can be whomever you are." Piper brushed her hand along the top of his. "We all love you." She couldn't think of anything else to say.

"Thank you." He brushed a tear from his eyes. "I didn't surprise you, did I?" Piper shook her head. "Beth told me that you already knew."

Piper squeezed his hand again. "I just knew there was something we should share, talk about." She shook her head. "I don't know. I've only been a mother for twenty-five years. I guess I'm still learning." She ran her fingers through his hair. "About you and Beth. I am curious. The two of you seemed to fit together and not fit at the same time. You and she are an interesting friendship."

Bryce nodded. "We both think we don't fit in here. But we love our families and the life here. I told her that I'd help her move to her new job and she promised to visit me and my friends if I ever find where I do fit." He chuckled. "I think she's my best friend."

"Honey, your place is here as long as you need us." The mother of twenty-five years knew one thing for certain. Love your kids forever. And she thought about the story of Mrs. Hennessey that Sean and Lee had shared. Mothers really do love their children forever.

\* \* \*

"I can't believe how much happens in a lockdown." Lynn thought about change - Tim and Janet home; Doyle and Lori engaged. Career paths ended, or put on hold, or new ones beginning. Kids going to school on computer. Everyone making changes to adapt to the times.

"Tell me about it!" yawned Dusty. He knew what he saw every day. He tried to keep people from getting too crazy. Bergy was finally under control. But all those people worried about sick relatives were causing problems at nursing homes and at the hospital. He just knew her days were not like his. He told her about some of the antics he dealt with.

"I'm sorry," she kissed his cheek. "But I was thinking of all the positive things. You made Emily and the children safe. We zoomed Sean's wedding. Have you forgotten?" She snuggled, distracted by another thought. "I wonder where they went for a honeymoon?"

"Hank's cabin."

"Hank's cabin? How do you know that?" She sat up and stared at her husband.

"The regional drug task force uses it to watch a neighboring cabin. Hank told us it was off limits for a week or two." He rolled on his stomach and punched his pillow. "Then Mars talked to Hank and booked the cabin for Trina and the baby."

"The baby's isn't due for a few more months."

"I know," groaned Dusty. "Have I told you how crazy Mars is getting? He's worried about Trina birthing in the hospital. This last week when she was sick, he was worthless. His mother is trying to escape from London. I think he plans on having Trina and the baby stay with him at the cabin for a few days, sort of a quarantine. Lucia's friend will stay at the house and watch the other two kids." He punched the pillow again. "That baby can't get here too soon."

She snuggled up again and hugged him. "Mars will be calmer once it's here. Is Tee still in hot water with the sheriff?"

"No, Doug did such a great PR job, the sheriff thinks it was all his idea." Dusty was still amazed at how Doug worked all the drama into a story worthy of a movie script, with the sheriff as the mastermind behind Dawson's capture and Tee's Indiana success. "Do you have crazies coming to the Philanthropies office?" He was trying to be a concerned husband.

"My office is running smoothly. Rory is working out well. He's great with numbers and knows everyone and has been able to help folks with the grants they've received. He likes to be at the office instead of working from home." She chuckled. "He said at home he spends more time eating than working."

Dusty chuckled. "Tee tells me the same thing. She's having a hard time working and managing her kids. We've fixed her schedule so she comes into the office when Lonzo has his days off. She's worried about her mother getting sick."

"I hope this vaccine moves us back to normal," sighed Lynn. "I miss hugging Dad."

"Maybe that's what we'll learn from all this," proposed Dusty.

"What?" She liked these late nights snuggled with Dusty.

"We'll learn how important hugging is and we should do a lot more of it."

And he did.

## THE END

# Caught

## The River Bend Chronicles - Book 21

The story opens in vaccination spring. Folks are getting vaccines and coming back – resigned to living a cautious, but quasi-normal life. Lynn is drawn into the marriage problems of several of her friends in River Bend. She tries to be supportive. But the husbands involved are caught up in a drug raid as distributor, user, and innocent onlooker. Dusty and the FBI pursue the investigation into local drug operations and soon suspect a leak of information in the regional drug task force. As the investigation continues, Lynn helps her friends work through the impact of drug arrests on families and futures. Life in The Heights revolves around returning to normal as they plan college graduation and a pending wedding.

# About The Author

Renee Kumor was a stay-at-home mom for several years developing a personal ethic of community service. She began writing a political opinion column for the local newspaper, but retired from writing when she announced her candidacy for local political office. After eight years as a county commissioner, she returned to non-profit service and began writing a monthly column for the newspaper on non-profit management and service issues. The setting for the *River Bend Chronicles* series reflects her early life in Ohio and her later years in western North Carolina.

Thank you for reading. Please review this book. Reviews help others find Absolutely Amazing eBooks and inspire us to keep providing these marvelous tales.

If you would like to be put on our email list to receive updates on new releases, contests, and promotions, please go to AbsolutelyAmazingEbooks.com and sign up.

For sales, editorial information, subsidiary rights information
or a catalog, please write or phone or e-mail

AbsolutelyAmazingEbooks
Manhanset House
Shelter Island Hts., New York 11965, US
Tel: 212-427-7139
www.AbsolutelyAmazingEbooks.com
bricktower@aol.com
www.IngramContent.com


For sales in the UK and Europe please contact our distributor,
Gazelle Book Services
White Cross Mills
Lancaster, LA1 4XS, UK
Tel: (01524) 68765 Fax: (01524) 63232
email: jacky@gazellebooks.co.uk

www.ingramcontent.com/pod-product-compliance
Lightning Source LLC
Chambersburg PA
CBHW070838030726
47504CB00005B/1142

* 9 7 8 1 9 5 5 0 3 6 5 0 4 *